the
hope chest

Also by Viola Shipman

The Charm Bracelet

the
hope chest

viola shipman

THOMAS DUNNE BOOKS
St. Martin's Press
New York

THOMAS DUNNE BOOKS.
An imprint of St. Martin's Press.

THE HOPE CHEST. Copyright © 2017 by Viola Shipman. All rights reserved. Printed in the United States of America. For information, address St. Martin's Press, 175 Fifth Avenue, New York, N.Y. 10010.

www.thomasdunnebooks.com
www.stmartins.com

LIBRARY OF CONGRESS CATALOGING-IN-PUBLICATION DATA

Names: Shipman, Viola, author.
Title: The hope chest : a novel / Viola Shipman.
Description: New York : Thomas Dunne Books, St. Martin's Press, 2017.
Identifiers: LCCN 2016043273| ISBN 9781250105073 (hardback) | ISBN 9781250137630 (Canadian edition) | ISBN 9781250105080 (e-book)
Subjects: LCSH: Domestic fiction. | BISAC: FICTION / Contemporary Women. | FICTION / Family Life.
Classification: LCC PS3619.H5788 H67 2017 | DDC 813/.6—dc23
LC record available at https://lccn.loc.gov/2016043273

Our books may be purchased in bulk for promotional, educational, or business use. Please contact your local bookseller or the Macmillan Corporate and Premium Sales Department at 1-800-221-7945, extension 5442, or by e-mail at MacmillanSpecialMarkets@macmillan.com.

First U.S. Edition: March 2017

First Canadian Edition: March 2017

10 9 8 7 6 5 4 3 2 1

For My Father

I miss you every day, but know that you are near.

You taught me hard work and perseverance pay off,

and never, ever to give up. And I won't.

For My Uncle Don

Who valiantly battled ALS for a decade

and taught me—in the midst of his horrific struggle—

what strength, grace, and hope truly mean.

For My Grandmothers and Great-Aunts

The items from your hope chests

remain an important part of our family,

and are a prime reason my house is always a home.

For Anne Lamott

Your birthday wish (and drawing) inspired me,

as does your writing, each and every day.

Barbara's face was set now, almost like a mask, like something the wind is blowing hard against, and she'd lost a lot of weight, so you could see the shape of her animal, and bones and branches and humanity.

Yet she still had a smile that got you every time, not a flash of high-wattage white teeth, but the beauty of low-watt, the light that comes in through the bottom branches: sweet, peaceful, wry.

—Anne Lamott, on her friend's battle with ALS,
from *Small Victories*

prologue

The Scent of Cedar

May 2016

I think that's about the last box, sweetheart. Do you need a few minutes alone to say goodbye?"

Mattie Tice scanned the room and then looked at her husband, Don, before nodding yes.

How can I properly say goodbye to the home I love when I can barely even talk anymore? Mattie thought.

After nearly fifty years together, Don could read his wife's thoughts by instinct. He walked over to Mattie, knelt in front of her wheelchair, and leaned in close, until her white-blond hair tickled his tanned face.

"It will always be our lake home," he whispered, his breath smelling sweet like the toffee lattes he loved to drink, especially when he was tired. "Our home is wherever we are."

Mattie knew his words were meant to comfort her, but she was too upset for them to help. She opened her mouth to talk, but even if she screamed, no one could hear her.

My voice is getting weaker, Mattie thought.

"Say it again, sweetie. For me," Don said softly, lifting the tiny mic that dangled in front of his wife's face to amplify her voice.

"That's . . . B . . . S," Mattie said slowly. "Just . . . like . . . A . . . L . . . S."

Don laughed at her pluck and kissed her cheek.

"I know," he said. "I'm sorry. I know how much you hate platitudes."

"You know what they say about death and moving," Mattie said, one garbled word at a time. "Very stressful."

The word "death" hung in the silence of the now empty cottage and rattled around in Don's mind.

He smiled and bit the inside of his cheek—it was the only way he could keep himself from crying in times like this.

Don put his hands on his wife's shoulders and massaged them.

"Right up there with taxes," Don said. "I know how hard this is, my love."

Mattie leaned her head to the right until it was pressed against her husband's hand. *He is a warm man,* she thought, *inside and out.*

"Don't beat yourself up," she said to her husband, knowing his every emotion. "I'm a big girl."

Mattie Tice was the strongest person Don had ever known and that strength had willed her through five years of living with ALS.

But now their beloved lake house was simply too much for her to navigate.

It's too big, and I'm too small, Mattie thought, looking around the cottage she'd been coming to since she was ten years old.

Two movers suddenly came barreling down the narrow staircase carrying a box. Mabel, the Tice's beloved mutt, barked her disapproval.

"I thought that was everything?" Mattie asked before they could exit the front door. "What's in there?"

The two young men—broad shouldered, barrel-chested—stopped, unable to understand what she was saying.

"She's wondering what's in there," Don restated for them.

"OF COURSE, MA'AM!" one of the movers, who was maybe twenty, yelled. He walked over, gesturing for his friend to follow, and stopped in front of Mattie. "WOULD YOU LIKE TO SEE?"

He put the box on the floor with great animation and opened it, as if he were pantomiming a children's story to a group of kindergarteners.

Don tried hard not to roll his eyes.

People always talked to his wife as if she were a baby, or deaf. They shouted, they cooed, they were nervous, they even invented their own language.

Why are people always so uncomfortable around someone with a disability? Don wondered, his mind screaming: *She has ALS! Her brain, ironically, is as strong as her body is weak.*

Instead, Don smiled politely and remained quiet. His wife hated scenes.

The box was filled with big, old scrapbooks, and the mover pulled one out and placed it on Mattie's lap. Don walked over quickly to open the ancient, hardbound album for her.

"My flowers," she said. "Oh!"

Over the years, Mattie had created these albums, documenting every start of every flower that every person had ever given her: Latin and common names of the plants and flowers, their colors, and years they were gifted and planted.

Alongside, Mattie had made a watercolor of each plant. Years later, when the plant was mature, Mattie would paint another watercolor of it in full bloom.

These books had also served as Mattie's professional signature: She gave elaborate drawings of her garden designs to her landscape clients, returning years later—often unannounced—to paint the now fully grown gardens she had envisioned. Mattie's clients had included CEOs, politicians, famous actors, and musicians.

The earth centers us all, Mattie thought.

Mattie ran a trembling finger over a watercolor of a white peony with a pink center, one of her favorite flowers. It transported her back in time. She could feel her hands in the earth. She could feel a connection to the world.

I could feel, Mattie thought.

"Thank you," Mattie said suddenly, and Don instantly closed the book. "Alone . . . now . . . please."

"Of course," Don said. "Let us know when you're ready."

Mattie could still hear her husband's Ozarks accent living deep within his well-polished city-speak. It unknowingly reared its head when he was stressed. He'd try to hide it, but the give away, "ready" always came out in three syllables: "re-uh-dee."

"Go," she said, forcing a smile.

Don was often the only one now who could easily understand his wife without intense concentration. He knew by heart her vocal cadences and rhythms, her every grunt, grumble, cough, choke, inflection. He could nearly read her mind by staring into her hazel eyes, those verdant flecks reminding him of the sea grass waving in the distance on the sandy dunes leading to Lake Michigan.

Don kissed the top of his wife's head, stopping for a second to inhale her scent.

She always smells like sunshine, Don thought.

Mattie smiled, lifted her head a few inches off the headrest of the wheelchair, and nodded, before reclining it slightly to watch her husband—still so young, so strong, so vibrant—as he walked out the front door. A spring wreath hanging on the door looked like a happy halo over his head as he passed by.

She heard the birds sing before the door closed, their song like a summer chorus. Don always told Mattie that her voice, even now, sounded like a bird's song.

Still beautiful, he told her every day.

Mattie pressed her right index finger on the wheelchair's control and slowly rotated in a circle around her living room before toggling the joystick forward and stopping the wheelchair in front of the large picture window overlooking the lake.

The window was open just a touch—"to air out the home as well as its ghosts," Mattie had joked earlier. She closed her eyes, listening to the whistle of the breeze as it transitioned from water to dune to land. Mattie opened her eyes again and rolled her head to the left, watching the breeze ripple the dune grass before causing the peonies, fox glove, delphinium, and arctic orange poppy blossoms to dance. When the wind finally reached her, the dainty collar of her white shirt rippled and her matching hair took flight.

She rolled her head right and watched Don load hundreds of little pots into the back of their "handi-capable" van.

Mattie's heart broke.

Pots! Now all I will have are pots? she thought. *Potted plants. Just like me.*

When Mattie was diagnosed with ALS, her life in her beloved garden—and career as a landscape architect—quickly disappeared.

For decades, she had worked alone, in her garden, in other people's gardens, and in the attic office she could no longer reach. Those were her private places.

Now, she was never alone: Everyone hovered around like ghosts, worried about every cough, breath, sip of water.

Nothing to take root ever again, to grow, to bloom. Forever trapped in this chair, Mattie thought, slamming her fists down on her wheelchair.

Mattie negotiated her wheelchair from the living room into the dining room, Mabel following closely behind. She stopped in the middle, where the grand table had long anchored the room. She could hear the voices of her family and past celebrations—anniversaries, birthdays, Thanksgivings, Fourth of Julys—ring in her head.

She moved into the kitchen and thought of all the dinners she had prepared, the cookies she had baked, the picnic baskets she had packed. Vintage lake blue tiles she'd bought from Pewabic Pottery—Michigan's historic ceramics studio—reflected the sunlight and filled the room with a warm glow.

Mattie moved her chair into the family room overlooking the lake, and the smell of smoke from the floor-to-ceiling fireplace engulfed her. She smiled at the beautiful, polished Michigan stones—gathered by her father and husband from the lakeshore—that comprised the fireplace.

Mattie remembered the first night in this house—a bone-chilling June night—when her father had just purchased the cottage.

He had lit a fire with birch limbs he had picked up in the woods—and nearly lit himself and the house on fire as well—not yet realizing that some woods were made for burning and some were not.

Mattie smiled and looked at the faded square over the mantel. She had framed a picture for her father decades ago of "The Firewood Poem," and she could recite it line by line even though it was no longer in its sacred place.

> *. . . Birch and fir logs burn too fast*
> *Blaze up bright and do not last . . .*
> *But ash green or ash brown*
> *Is fit for a queen with golden crown*

Poplar gives a bitter smoke
Fills your eyes and makes you choke
Apple wood will scent your room
Pear wood smells like flowers in bloom
Oaken logs, if dry and old
Keep away the winter's cold
But ash wet or ash dry
A king shall warm his slippers by

Mattie turned her chair toward the screened porch that overlooked her massive backyard gardens, patio, and pool.

Her giant ferns were unfurling everywhere—like sleepy dancers stretching after a long winter's hibernation. She stared out at the lake, the entire sandy coast of Michigan in the distance, the water's horizon draped in clouds, almost like a mirage.

So Wuthering Heights, Mattie thought. *I will miss you.*

Mattie watched the wind sway through the branches and tender leaves of the sugar maples. Suddenly, a gust off the lake swept up and over the bluff, and a smell overwhelmed her. She shut her eyes and inhaled.

The scent of cedar.

Without warning, Mattie's heart began to pound. She stared at the reddish-brown trunk of the ancient tree that sat at the edge of her garden.

How long ago was it? she thought, trying to remember how old she was when she took a sapling from her parents' home in St. Louis and planted it here with her father.

The cedar's arms reached toward the heavens. It was old, some of its lower branches sparse, and it stood in contrast to the willowy white birch she had also planted long ago. But the ancient, aging cedar had an unmistakable grace.

Just like me, Mattie laughed.

Mattie lifted her nose and sniffed again, Mabel doing the same. Mattie unconsciously moved her wheelchair until she was up against the screen.

The scent triggered something in Mattie, something powerful, ancient, unforgettable.

Mattie's mind whirled, and she could suddenly hear the voice of her father.

"How big do you think this will get, Dad?" she remembered asking him when they planted it.

"How big are your hopes and dreams?" he asked, shovel in hand.

Mattie's heart began to pound even faster, and a tear popped into her eye. She immediately tried to blame it on allergies, but knew better.

Easter 1950

"I found it! I found it!"

Madeline Barnhart zipped through her sloping backyard in St. Louis, down the hill, and directly toward a dyed pink egg nestled in the crook of a redbud tree.

Her parents laughed as she jumped up and down in her Easter dress—white with little pink bows that her mother had made, and patent leather shoes—holding up the matching pink egg for them to see.

While his daughter was looking, Joseph Barnhart secretly pointed behind his wife's back toward the next location—a squirrel hole in an old oak—and Mattie giggled, racing off to the next hiding spot with her basket bursting with bright green plastic grass, chocolates, and colorful eggs.

Joseph put his arm around his wife.

"Perfect Easter," he said, kissing her cheek.

"Looks like *The Wizard of Oz* with all the color, doesn't it?" Mary Ellen asked.

As the Barnharts stood on their deck, they could survey not only their sprawling suburban yard but also those of their neighbors. They could see neighborhood kids rushing around their yards with baskets, too, while Harry Caray's unmistakable voice boomed over radios broadcasting the Cardinals game.

The dogwoods and redbud were in bloom—white and pink dotting the lush green—and most of the trees, save for the stubborn oaks, were nearly full of leaves. Tulips encircled the trees—a Crayon box of colors—while sunny daffodils lined the fence.

It was April, and St. Louis was downright hot: The air was thick and moist like a rain forest. The earth smelled alive.

Mary Ellen dabbed at her brow with the Kleenex she pulled from deep within the top of her own Easter dress.

"You're like a magician," teased Joseph. "Always pulling Kleenex from a purse, a sleeve . . . anywhere."

Mary Ellen draped the Kleenex over her husband's face. "Sometimes I wish I could make you disappear," she said laughing, before returning it to her forehead. "Humidity's already back. It's going to be a hot summer, I can already tell."

Joseph waved his arms in front of his wife, pretending to be a fan.

"That's not going to cut it," she laughed.

He walked over and took a seat in a lawn chair on the patio, as his daughter continued her hunt.

"We should think about a summer house," he said. "A place where we can get out of this heat."

"Really?"

Mary Ellen beamed expectantly.

She looks just like Doris Day, Joseph thought. *And Mattie looks like a mini-Doris. Both blond, happy rays of sunshine.*

"We could do it, especially with the extra money from my raise," Joseph said of his accounting job at Anheuser-Busch. "All the fellas from the brewery are buying in Wisconsin and Michigan. And I have nearly a month off now. We could make it work."

Mattie's happy shrieks echoed throughout the yard, and the ten-year-old zipped past the birdbath toward her parents, sending a pair of fat robins flying into the sky.

"Too much chocolate," Mary Ellen said, plucking another Kleenex from her dress and wiping down her daughter's face. "You are too excited."

"It's Easter!" screamed Mattie. "I love my Brach's!"

"Well, we have one more surprise for you today . . . *if* you stay calm," her mom said, unable to hide a smile. "Follow us."

Mary Ellen and Joseph led Mattie into the family room of their sprawling red brick ranch, and their daughter gasped: A trail of jelly beans me-andered past the kidney bean–shaped coffee table and burnt orange amoeba lounge chair and ottoman.

"Where's it go?" Mattie giggled.

"Follow it and find out," Joseph said.

"Follow the yellow brick road," Mattie sang, giggling, before changing the lyrics. *"Follow the jelly-bean road!"*

Mattie took off in a flash—Easter basket still in the crook of her arm—her parents running to keep up, the trail of jelly beans leading across the kitchen linoleum, past the Hotpoint appliances, and into the formal living room where smack-dab in the middle sat a large package wrapped in colorful cellophane.

"That's a big Easter basket," Mattie said, her hazel eyes wide.

Joseph laughed, running a hand through his thick, black hair, which was slicked back and parted on the side. "Open it," he said, kneeling down in front of his daughter. "I'll help you."

The two began to unwrap the layers of cellophane, the loud crinkling causing Mattie to giggle even more.

"What is it?" Mattie asked as the gift was revealed, her mouth hanging open.

"It's a hope chest," Mary Ellen answered, taking a seat on the carpet next to her daughter.

"A what, Mommy?"

"A hope chest," she said. "It's sort of like a jewelry box, except bigger, for your dreams."

Mary Ellen sat on her knees next to Mattie and smoothed her daughter's short blond hair.

"This was mine when I was a little girl, and your dad and I thought it was the perfect time to pass it on to you."

"Why?"

"Because I want to help you fill it before you're all grown up."

"With what?" Mattie asked.

"Well, a hope chest is filled with lots of things," Mary Ellen said, continuing to smooth her daughter's hair. "It's filled with blankets and linens to keep you warm. It's filled with household items, like glasses, dishes, kitchen towels, and bakeware, so that your future house is truly a home. It's filled with memories, like scrapbooks and family pictures, teddy bears and dolls, so that you can pass those along when you are married and have a family. It's a way to connect your past with your future."

Mary Ellen stopped and looked at her husband. "But, mostly, a hope chest is filled with love, and the hopes and dreams that parents have for their daughters, that we have for you."

"It's so pretty," Mattie exclaimed, touching the chest, whose wood was burnished and the color of gold, the lid shiny and smooth from use.

"Your father wanted to add something, too," Mary Ellen started, "so he carved these beautiful spring flowers onto the front."

"They're all your favorites: tulips and daffodils and dogwood blooms," Joseph said. "I thought you'd like that since we love to work in the garden together. And those flowers represent spring, the season of eternal hope."

"Thank you, Daddy," Mattie said, standing to give him a big hug.

"Open it," Mary Ellen said. "I have something in there for you, too."

Mattie tried to lift the lid, but it wouldn't budge. "I think it's jammed," she said, turning to look at her parents. "Or broken."

"Oh, I forgot," Mary Ellen said. "See the lock? There's a special key— the only one like it in the world—that goes with it that only you will have. So you need to keep it in a secret place, okay?"

"Where is it?" Mattie asked.

"Would you help me?" Mary Ellen asked her husband.

"I don't know where the key is, either," Joseph said.

"The last place anyone would ever look," she said, grabbing one end of the chest and nodding at her husband to grab the other. The pair tilted the chest up and taped to the bottom was the key. "The most obvious."

Mattie giggled.

"Grab it, sweetheart," Mary Ellen said.

Mattie took the key, her parents tilted the chest onto the floor again, and Mattie carefully inserted the key into the old lock.

As she lifted the lid, she asked, "What's that smell? It's like we're in the woods."

"That's cedar," Mary Ellen said. "That smell never goes away. It smells exactly the same way it did when I was a little girl. You'll never forget that scent. Did you find anything in there yet?"

Mattie bent over the chest. Its lid had a lined drawer with compartments that ran the entire length of the chest. In the bottom of the deep chest sat one item: a wooden plaque.

Mattie carefully lifted it out of the chest.

"It's a 'Home Sweet Home' plaque for *your* future home," Mary Ellen said. "I wrote the poem on it just for you, and your father engraved the plaque."

Mary Ellen took it from her daughter's hands and held it up for her to read.

Hope Is Only One Short Letter From Home
H is for Hope
Now and for always

O is for the Overwhelming love
I have for you

P is for the Practical items
That will make your house a home

E is for the Eternal memories this chest will provide
Every time you open it up

You are my hope, and my home, in this world
My daughter, my love

As Mattie read, Mary Ellen's eyes grew misty, and Joseph put a reassuring hand on her shoulder.

"And, see," Mary Ellen said with a shaky voice, "on the other side of the plaque your father engraved the word 'home' and trailed your name down from the *m*. Like the title, my mother always told me that hope is only one short letter from home."

"Thank you, Mommy!" Mattie said. "I love it! When can we start filling it up?"

"We have all the time in the world, my angel," Mary Ellen said, laying the plaque back into the chest. "We'll have it overflowing by the time you meet the man of your dreams and have your first little girl."

Mary Ellen stopped and pulled her daughter close. "Can I tell you something important?"

"Of course." Mattie nodded.

"Always remember that hope is something you carry with you forever, not only in this chest but also in your heart. So look inside it and inside yourself when you need hope the most, and it will guide you, and remind you of what was and what is to be."

Mattie looked at her mother, considering her words. Then she nodded and dropped the key into her Easter basket, before reaching back in and grabbing a little chocolate egg. She unwrapped the candy and popped it into her mouth.

"Okay!" she said. "But I don't think there will ever be a time when I'm sad. I have oodles of hope!"

Mattie popped another chocolate into her mouth, hugged her parents, and skipped out of the room with her Easter basket.

"Later, gator!" she giggled, leaving five chocolaty fingerprints on the inside of the white frame of the door, just below the pencil marks that measured her growing height.

"Almost forgot this!"

The shouts of the movers startled Mattie.

"Found it in the attic," one of the men was saying. "What is this old thing?"

Mattie heard a thud as they placed it down behind her, and she turned her wheelchair around to see what they had discovered.

Her heart stopped.

"That's my hope," Mattie gasped, her voice choking, stopping short of adding the word "chest."

Before she could say anything further, the young movers were already trying to open the chest.

"Thing's jammed," one of the movers said. He turned to Mattie. "Sorry."

Mattie smiled. "Key," she said. "Taped underneath."

The movers tilted the hope chest up a little, and an old key glimmered in the sunlight.

"Well, I'll be," one of the men said. "Pretty clever. Last place I would have looked."

He took the key, inserted it into the lock, and opened the chest.

"Wow," one of the young men said, before standing in front of the chest, which was overflowing with family heirlooms. "Smells great. What is all this stuff?"

Mattie's eyes instantly filled with tears when she looked at the contents: a cloth doll, family photos, china, Christmas ornaments, a Bible, a scrapbook, an embroidered pillowcase and apron.

One of the movers saw Mattie's tears and smiled at her.

"Must be for your kids or grandkids, huh?" he asked. "That's real sweet. Glad we found it."

"Please put it in the back of our van," Don said quietly from the front door, before walking over to take the key and whisper to his wife, "Honey, are you okay?"

"How could I have forgotten that?" she asked, her voice weak and trembling. "How?"

"It was in the attic," Don said. "It's been there a long time."

"I never would have forgiven myself," Mattie said.

The smell of cedar rushed on to the screened porch.

"Can we leave now? Please," she begged.

Don leaned in to kiss his wife.

"Of course," he said, softly kissing Mattie's cheek. Don put his hand underneath her chin and looked into his wife's eyes. "I love you."

"Me, too," she replied. "Time to go."

"Here," Don said, putting the key into her hands. "For luck. To remind you that memories can never be locked away."

Mattie tried to smile, but nothing came. Instead, she navigated her wheelchair out of the house, down the ramp, and to the van, silently screaming inside.

I'm saying goodbye to everything, Mattie thought. *My family. My history.*

Mattie stopped.

My life.

Mattie squeezed her eyes shut, until her chair had been lifted and locked into place and she could hear the gravel of the long driveway crunch under the tires.

Mattie tried to keep her eyes closed, but she couldn't help herself, and she opened them at the final moment, just in time to see the wood-carved sign that announced the name of the family cottage to visitors for years— HOPE DUNES—swinging in the lake breeze on a log post attached to two stone pillars.

Mattie closed her eyes again and rubbed the key, but she couldn't shut out the smell of cedar seeping from the chest or the fact that the only thing worse than remembering a time once filled with hope was living when there was none at all.

part one

The Cloth Doll

One

May 2016

Rose Hoffs leaned in to her bathroom mirror and pushed at the bags beneath her eyes.

She sighed and reached for some moisturizer and then for the foundation.

More water, more sleep, more exercise, more . . . everything, Rose thought. *I'm 27 going on 107.*

Rose took a deep breath and an even bigger swig of coffee and continued to "put on her face" as her mom used to say. Her nose twitched instinctively, just like a rabbit, and she sniffed the air.

Spring, Rose thought. *The town is alive again!*

It was a beautiful spring day in Saugatuck, Michigan, and the windows were open in Rose's tiny five-room cottage, letting in the warm air that Michiganders wait so long for after interminable winters. Carried along on the wind was the sweet scent of blueberry streusel muffins, cinnamon scones, and roasting beans from Lake Effect Coffee located a few blocks away.

Rose's mouth watered.

Rose's cottage on Butler Street sat perched behind a row of larger resort homes, almost like a carriage house. But it wasn't. The home was one of the town's original fishing cottages—which came with a tiny square lot big enough for some rhododendrons and a couple of bikes. The Hoffs never dreamed resorters would come in droves to the little artists' colony on the dunes of Lake Michigan, buying every available plot of land and building houses that reached up, up, up for seasonal peeks of the river and lake.

In fact, the Hoffs' house had become known in town as the "Up" house (the level of sarcasm or affection for the nickname depended on whom you talked to and their net worth) because their adorable little cottage sat in the midst of gentrification just like the elderly widower's home in the Disney movie.

The film *Up* came out just before Rose's mother died, and she had loved the movie and moniker.

"Up," she would say, laughing every time the cartoon movie house took flight thanks to the hundreds of helium balloons attached. "Our house is like that one: filled with hope and adventure."

The wind again wafted the scent of freshly baked treats into Rose's house—*Those are definitely blueberry muffins,* she thought—making her mouth water again. Rose wondered how many blueberries her parents, Dora and Dave, had sold over the course of their lifetimes from their tiny farmers' market on Blue Star Highway.

We couldn't afford to buy this house today, Rose thought. *I couldn't even afford to keep their stand going. I can barely pay the taxes.*

Rose's mind drifted to all the resorters who owned land around the Hoffs' house and their offers to buy the house and property.

How much longer can I hold out? Rose wondered. *My mother would never forgive me if I lost it. I need this job.*

Rose shook her head and reached for her lipstick.

"How about this one, Mommy?"

Rose looked over at her daughter, Jeri, seated on a cushioned chair at the vanity, happily holding up a tube of lipstick. In the few minutes Rose had not been paying attention, her seven-year-old daughter had painted her whole face pink, her favorite color. She resembled one of the Doodlebops, from the cartoon she loved to watch.

"Very Deedee Doodle," said Rose, smiling, despite Jeri's misbehavior, referencing one of the colorfully painted children's band members who teach kids social lessons.

"Yeah!" giggled Jeri. "Better than one of the boys."

Jeri stopped and looked at her mom with a serious expression. "How come I'm named after a boy? All the kids in Mrs. Hooper's class made fun of my name this year. I'm glad it's summer vacation!"

"Well . . . ," started Rose, who always had trouble explaining this fact to her seven-year-old.

Do I tell her that her father had wanted a boy? And that he had been disappointed with a girl? And with me? And with pretty much everything in his life? And that her name was a compromise to keep him happy?

"We wanted a name as unique as you," Rose said, reaching over to muss her daughter's curly red locks. "Don't worry. You'll grow into it. It wasn't easy being named after a thorny flower, either."

Rose dampened a washcloth and leaned down to clean her daughter's face.

That won't cut it, Rose thought, before grabbing some makeup remover as well as some makeup remover towelettes. As she was scrubbing Jeri's pink, round cheeks, her daughter said, "A rose is beautiful, Mommy. Just like you."

Rose's lip quivered, and her eyes filled with tears.

"You're so sweet. Thank you. You're going to make me cry."

"Don't cry, Mommy," Jeri said. "It's a very big day."

Rose nodded, as she finished scrubbing her daughter's face. "Yes, it is," she agreed.

She was putting on her lipstick when Jeri asked another question.

"Are you nervous?"

Rose stopped with her lipstick in midair, as if she were conducting an invisible orchestra. Her lip quivered again.

"I am," she said. "It's a very big interview for me . . . for *us*."

"Wait here," Jeri said, hopping off the little seat at the vanity. Rose could hear Jeri's padded footsteps run into her bedroom. A few seconds later, her daughter was back, her tiny hands hiding something behind her back.

Jeri's face broke into a wide smile.

"Here!" she said with conviction, handing her mom her favorite doll—a beat-up, hand-me-down Raggedy Ann cloth doll. "She was sleeping, but I woke her up. I think you need her more than I do today."

Rose smiled and, without thinking, hugged Jeri and the cloth doll tightly.

"Thank you, sweetie," she said.

"I want you to take Ann with you on your . . . what's it called again?" Jeri asked.

"Interview," Rose said.

"Yeah, inner-blue," Jeri said. "She'll keep you company."

Rose smiled at her daughter, feeling calm for a split second, before she felt her nerves kick in again.

I have no friends or family to watch Jeri today, Rose thought, *and no extra money for a sitter. I'm a bad mother.*

"Remember, you're going to have to babysit Ann in the car while I talk to the nice people for a few minutes today, okay?" Rose said to her daughter. "You're going to have to be a very big girl today."

"I will! I promise!" Jeri said. "And you're gonna have to be a big girl today, too!"

Rose smiled and again hugged the doll, which smelled of her daughter.

I can't recall a time Ann hasn't been part of my life, Rose thought.

"I promise to be a big girl, too," Rose said. "But now I have to find some big girl clothes to wear. We've got to hurry."

Rose and Jeri scurried over to the closet, and Rose began to scour through her clothes, tossing slacks, suit jackets, and blouses onto her bed.

Jeri's words—*You're gonna have to be a big girl today*—ran through Rose's head as she tried to pick out something to wear.

Why do I still feel like such a little girl? Rose thought, still clutching the red-haired doll that looked so much like her and her daughter.

Two

February 2010

Rose watched her baby daughter sleep, nuzzling her beloved doll, which was nestled into the curve of her chubby body.

As Jeri slept, she unconsciously gummed the cloth doll's hand, something Rose had done to the same doll as an infant, her mother had told her.

Rose reached out to caress the downy reddish curls that swept like little waves over her daughter's head, but stopped at the last moment, lowered her head, and wept.

I have everything, Rose thought. *I have nothing.*

In two short years, Rose's life had turned upside down. She had quit school, married her boyfriend, gotten pregnant, gotten a divorce, had a baby, and lost her mother.

In the distance, bells of the neighborhood church chimed. Rose thought of the day she married Ray Rhodes.

"I don't hear joyous church bells ringing today," her mother had said. "I only hear alarm bells."

She had been right, of course, Rose thought. *About everything.*

The church bells echoed throughout Rose's tiny home, making the old, wavy glass reverberate in the windowpanes of the house in which she had grown up. She looked around the nursery—once her bedroom—and watched tiny yellow ducks happily marching in rain boots around the border that lined the walls of the room.

"*Happy,*" Rose thought, staring at their smiling beaks. *What's that?*

She swung forward in her rocker and gently eased the Raggedy Ann doll from the crook of her daughter's body.

I must look like the Grinch when he stole all of the Whoville children's Christmas gifts, Rose thought, slinking the doll out of the crib without waking Jeri.

Rose wrapped her arms around the tiny doll and hugged it. Raggedy Ann had faded from years of play and washes, her red triangle nose, string hair, gingham top, and striped legs now more pink in color.

"Life sure puts us through the wringer, doesn't it?" Rose whispered to the doll. With Rose's coaxing, Raggedy Ann nodded her head in agreement.

Rose looked into the doll's eyes. Ann had two mismatched button eyes, one the original large black circle, the other a small blue button from . . .

A sob emerged from the depths of Rose, and she covered her mouth to stop herself from waking Jeri.

Oh, Mom, she thought. *I miss you.*

I hate cancer, Rose said to the doll, who had lost its original eye when Rose—overcome with grief—had nervously twisted it off and then lost it during her mother's illness. She had plucked the new button off the back of her mother's blue Easter dress when she picked it for the funeral and added it to the doll as a way to keep a part of her mother with her forever.

Cancer has taken both my parents and both of Jeri's grandparents. I'm too young to have no family.

"I love blue!" her mother had chirped every Easter as she walked to the stone church on the hill in Saugatuck, rain or shine or snow. "Blue spring skies, bluebirds, blooming blue bells, and blue moon ice cream. Blue is hope, Rose. Sunny skies ahead!"

Rose would always laugh at her mother's optimism because Easter weather in Michigan was iffy, at best. But, no matter the weather, Rose's mother made her feel safe, happy, hopeful.

"I have no future without you, Mom," Rose told Dora in her final days, when all her mom wanted to do was hold her newborn granddaughter and sleep.

"No," Dora responded one morning, before she fell into a coma from which she wouldn't wake, "you just won't have any backup plan anymore."

That morning, Dora patted the edge of the hospital bed for her daughter to come and sit. "You're such a wonderful mother and daughter. And you take such great care of me. You are neither helpless nor hopeless. You're just scared."

She continued with a sense of purpose: "Take some of my strength moving forward, and some of your daughter's strength. You should be a nurse. It's your calling. Go back to school."

Dora had stopped and kissed the top of Jeri's head. "And never forget," she said, her voice shaking, "that the world is always full of hope and possibility simply because this precious angel is now in it."

The February wind rattled the window frames and Rose from her thoughts. She looked outside. It was ten in the morning, but it might as well have been midnight: The Saugatuck skies were black, and lake-effect snow was coming down in heavy bursts every half hour. Right now, Rose couldn't even make out the silhouette of a tree in her neighbor's yard. The little house moaned in the storm.

Rose shivered. It was a day just like this when she had moved out of this house.

"You're not taking that thing, too, are you?" Ray Rhodes had asked his new wife, as Rose clutched the doll against her pregnant stomach and looked over at her mother. "We got a tiny apartment."

"Yes! She's taking the doll," said Dora. "It was mine as a little girl, Rose's as a little girl, and one day it will belong to your little girl."

"Dolls." Ray had snorted. "Girls."

"Mom," Rose said sweetly. "Please. Don't."

"I'm paying for that place," Dora said, her words as icy as the winter weather roaring outside. "I think there's room for the doll and *three* girls—don't you?—considering I'll be there *all* the time."

Ray roared out of the Hoffs' house and into the swirling snow outside.

Why didn't I listen? Rose thought. *Why did I believe he would change? Ray and Rose Rhodes. I thought we fit perfectly. Why was I such an idiot?*

Rose shivered and realized she was still sitting in her daughter's nursery. She stood and checked the thermostat in the hallway.

Sixty degrees. And the heat was running nonstop.

Rose briefly considered cranking it up a notch but stopped, thinking of all the bills that were due.

Ray wouldn't help, she thought, *even if I knew where he was and he had two nickels to rub together.*

Rose was happy to have her mom's house—and to have retaken her family name after her divorce. Now, she needed a job to pay the remaining mortgage, the utilities, and the taxes. Her parents' tiny inheritance was already dwindling.

I have a baby, Rose thought. *I can't just go back to school. I need an income.*

Jeri began to squirm, and Rose walked back into the nursery, grabbing a throw and pulling it over her shoulders, still holding the doll.

Out the window, a sliver of blue sky—an oddity of the lake-effect snow machine—appeared. It can be a virtual whiteout and still sunny.

Mom? Rose thought. *Are you trying to tell me something?*

She walked over to an old chest of drawers. The paint was peeling and the dresser top was crammed with a mix of Rose's past and present: high school trophies and ribbons scattered amongst bottles and bibs.

Rose's ribbons were all "honorable mention" or team manager ribbons. One trophy from the basketball team read, "Best Sixth Man," while another from FHA read, "Always Gives It Her All."

Rose opened a creaky drawer in the old chest. She rifled through a pile of baby clothes, searching for a book. She gasped when she pulled out her senior yearbook. Rose opened it and began to read what her friends had written: "To the nicest girl ever"; "You were always there for me"; "To the sweetest girl in school."

Rose flipped through the yearbook, stopping at "Senior Superlatives." There was a color picture of Rose outside, smiling while embracing the trunk of a pine tree, the sun beaming through her red hair, making it look as if it were on fire.

"Most Likely to Give a Hug When You Need It—Rose Hoffs," hers read.

Rose gave her shoulders a hopeless shrug.

What did being nice ever get me? Rose thought.

Rose dug her hand back into the drawer and pulled out another book.

Ah, here it is, she thought. The *Raggedy Ann Stories by Johnny Gruelle.*

Rose opened the book and smiled. Her mother used to read it to her when she was little. Rose turned to the preface. The yellowed page was still bent at the corner, and she hugged her doll even more tightly.

"What lessons of kindness and fortitude you might teach could you but talk . . . No wonder Rag Dolls are the best beloved! . . . The more you become torn, tattered and loose-jointed, Rag Dolls, the more you are loved by children."

Rose smiled as her daughter began to coo.

I'm a walking Raggedy Ann, she thought, looking at the little doll and then at her little girl.

Rose walked over and pulled her waking baby into her arms, and Jeri clutched at the little doll's arms, before falling asleep again almost instantaneously.

Rose took a seat in her rocker and watched Jeri sleep. A ray of light pierced the darkness and illuminated the pink cheeks of her daughter and of the doll.

Blue skies ahead, Rose thought, thinking of her mom, her Easter dress, Raggedy Ann, and how the simplest of moments are often the most beautiful.

She tenderly kissed the top of her daughter's head. *Maybe things look up when you least expect it.*

Three

R ose stopped at the entrance to River Bend Estates. An enormous
metal gate—designed with endless curlicues to make it seem friendly
rather than imposing—stopped visitors.

"It looks scary," Jeri said.

Rose looked over at her daughter. She was clutching her doll nervously.

"It's not scary, sweetie," Rose said, entering the code that had been given
to her by the owner of There's No Place Like Home, the senior care group
she had been working for part-time the last few years. "It's just like a big
version of our front door."

"Oh," Jeri said, smiling suddenly, talking to her doll. "It's not scary, Ann.
It's like our front door."

As the gates opened, Rose immediately felt as scared and unsure as her
daughter.

I need this, Rose thought, checking her appearance in the mirror. *Don't
blow it.*

River Bend Estates was located about five miles inland from Lake
Michigan and the little resort towns of Saugatuck-Douglas. The develop-
ment sat on a bluff overlooking the river and the marsh that fed the lake.

It was divided into two parts: The right half was filled with large homes, while the left side was made up of smaller attached and detached homes and townhomes, some sprawling one-stories, and some towering two-stories.

Rose looked at the directional app on her phone and turned right.

There it is! 331 River Bend.

"Wow," Jeri said, as Rose parked her car. "It's pretty! And big as a castle! I'm glad I wore my special dress."

Rose smiled at her daughter. She had opted to wear a glittery pink princess dress as good luck for her mother. "It is big," Rose agreed.

The Tices' home was a sprawling one-story, with a stunning stacked stone entrance and wide windows. An endless array of potted plants and flowers filled the grassy yard, each one holding a specific place, as if waiting patiently to go home again.

Rose took a deep breath and picked up a folder nestled in the pocket of her car door. It was filled with information and forms about the Tices.

ALS. How horrible, Rose thought.

Mr. Baker, the owner of There's No Place Like Home, told Rose he had a "gut feeling" she might be right for this.

"They need somebody young and strong," he said. "Somebody nice. They're a very sweet couple."

"They also need someone who's even-tempered but full of life. I think you're ready for this. You've been so good with our patients and other care-givers. Your initial schooling in nursing and elder care is ideal." He had more confidence in her than she had in herself.

Rose shut her eyes, and remembered the last thing Mr. Baker had told her.

"It probably won't be a very long assignment, though, I'm sad to say."

Rose unbuckled her seat belt, leaned into the backseat, and grabbed a chapter book, a box of crayons, and a coloring book and placed them on the console. She grabbed her old iPod out of the glove compartment and unwound the earbuds.

"Promise me you and Ann won't leave this car until I come back, okay?" Rose said, rolling down the windows and looking at her daughter.

"I promise," Jeri said, already grabbing the coloring book. "How long will you be gone?"

"I'll be back before you've barely even begun to listen to *Frozen*," Rose said, holding out the iPod to her daughter. "Wish me luck."

"Good luck," Jeri said, lifting up the doll's arm so her mom could give it a high-five.

From the living room window, Mattie watched a young, red-haired woman in a rusting car give a little girl and a doll that looked just like her a kiss.

What on earth, Mattie thought.

Rose got out of her car and walked down the winding brick walkway, stopping briefly to admire a few of the trees: a small birch, a redbud start, a dogwood, and a cedar sapling.

"Do you like to garden?"

Rose jumped at the sound of a man's voice.

"Sorry to surprise you," he said, coming out of the garage. "Don. Don Tice."

"Rose Hoffs. It's so nice to meet you."

Don smiled warmly at Rose.

"And I do love to garden," she continued. "Although I don't really have the time or space to do it."

"Michigan is heaven for gardeners, isn't it? Everything grows to nuclear proportions. Gardening was Mattie's passion," Don said, his smile abruptly turning into a frown upon catching his error. "*Is* her passion. I just try to keep it going for her now. It makes her happy."

Don gestured for Rose to follow, and he led her around the house and through a white gazebo into the backyard.

"My gosh. How beautiful," Rose said, her eyes scanning the distance beyond their yard at the winding river and marshes where a blue heron was high-stepping through the water looking for fish.

"It is, but it's not Hope Dunes," Don said. "That's Mattie's lake cottage. We have it for sale, and she misses it terribly. The cottage was in her family forever. She's battling some depression now because this house is new, and Mattie prefers things with a history."

Don took a seat in a pretty striped chair on the brick patio. Rose took a seat next to him, her attention diverted by a wheelchair ramp exiting the patio door, and a small ramp leading to the yard. A wooden labyrinth wound throughout the grass and gardens like a yellow brick road.

"Mattie can't stand those aluminum ramps and walkways," Don said, picking up on Rose's thoughts. "She wanted to make her disability fit into the landscape. She designed all of this, dictating it to me. That used to be her career. She was a very famous landscape designer."

Rose smiled and studied Don's face. His eyes were puffy and red, his skin sagged and was the color of concrete. It looked as if part of his freckly face had been erased. His spirit was heavy.

I can relate, Rose thought.

"What did you do?" Rose asked.

"I was an executive at Herman Miller," he said. "Furniture. Mattie and I love the beauty and importance that objects and plants hold in people's homes and lives."

Rose immediately thought of her daughter's doll.

"I agree," she said.

"I'm tired," Don said suddenly, out of the blue, his voice instantly shaky, his brown eyes gazing over the yard. "I've tried to do it all by myself. I just . . . I just can't do it all anymore."

Don stopped and looked intently at Rose. "Your firm came highly recommended from our doctor, and our insurance has approved hiring a caregiver . . . respite care . . . in-home care. I'm sorry, I don't know what the right term is."

"It's okay," Rose said.

"I need someone during the day to help me get her out of bed, bathe her, change her, help her to the bathroom, feed her, keep her company."

Don hesitated. "I just need a break. I need to go to lunch. I need to see friends. I need to go to the gym. I need to . . ."

"Breathe," Rose said. "I understand."

"I'm sorry," Don said. "It's hard. I just feel so guilty for even saying that. She doesn't qualify for hospice yet since her breathing is still fairly strong. I've gone through the file that your agency sent me. I guess I thought you'd be more experienced . . . I mean, older." His cheeks flushed.

A dog barked, and Rose turned to see a long-haired mutt—sort of like a dark version of the Shaggy D.A.—wagging not just its tail but the entire back half of its body. Mattie sat just behind the dog in a small dining area off the patio, their images distorted by the screen door.

"That's Mattie," Don said. "And that's Mabel."

"Sounds like a singing group," Rose said. "Mattie and Mabel."

Don smiled.

"Can I speak with her?" Mattie asked.

"Of course," Don said, standing up to open the door, whispering to his wife, "Remember to speak slowly."

Mabel came flying out and leaped directly into Rose's lap. She opened her arms and threw them around the dog.

"You like dogs?" Mattie asked.

Her speech was garbled, but her diction precise and eloquent. Rose had been worried about understanding her, but there was a dignified cadence to Mattie's speech, almost like an aging jazz singer whose voice had been put through a synthesizer.

"Yes," Rose said. "I had dogs growing up."

"Not now?" Mattie asked into her mic, moving the wheelchair down the ramp and onto the patio.

"No," she said.

"Follow me," Mattie said, taking her wheelchair into the backyard and along the wooden path. "See you later, Don."

"That's my cue." Don winked. "I'll check back in a few minutes. I'll either be in the laundry room or the garage."

Rose stood and followed Mattie.

"Bleeding heart," Mattie said into her mic, nodding at a beautiful plant whose stems seemed to be weeping drops of tender, beautiful pink hearts.

"It's so pretty," Rose said. "Almost heartbreakingly so, pardon the bad pun."

"Perennial," Mattie explained. "Also called lady in the bath. Hold it up . . . press the petals together."

Rose hesitated.

"Go on," she said. "I can't do it."

Rose winced.

"I'm sorry. I have to joke about it, or I'd go crazy," Mattie said, before encouraging Rose to push the petals together. "You won't hurt it. What do you see?"

Rose smiled as she pressed the tender petals together. "A white lady . . . in a rose-colored bath!"

Mattie smiled and turned her face toward the sun.

"No Place Like Home," Mattie said slowly, referring to the name of Rose's company. "Sounds so . . . magical."

"I know. A little hokey. But I loved *The Wizard of Oz*!" Rose said with the enthusiasm of a child.

Mattie shut her eyes and thoughts of the jelly-bean path her parents had created that Easter long ago popped into her head, before Mabel came running over—a wet ball in her mouth—and nestled alongside Rose's legs.

"She wants to be petted." Mattie smiled. "I fall short with that."

Rose leaned down to pet the dog and when she did, Mabel's golden eyes shined with joy.

"Tell me," Mattie said slowly, "about yourself."

"Well, I grew up here. My mom and dad were Dutch, and they ran their own little farmers' market in the area. It was in our family for generations."

"Apple Blossom Farms, right?" Mattie said, smiling. "Oh, my gosh. I bought so many things from them: corn, tomatoes, blueberries . . . I made so many wonderful family dinners."

"They're both gone now," Rose said.

"Sorry. They were lovely," Mattie replied, remembering the kind couple.

"Thank you," Rose said, her voice halting. "The farm stand is gone now, too."

"Children?" Mattie asked.

"Yes," Rose said. "I have a seven-year-old daughter, and . . ."

"A daughter?" Mattie asked, her mind finally putting the pieces of the puzzle together.

"Yes. Her name is Jeri, and . . ."

Mattie interrupted her again. "Is she in the car?"

Rose's stomach clenched, and she began to stammer. "What? . . . Car? . . . Well . . ." Rose considered fibbing, but she had always been a horrible liar. "Yes, ma'am, she is."

I just blew it, Rose thought, her head spinning, the gardens in front of her spiraling. *Not only will I lose this job, I'll lose my job with the company.*

"Ask her to join us," Mattie said, smiling. "It's okay. I love children."

"Are you sure?" Rose asked, her heart slowing. "It's just that this interview came up at the last minute. I didn't have anyone to watch her . . ."

"It's okay," Mattie said again. "Go get her."

"I apologize," Rose said with a shaky voice. "I'll be back in a moment."

As Rose rounded the backyard, a hawk circled overhead, birds chirped, and Mattie could hear the soft rush of the river in the distance—before a bloodcurdling scream shattered the silence.

"DOGGIE!"

Mattie turned her wheelchair around just in time to see a blur of pink zipping around her backyard, giggling.

"Jeri!" Rose said in a panic, trying to grab her daughter. "Keep your voice down! We're guests here. This is no way to behave!"

Jeri finally slowed down enough for Rose to grab her hand. "Mrs. Tice, this is my daughter, Jeri. Jeri, say hello to Mrs. Tice."

"Hello," Jeri said with a curtsy.

"You like dogs?" Mattie asked.

Jeri tilted her head, a look of confusion crossing her face. She looked at her mother, who repeated Mattie's question.

"I love dogs!" Jeri squealed. "But we can't have one. House is too small, like our bank account."

"Jeri!" Rose said, a horrified look coming across her face. "You're being rude."

"But you say that all the time, Mommy," Jeri said.

Mattie smiled. "I love your dress. Very pretty."

Jeri again looked at Mattie, confused, before looking up at her mother. "She said she likes your dress," Rose explained.

"Thank you," Jeri said, smiling, smoothing the silky sequined skirt, which swished with every move the little girl made. "It's good luck for my mom. She's nervous."

"Jeri," Rose admonished again, before looking at Mattie. "She had too many Pop-Tarts this morning."

Rose ducked her head and added, "I was in a hurry."

"Ah, sugar." Mattie smiled at Rose, again remembering jelly beans and chocolates. "Loved it when I was a little girl, too."

Jeri was studying Mattie closely when, suddenly, she reached out to touch her wheelchair and then her face.

"What's wrong with you?" Jeri asked Mattie innocently, tilting her head, her curls bouncing.

"I'm so sorry, Mrs. Tice!" Rose said, mortified.

"It's okay," Mattie said, looking Jeri squarely in the eyes. "I'm sick."

"I'm sorry," Jeri said, her big eyes growing wider. "I don't like to be sick."

"Me, either," Mattie said.

Jeri looked at Mattie and, without hesitation, reached in and gave her a hug. "I hope you get better real soon."

Mattie's eyes filled with tears, and she looked away. Rose walked up behind her, put her hands on her shoulders, and began to massage them.

"Mommy, can I go to the bathroom?" Jeri asked. "I . . . have to . . ."

Rose stopped and walked in front of Mattie's wheelchair. She hesitated, embarrassed by another distraction.

"Through the kitchen," Mattie said. "First door on the right."

"I understood you!" Jeri said before taking off toward the porch, Mabel following. "Don't worry. I'm a big girl," she shouted back to her mother. "I can do it all by myself."

"Jeri," Rose yelled, before her daughter turned and shot her a look of little girl independence.

That confidence and strength must have skipped a generation, Rose thought, looking at her strong-willed daughter.

"I can't apologize enough, Mrs. Tice," Rose said. "I never dreamed that . . ."

"Bet this makes you less nervous," Mattie smiled.

"Until a few seconds ago," Rose laughed.

For a second, there was silence. An iridescent blue hummingbird suddenly darted between the two.

Mom? Rose thought. *Is that you again with the blue?*

"Are you okay?" Mattie asked.

"Yes . . . no . . . I don't know. It's just that, to be honest, we really need this job. I've been working part-time at the agency, and I need full-time hours. I worked for two years before that at an assisted living facility."

"Am I your first full-time patient?"

"No," Rose said, words just spewing forth, as if she were reading a book to her daughter. "My mom died of cancer. And I was with her every single day. I did everything for her . . . everything."

Mattie looked up at Rose.

What a fragile flower, Mattie thought. *Like a bleeding heart.*

"You can never replace your mother," Rose continued.

"You can't," Mattie agreed.

Without thinking, Rose again put her hands on Mattie's shoulders and caressed them.

"Thank you," Mattie said, sighing. "That's nice."

After a few seconds, Rose began to worry. *What's taking Jeri so long?*

"I'm sorry, Mrs. Tice," Rose said. "I should go check on my daughter. Do you mind?"

"Go on," Mattie said.

Rose walked to the porch, opened the screen door, and stepped in to the breakfast nook.

"Jeri? Hello?"

Rose walked in to the kitchen, then the dining room, before she heard a muffled giggling coming from down the hall. She walked to the edge of a doorframe. Jeri was sitting on the ground, playing with a doll, Mabel laying beside her.

"What are you doing in here?" Rose asked. She looked around the room and realized the walls were filled with framed photos of the Tices.

This is their bedroom, Rose thought, alarmed.

"This isn't your house or your bedroom, young lady," Rose said. "What's gotten into you today?"

"I'm sorry, Mommy," Jeri said. "I got bored."

Rose stepped in to the bedroom to get her daughter but was caught by a framed photo of the Tices, sitting on the dresser.

Oh, my gosh, Rose thought, staring at a picture of the couple when they were young and standing on the beach, the sunset not only illuminating their tan faces but seeming to reveal their souls. They were holding glasses of wine, and Don was kissing Mattie's cheek.

She was so beautiful, so healthy, so vibrant, Rose thought, picking up the photo.

Rose lifted her eyes from the picture and finally noticed the hospital bed that filled much of the otherwise beautifully appointed room. It was equipped with electric controls and covered with a large mattress that resembled an egg carton. A hydraulic lift sat to the side of the bed, along with a small twin bed that looked as if it had never been used.

"Everything okay?"

Rose jumped at the sound of Mattie's voice, her heart racing. She was still holding the framed photo.

"I'm so sorry, Mrs. Tice," Rose said. "I found Jeri in here. I don't know what to say."

Rose braced herself, but Mattie just said, "You found my favorite photo." Mattie eased her wheelchair into the bedroom.

"Look what *I* found!" Jeri said excitedly to her, holding up a doll.

It was then Rose realized a chest at the end of Mattie's hospital bed was wide open, and many of its items were scattered across the floor.

"Jeri!" Rose said. "What did you do? This isn't your room and those aren't your belongings."

"But it was unlocked. And I found a doll just like Ann!" Jeri said. "Now she has a sister."

Mattie laughed and eased her wheelchair next to Jeri. "My doll," she said. "I forgot about her."

Mattie stared at the doll, lost for a moment. "My mom made her," she said slowly. "Her face is from an old cloth my grandma sewed. Her hair is my grandma's yarn. Homemade Raggedy Ann."

"I have one just like her!" Jeri said, standing excitedly. " 'Cept her eyes don't match."

"Is this a hope chest?" Rose asked.

Mattie nodded.

"I haven't seen one in ages," she said. "My grandma had one. She told me when I was little that *Seventeen* magazine used to have ads for these chests. I have no idea where hers went."

"My mom gave me this," said Mattie. "Was going to give it to my daughter and granddaughter."

"Do you have children?" Rose asked. "Grandchildren?"

"No," Mattie said sadly, shaking her head. "I wanted them. Very much."

"Here," Jeri said, giving Mattie the cloth doll. "Now you do."

Mattie stared into her doll's button eyes. It was one of the first items her mother had placed in her hope chest, right after they gave her the chest on Easter. Her mom had hidden it in there for her birthday, and Raggedy Ann and Mattie became instantly inseparable: The doll had accompanied Mattie to the beach, Cardinals baseball games, and tea parties. She had been her best friend, often when Mattie felt like she didn't have a friend in the world.

Mattie could feel herself hug the old doll, even though her body wouldn't follow her mind's orders.

Mattie stroked the doll's red yarn hair and little cloth face with her finger.

"Dolls always make everything better, don't they?" Jeri asked, studying Mattie's face.

"They do," Mattie replied.

"I always wished I had my grandma's hope chest," Rose said, watching Mattie smile at the old doll. "They may seem a little old-fashioned, but their purpose is even more important in an age where we seem to have lost our connection to our family, our history, each other."

Rose continued, "Most importantly, memories never die. Neither does hope."

"That's beautiful," Mattie said without thinking.

"There's so much cool stuff in here," Jeri continued, looking into the chest. "And it smells like the woods!"

The little girl's words catapulted Mattie back in time.

She thought of the day she had gotten the chest, and the "Home Sweet Home" plaque sitting somewhere inside.

Jeri pulled an old embroidered apron from the chest and tied it around her pink princess dress, before nabbing an antique teacup. She plopped on the floor and pretended to sip from the teacup, her pinkie finger extended.

"I just love tea parties, don't you, Ann?" Jeri asked the doll on Mattie's lap.

Mattie was staring at the little girl, a lost look on her face. Rose's heart dropped.

"Jeri, that's enough," Rose said. "Put Mrs. Tice's belongings back in her hope chest and apologize. I think we've caused enough commotion for the day."

"I'm sorry," Jeri said, ducking her head and taking off the apron before folding it and laying it back in the chest along with the little cup.

Mattie smiled at the girl, continuing to stroke the doll's hair with her finger.

"No. It's nice to see it being used again," Mattie said, thinking to herself, *I'm glad there's no attic in this house. And I'm glad I didn't lock it back up again.*

"What's going on in here?"

Don's voice startled the group. Rose looked at Mattie—a look of horror etched on her face—seeking guidance.

"This is Rose's daughter, Jeri," Mattie said sweetly.

"She was waiting out in the car," Rose explained, her words coming out in a rush, "and your wife was kind enough to invite her in."

Rose halted. "Though not into your bedroom."

Don laughed. "I miss everything folding laundry."

He looked at Jeri and gave her a big wave. "We love children," Don said. "Just weren't blessed to have any of our own."

Don walked over and kissed his wife gently on the cheek. Rose looked down at the photo she was still holding.

"I like to kiss my wife, I guess," Don said shyly, nodding at the photo.

"We really didn't mean to snoop," Rose said, setting the picture back on top of the dresser. "Are there any more questions you have of me before we get out of your hair?"

Mattie and Don looked at each other, as if they were reading one another's minds.

"When can you start?" Mattie asked.

"What?" Rose asked, her voice squeaking with excitement. "Are you sure?"

"Are you?" Don asked.

"Yes!" Rose said, giving a little jump.

"Does this mean we got the job?" Jeri asked her mom, a quizzical look etched on her face. "The inner-blue went okay?"

"I think so," Rose said.

"Yeah! I'm glad I wore my lucky dress, then," Jeri said, before turning in a circle to make it twirl.

"I'll call the agency," Don said. "We'll set up a training period and start date."

"Next week would work well," Rose said. "I need to line up somebody to watch Jeri."

"She's welcome any time," Mattie said.

"Yeah!" Jeri yelled again. "How 'bout tomorrow? It's summer vacation!"

The Tices laughed.

"You know," Jeri continued, frowning, her eyes sad, "I don't have any family."

Silence engulfed the bedroom. For a long beat, no one said a word, until Mattie finally filled the gap.

"Hope is only one short letter from home," she said very slowly, her eyes closed, emphasizing each word to ensure Jeri could understand her. "Remember, hope is something you carry with you forever . . . Look inside when you need hope most, and it will guide you, and remind you of what was and what is to be."

When Mattie opened her eyes, they were filled with tears.

"Honey, are you okay?" Don asked.

Mattie nodded.

"Now that was beautiful," Rose said.

"Nice to meet you, Rose," Mattie said. "See you soon, Jeri."

"Want me to put your doll away now?" Jeri asked her.

"Think I'll hang on to her," Mattie said.

From the front window, Mattie watched Rose and Jeri head to the car, skipping the last part of the way.

Afterward, Mattie returned to her bedroom and stopped her wheelchair in front of her hope chest. She stared at it for the longest time, a smile crossing her face.

Maybe that's why I kept you all these years, Mattie thought.

part two

The Beach Glass Pendant

Four

June 2016

W e have to stop meeting like this."
    Don awoke and saw his wife looking at him, a sad, soft smile etched on her face.

"I can't sleep without you," he said, yawning.

He sat up in Mattie's hospital bed.

"I mean it," she said. "You're not resting."

Don smoothed her hair. He could literally count on two hands the number of times the pair had not slept together during their marriage. Even when Mattie's legs thrashed before her diagnosis, even when she was hospitalized, Don would crawl into bed with her. He had to be near her, beside her. He could not breathe without her. And as they approached their fiftieth wedding anniversary, Don refused to spend even one night apart from his wife.

How many nights together do we have left? Don thought, reaching for his wife's hand, his fingers unconsciously rubbing her wedding ring.

"For better or worse," Don said.

"This is the 'for worse' part," Mattie replied.

"What do you want for your fiftieth wedding anniversary?" Don asked.

The windows were cracked, and Mattie laid her head back on the inclined mattress and neck pillow and looked out at the row of tall pines swaying in the breeze, just enough sun glinting through the overcast day to make the marsh appear golden and glimmering.

Mattie then looked deeply at her husband but didn't say a word.

Don bit the inside of his cheek, hard, and smiled at her, willing the lump in his throat to retreat.

"And if I ever lost you, how much would I cry?" Don began softly and tenderly, singing the lyrics from their wedding song.

"Don," Mattie said. "Please."

"How deep is the ocean . . . " he continued.

"My beautiful husband," Mattie said, tears filling her eyes. "What am I going to do with you?"

What am I going to do without you? Don thought.

"Okay, let's get you up and ready for the day," he said instead.

Don eased out of bed and walked around to elevate his wife's side, lifted her to the edge of the mattress, and attached the sling around her top half before attaching it to the hydraulic lift.

"Lift off," he said.

Don helped Mattie settle onto the portable toilet, then cleaned and washed her before dressing her and relocating her to the wheelchair for the day.

When she was ready, nearly an hour later, he kissed her cheek and then reached into his pajama pocket.

"Surprise!" he said. "I found this last night before I crawled in bed with you."

He pulled out a beautiful beach glass pendant and held it in front of his wife's face.

"I didn't mean to snoop," he said, "but I saw it glimmer when Jeri was playing in your hope chest. I knew what it was immediately."

"Oh, Don," Mattie said. "I'd forgotten about this. How could I have?"

"You've had a few things on your mind lately," he said. "Consider it a pre–fiftieth anniversary gift. Even the chain is gold. I think it's meant to be that we found your old hope chest. I wouldn't have found this."

Don carefully attached the necklace around his wife's neck and gave her a kiss. "Remember?" he asked.

"How could I forget?" she replied.

"You're still just as beautiful as that young girl."

Five

June 1962

"My veil! It's still in the car!"

"I'll get it. Don't worry."

Two voices—one panicked, one calm—drifted through an open window of the Stone Chapel, a gorgeous old church on the Drury College campus in Springfield, Missouri.

To Don, the rocky church seemed to rise from the ground toward heaven like the beautiful bluffs that hovered over much of the Ozarks.

A pretty, petite blonde in a yellow bridesmaid dress tied with an electric blue sash came flitting out of the church and down its stony steps as elegantly and weightlessly as if she were a monarch butterfly.

Don's heart jumped.

Madeline Barnhart! he knew immediately.

Don watched as she floated into the parking lot to retrieve the veil. As she was closing the giant trunk on a red, two-door, bubble top Chevy Impala, a boom of thunder rolled overhead. She began to sprint back toward the church, but she couldn't outrun the heavy, wet raindrops.

"My hair! My dress! My makeup!" she yelled, running with the veil. "Of course! Perfect timing!"

Suddenly, she heard a whoosh, and an umbrella—as magical as any owned by Mary Poppins—appeared over her head, shielding her from the rain.

"At your service," said a muddied young man, bowing.

"Thank you," she replied, taken aback.

"You're Madeline, right? Madeline Barnhart?"

"Mattie. Yes," she replied. "I'm sorry. You are . . . ?"

"Don Tice," he said. "I've seen you in Advanced Lit. I sit in the back. *Way* in the back."

Mattie chuckled. "I'm sorry I didn't recognize you. I don't have my binoculars today. What are you doing here?"

She was about to ask if he were attending the wedding, but she looked at his dirty work pants, his stained T-shirt, and muddy, gloved hands, and thought otherwise.

"No, I'm not attending," he said and laughed, reading her mind. "I do work study for the grounds crew at Drury. Helps pay my tuition." He stopped. "And I really love it."

Don walked Mattie to the steps of the chapel. When she was safely in the stone entryway, he lowered the umbrella in a single, swift move.

"I asked if I could spruce up the chapel's grounds before the wedding," Don said, his deep voice echoing in the entryway, giving Mattie the feeling they already shared a common history. "I need the extra money. And," he added shyly, "I'm a little bit of a romantic."

Don suddenly shot down the stony steps in a single bound and beelined to a wheelbarrow. When he turned, he was holding a lovely, delicate bunch of bright blue flowers.

"I asked about the colors of the wedding," he said. "This is called love-in-the-mist. I just thought, you know, that it was perfect, in color and name."

Mattie caught her breath, and the veil shook in her hands, the lace tickling her arms.

"I love flowers, too," Mattie said. "My father and I garden all the time in St. Louis and at our summer cottage in Michigan."

"I just thought these would match your dress and your necklace," Don said, ducking his head. "It's beautiful."

Mattie gently touched the small pendant dangling on a delicate gold chain. "It's beach glass," Mattie said. "My parents and I look for it on the beach in Michigan. It's like a treasure hunt. This blue color is very hard to find."

Mattie stopped and lifted the pendant, smiling as she felt its smoothness. "This probably started as a discarded bottle, and, over decades, the waves of Lake Michigan polished and smoothed it, and turned it this beautiful color. My dad and I found this piece right after he bought the cottage in Saugatuck, and my mom made it into this necklace and put it into my hope chest. She made me promise I wouldn't wear it until I got married. You know . . . something old, something new, something borrowed, something blue. This would be the blue part."

Mattie laughed and looked into Don's eyes. "She would kill me if she knew I was wearing it right now, but I couldn't resist. It's my best friend's wedding! And this beach glass reminds me of my parents. My dad says you have to search long and hard to find love—just like beach glass—but sometimes finding it is as easy as simply being aware of what's right in front of you, keeping your eyes open during the search. Because—*boom!*—like beach glass, it will be right there."

Don's face turned crimson.

"That's a lovely story," he said. "And I won't tell your mom . . . I mean, if I were ever to meet her."

Mattie smiled. "You'd love my parents. My dad also polishes stones he finds on Lake Michigan. He jokes they're like people: Sometimes you have to work real hard to see the beauty that's inside."

"You're something else," Don said without thinking.

This time, Mattie blushed.

"Did you have a good semester?" Mattie asked. "What are you studying?"

"I did. And I'm studying business," Don said. "But I love art, too. I hope there's some way to integrate the two. How about you?"

"I had a great year. I can't wait to be a senior!" Mattie said. "And I'm studying architecture, but not for homes. For gardens."

"Really?" Don asked. "Wow."

"Everyone seems to think it's a silly pursuit, but I think it will be a big business one day. I think women can do anything!"

Don leaned toward Mattie. "They can," he said. "And beauty is *never* silly. Art is never silly." He stopped. "It's what makes us aspire to be better people."

Mattie felt wobbly on her feet, and she took a small step back.

"MATTIE! WHERE ARE YOU?" suddenly came from inside the church.

"I think someone's looking for me," she said. "I best go."

"Yes, you better go help her finish getting ready," Don said. "Only a few hours until 'I do.'"

Mattie smiled at Don's Ozarks accent. "Ready" came out in three syllables: "re-uh-dee."

Mattie began to turn but stopped, fidgeting with the veil and whispering, "You know, I'm supposed to be the maid of honor, but I feel like the word 'honor' has been dropped from the title."

Don laughed, and as Mattie turned to leave again, he suddenly said, "You're as pretty as your pendant."

The two looked into each other's eyes, before Mattie ducked her head.

"That's so sweet," she said. "Thank you."

Mattie looked at Don and smiled, before again turning to head inside the chapel.

"Oh, here. Don't forget these," Don said, handing her the small bouquet of love-in-the-mist.

Mattie blushed again, took the flowers, and dashed back inside the chapel. But once inside, she hesitated and then stopped for a moment longer before making her way over to the ornate oval window that overlooked the grounds.

She peeked and saw Don kneel to the earth and begin to plant.

He's not like the St. Louis prep school boys I've always dated, she thought. *He's genuine, driven to make something of himself.*

She squinted her eyes and stared at Don. *And he's cute, in a sort of wholesome Andy Griffith way,* she thought, looking at the freckled, sandy-haired young man with his hands in the dirt.

Mattie instinctively felt for her necklace. *Why didn't I notice him until now?*

For a second, Mattie's heart stopped, and then she scurried off.

Don didn't let on, but he saw Mattie sneak one last glance at him. His heart had stopped, too.

Is she my beach glass? he wondered.

Four years later, they were married, and Mattie wore "something blue."

Six

G o," Rose told Don soon after she'd arrived later that morning. "Go get a coffee. Go for a run. Go to the gym. Go do something. It's okay."

Don looked over at his wife.

"Go," Mattie said.

Don put on some workout clothes and a brave face as he pulled out of River Bend Estates, smiling and waving goodbye at his wife, but his mood was as grey as the cloudy, cool June Michigan morning. He was overcome with guilt leaving Mattie for the first time in years.

Maybe I do just need a good workout to clear my head, Don thought. *But maybe my head needs coffee first.*

He drove into downtown Saugatuck. The sidewalks and streets were already glutted with early morning runners and dog walkers, and all the shop owners were propping open their doors, raising their blinds, and putting out colorful welcome flags on their brightly painted storefronts.

People nodded at Don as he drove by in his vintage T-bird. He had rarely taken the car out since Mattie had been diagnosed with ALS. There was no room for her wheelchair.

She used to love this car as much as me, he thought. *The sunshine shining on my sunshine,* he recalled saying to her as they sped down Blue Star Highway past all the farmers' markets, antique shops, ice cream stands, and restaurants.

Mattie had asked Don to sell their beloved Chris-Craft when she could no longer get onboard with a cane and after being knocked to the floor of the small boat numerous times while attempting to board it. Even with assistance, the rocky waves were just too much for Mattie to handle, and she knew she was one fall away from being even more incapacitated. She was also embarrassed. Mattie couldn't move on the boat, or help out, as she always used to do.

"It haunts me sitting there at the dock," she told Don one perfect July day, as the vintage wood boat bobbed on the waves in the marina, its hull gleaming in the sun, its American flag flapping in the breeze. "No more sunset cruises. No more champagne with friends. No more jumping into the lake. No more kissing you at the end of the dock. It's a reminder of everything I can't do anymore."

It nearly killed Don to sell the boat—which the couple had bought, restored, and christened *Flower Power* after Mattie's business had boomed—but he couldn't part with his beloved bird.

Despite the chill in the air, the top was down on his turquoise T-bird, while classical music rolled in waves out of the convertible's speakers, as if an entire symphony were riding shotgun with him.

The lake air feels good, Don thought, inhaling, the smell of the lake filling his lungs. *Makes me feel alive.*

Don rounded the corner to Water Street and pulled into an open spot on the town's main street, which paralleled the channel that fed Lake Michigan. He sat for a moment staring at the town's boardwalk and the water, at all the people strolling along with muffins, jogging, or taking their boats out for an early ride on the lake.

We take all of this for granted, he thought. *A simple walk. A day out. Our health.*

"Where's the rock music, man? Zep? The Stones? Pink Floyd?"

Don looked up to see Vinnie DeMuccio, the hippie turned Wall Street exec turned owner of Lake Effect Coffee.

"Classical music? In this car? Hell, I'll even take the Eagles over Shakespeare."

"You know me, Vin," Don smiled, crawling out of the low-slung car. "I'm pure class."

Vinnie chuckled and pulled Don in for a bear hug.

"And it was Vivaldi, not Shakespeare," Don teased.

"It's good to see you again, man. Really."

Vinnie shook Don's shoulders, causing the coffeehouse owner's long, thinning, greying hair to shimmy like a grass skirt on a hula dancer. Vinnie opened his mouth to say something, but he froze, a painful expression etched on his face.

"So good to see you," Vinnie repeated, shaking his head.

Don could tell Vinnie wanted to ask about Mattie, but everyone was always uncomfortable doing so.

People will ask me about anything, Don thought. *My dog. My car. My art. My last doctor's appointment. Everything except my sick wife.*

"Coffee on the house!" Vinnie said, breaking the silence. "Isn't it good to have connections?"

Vinnie walked up the steps of Lake Effect, where a line of java seekers wound out the old doors, down the stairs, and on to the sidewalk. Don was always a little uncomfortable when Vinnie did this, but it was better than waiting forty-five minutes and, to be honest, the shop likely wouldn't be here today without Don and his wife.

"Every resort town needs a great bookstore, a good coffee shop, a terrific restaurant, and a knowledgeable nursery," Mattie had said decades ago, at a time when the town had gone through a period of economic decline.

Mattie and Don had backed them all, at one time or another, and Mattie's career alone kept the nursery booming.

"Toffee latte?" Vinnie asked, as if he didn't know.

Lake Effect had the best toffee lattes in the world, Don firmly believed, largely because they made their own toffee and roasted their own beans.

"Extra shot, skim?" Vinnie continued. "Whip?"

Don winked and gave Vinnie a confident nod that lied, "I'm okay."

Don took his latte and sipped it in the back garden only the locals knew existed behind the coffee shop. The tiny garden held maybe five tables, and was surrounded by pots filled with blooming zinnias and begonias as well as fresh herbs, which the coffee shop used in their savory scones, soups, and egg bakes.

This used to be Mattie's favorite spot in the world, next to Hope Dunes, Don thought, sipping his latte. *I wish she were with me right now.*

A friend once accused Don and Mattie of being codependent, implying that was so because they had never had children. Don had scoffed at the friend—now *former* friend—and said, referencing his college lit classes, "'Co' means together, mutual, partnership, equality. To complement."

He had stopped before proudly telling the friend, "Then I guess I'm willfully and blissfully codependent, and always will be. Love *is* being dependent on another, in life and spirit. That's a rare blessing, isn't it?"

Don left Lake Effect and began to head to the gym, but as he drove along the water, the memory of Hope Dunes called him to the lakeshore like a siren.

Don parked at the public beach a few blocks from their former cottage. The lot was empty on this chilly, overcast day.

I'll have the beach all to myself, Don thought happily, pulling a St. Louis Cardinals hoodie over his workout shirt and looking out at the lake below. He put the top up on his T-bird before taking the steep, winding, warped wooden steps down to the beach, stopping at a landing along the way that looked out at one of his favorite vistas. The lake was barely visible through the limbs of two old aspen trees. Their leaves whispered in the wind. To Don, the view captured what he loved most about the Michigan lakeshore: It was unspoiled, breathtaking, alive, colorful. Today, the lake was steel grey and green, the churlish waves white, the sand golden, the sky like concrete, while on the horizon there was a clearing line of . . .

Beach glass blue, Don thought.

Don walked down the last flight of steps and headed toward the shoreline. His presence startled a group of white seagulls whose feathers were being ruffled by the stiffening breeze.

"Sorry, fellas," he said, as the wind whipped the grey hair around his head.

Lightning flashed in the distance—a magical strobe light over the lake—and Don realized a storm was brewing. He could hear no boom of thunder yet, so he knew: *I still have time.*

He immediately began to scan the beach for rocks. Mattie's love of gardening came from her father, and so did Don's love of rock collecting.

Equal parts patience and inspiration, Joe used to tell Don as they searched for stones to cut and polish. *Like fishing, but better.*

Don felt it was an honor to carry on the craft from Joe, a man he had come to love deeply, and the cottage's fireplaces were made of the stones he and Joe had collected. Don had loved Joe and Mary Ellen as much as his own parents, and he missed them in his life.

They blessed us with their home, their hopes and dreams, Don thought. *Why couldn't we have blessed them with a grandchild?*

Lightning flashed over the lake, followed by a boom of thunder, which echoed and reverberated like a bass drum over the water, a sound that made Don feel as if he were listening to great classical music in an auditorium with perfect acoustics.

This water, this lake, is my heaven, Don thought, *like Mattie's gardens are to her. The earth centers us both.*

Don stopped and looked out over the churning waters. A layer of fog—eerie and ghostly—was beginning to roll in off the lake.

Ghosts, Don thought. *They're everywhere.*

He was staring at the water when he saw a flash of blue. At first, he thought it was a fish. Don searched the surf, waiting for a wave to pass, when he saw it again.

Without thinking, Don removed his socks and shoes and tossed them onto the beach, before taking a few steps into the freezing lake, which just eight weeks ago still had chunks of ice in it. He bent down, and this time he saw it wasn't a fish: A large piece of blue-green beach glass—almost the same size as Mattie's pendant—tumbled in the waves and the sand. Don's heart leapt.

A miracle, he thought. *The perfect anniversary gift! How lucky am I?*

Don waded a bit farther, his workout pants getting soaked, and reached into the water to grab the beach glass, but it floated away quickly, slyly, as if to tease Don.

"I'm going to get you!" Don told the glass.

He leaned down again, just as thunder clapped in the distance and an unexpectedly large wave whipped up by the growing wind hit Don and sent him tumbling into Lake Michigan.

He yelped underwater, shivering.

There you are, he thought, opening his eyes to find the piece of beach glass still bobbing just beyond his grip.

He came up for air, gasping.

What the hell, Don thought. *I'm already wet.*

He dunked back down into the water. Eyes open, Don found the beach glass, swam forward, dove, and grabbed a healthy dose of sand. He came up for air, coughing up cold water.

"Brrrr!" Don yelled, opening his hand, a fistful of wet sand falling out in a big clump.

The beach glass was not in his palm. He pawed through the sand.

"No!" Don yelled, before searching the waters again. "No! It's gone."

Thunder clapped, and, in the near distance, Don could see a curtain of rain quickly approaching with the fog. Lightning flashed over the water.

Don trudged back through the water, grabbed his shoes and socks, and began to run along the beach, toward the steps, the parking lot, and his car.

He made his way barefoot up the winding, wooden steps to the road, and when he reached the top, he was winded, wet, sandy.

Suddenly, the storm was on top of him, and torrents of rain pushed down over his body. Don jumped into his convertible, dripping, and slammed the door, turned on the engine, and cranked the heat.

Don drove down Lake Shore Drive to check on their old cottage. The tiny two-lane road that sat on a bluff overlooking Lake Michigan was dark and empty, just like Hope Dunes.

Don stopped on the side of the road and stared at the shake-shingled cottage in the rain. Suddenly, lights clicked on in the home.

Only gone a few weeks and somebody is already looking at it? Don thought.

He turned off the car, his wipers stopping in the middle of his windshield, and killed the engine and the lights, watching like a cat burglar as figures moved around the cottage.

Our cottage, Don thought.

He squinted and, through the rain, could make out their realtor and a couple walk into the kitchen, before heading up the stairs. Don stared, moving closer to the glass, until his face was against it and his breath fogged the window. He wiped it and continued to watch.

A few minutes later, the lights went out and headlights appeared. Don slinked down in the driver's seat, until his face was near the steering wheel. When he heard tires on gravel, he lifted his head and peeked out.

An older couple, about Don's and Mattie's ages, laughing, sipping coffees, drove by, followed by the realtor.

It's not fair, he thought. *It's not fair.*

Don sat in his T-bird, the rain smacking hard against the top of his convertible. He could feel Hope Dunes calling, clearly hear Mattie's and Joe's voices saying the same thing:

You have to search long and hard to find love—just like beach glass—but sometimes finding it is as easy as simply being aware of what's right in front of you, keeping your eyes open . . . because—boom!—like beach glass, it will be right there.

Don looked at the "For Sale" sign at the edge of the driveway.

Will Mattie even be here for our fiftieth wedding anniversary? Don wondered.

Suddenly, Don threw open the car door and stepped out into the rain. He stood in the middle of Lake Shore Drive watching little rivers run across it and then off the edge of the bluff.

Don looked out over the lake and remembered the beach glass that had eluded him.

Everything is slipping away, he thought, before amending that: *No, Don, she's slipping away.*

Don remembered all the ALS grief counselors and therapists he had seen the past few years. All had told him it was necessary to cry, to release the emotion that had been building since his wife's diagnosis, but he'd never been able to do that—*I have to remain as strong as my wife*—until this very moment.

Don lifted his head and screamed into the thunder. Tears fell down his cheeks and were absolved by the rain.

"It's not fair, God," he yelled to the heavens, his face toward the sad sky. "Help me! Please help me! I can't live without her!"

Then Don got back into his car, took a deep breath, and prayed for something, *anything*, before returning home to the woman he loved more than his own life.

part three

The Desert Rose Dishes

Seven

June 2016

Rose placed two bananas, a cantaloupe, and a red colander filled with even redder strawberries in the center of the big butcher's block of the Tice kitchen. She began to carefully chop the bananas and berries into nearly microscopic pieces.

Mattie sidled her wheelchair up next to the island—Mabel following closely behind her—and watched Rose slice and dice. Mattie knew why she was cutting things so carefully, but she smiled at Rose, keeping her thoughts to herself.

I hate feeling like a child, she thought. *A choking hazard. A danger. A burden.*

"Where's Jeri?" Mattie asked instead.

"With one of her friends," Rose said. "They're watching *Frozen*. Again. For the hundredth time."

Mattie smiled. "*Let it go*," she tried to sing.

"I wish she would," Rose said. "I actually have nightmares about that song now."

Rose turned to the stove and checked the boiling pot. She measured out some oats and added them to the water.

"How do you like your oatmeal?" she asked.

"On someone else's plate," Mattie said.

Rose smiled while paying close attention to the simmering oatmeal and the words Mattie was saying.

Plates, Rose thought, thinking of what Mattie had just said and pulling the oatmeal off the burner.

Rose turned to scan the kitchen cupboards. A piece of masking tape adhered to a lower cabinet caught her eye. She bent down. The words "Mattie's Dishes" had been scribbled onto it with a Magic Marker.

Don had specified that Rose use these dishes for Mattie.

"She still prides herself on trying to feed herself every day," Don had told Rose during her training. "She broke a dozen dishes before I turned to plastic."

"Just be prepared," he'd continued, sadness tingeing his voice. "It's like watching a helicopter propeller trying to eat. And be prepared to help if she chokes."

Rose kneeled and rotated the lazy Susan in the cabinet, before plucking a small plastic coffee cup from a small stack and a large sippy cup with a seal top and long plastic straw that was lying on its side. She turned the lazy Susan again and found on the other side a stack of plastic plates with rounded edges split into four compartments, much like a TV dinner tray.

These are exactly like the plates Jeri eats her lunch off of at school, Rose thought.

"Skim? Half-and-half?" Rose asked Mattie, opening the refrigerator.

"Half-and-half," Mattie said. "Cinnamon. Brown sugar."

Rose looked at Mattie, confused.

"Cin-na-mon," Mattie said slowly. "Buh-rown sug-ur."

"Sorry," Rose said, scooping some oatmeal into the largest section of the plastic plate, before adding some strawberries, melon, and bananas into the three smaller compartments.

"Didn't know if you liked things to touch," Rose added, showing Mattie her plate, as if to make her efforts look intentional.

"I'm a gardener," Mattie said. "Okay for things to touch."

Rose attached a tray to Mattie's wheelchair and set the plate on it, along with utensils and the cups.

Mattie took a deep breath as if she were steeling herself for the war ahead.

Rose had read much about ALS patients before starting this job. Eating was a challenge, as patients experienced fatigue when doing so, due to the difficulty in chewing. Muscle weakening for chewing and swallowing led to patients not wanting to eat, which led to poor nutrition, weight loss, and . . . Rose's heart dropped.

A feeding tube, Rose thought, remembering what she had read.

"Here we go," Mattie said. "Choo-choo!"

She shakily filled a spoon with oatmeal and tried to bring it to her mouth, her arm flinching and shaking, as if a drunken crane operator were trying to do it for her. Rose fought every motherly instinct in her body against rushing over and doing it for Mattie.

After a few long, agonizing seconds, the spoon made its way into Mattie's mouth, where she slowly gummed the tiny glob of oatmeal until it was nearly nonexistent before lowering her head a few inches to the giant straw for a long sip of water.

"You should see me with soup," she tried to joke, before looking down at Mabel. "She never used to beg. Knows an easy target."

Mattie forked a piece of banana and followed the same process. "Sorry, Mabel. Nothing fun."

After a while, Rose couldn't help sneaking a peek at the ornate grandfather clock that stood in the living room.

In the past ten minutes, she's eaten maybe five bites, Rose thought.

"Life gets in the way of living, doesn't it?" Mattie suddenly asked, as if she were reading Rose's mind.

Rose nodded.

Mattie took a sip of coffee from her plastic cup, sloshing some of the dark liquid onto her front and down her sleeve. "Mmm. You make a nice cup."

"I live right by Lake Effect Coffee," Rose said. "You can't make a bad cup of their coffee."

Mattie beamed. "Owner is a good friend. I loved to sit in their garden and sketch."

Mattie stopped. "I miss that. My routine."

"You can still have a routine," Rose said hopefully. "Go to the places you love."

Mattie shot Rose a look sharper than the knife she'd just used to cut up breakfast.

"I can?" she asked. "And navigate crowded sidewalks? And try to go up and down stairs? And have a cup of coffee without people staring? Or a nice dinner? Try on clothes perhaps, or sketch outside? Go to a public restroom? Repeat everything ten times so someone can understand like I'm doing now?" Mattie coughed and took a deep breath. "Not to mention this wheelchair is the size of a smart car."

Rose winced and Mattie softened, before continuing, slowly. "Sorry." She took a deep breath. "You know, ALS only attacks motor neurons, so my senses aren't affected. Unbelievable. That's why I miss plants, food, . . . life."

Mattie took another slow, unsteady sip of coffee.

"That's how all this started," Mattie said with a sad expression, her eyes fixed on a cardinal in a pine tree out the kitchen window. "Just lifting a coffee cup."

Mattie watched as the redbird chirped on the green limb. "Just thought I was tired."

Mattie picked up her spoon and knocked at her plate as if she were trying to shoo away a snake.

"I hate plastic," she said. "It's . . . just so . . ."

"Not special?" Rose asked.

"Disposable," Mattie said. "Ordinary. No elegance in my life anymore. Sweats and sippy cups."

She looked at her plastic cup and shook her head. "My favorite dishes were desert rose . . . like the cup Jeri was playing with."

Mattie stopped. "Rose. Like your name. Coincidence?"

Rose smiled at her, and patted her lap. Mabel jumped into it and curled up without hesitation.

"Loved those dishes," Mattie said, smiling. "My mom put them in my hope chest."

Mattie stopped and felt for the beach glass around her neck.

She lifted the plastic cup and looked out the window at the cardinal in the tree. "The pink and soft green are so pretty together," she said, as if in a trance.

Eight

June 1972

"How do you want your steak?"

Mattie rolled her eyes at her father's question, a gesture that was instantly mirrored by her mother.

It was an old joke.

If Joe Barnhart asked how you wanted your steaks grilled and you replied anything other than medium rare, he'd still cook them leaving the center pink and juicy, if not overly red. He had pulled this trick on Don before, but he still fell for it every time, especially after a beer.

"Medium well," Don yelled through an open window down to Joe where he was barbecuing on the back deck of Hope Dunes.

Mattie and Mary Ellen smiled at each other—holding their fingers over their mouths to keep quiet. Don obviously hadn't been fully indoctrinated into Joe's grilling game.

"Did you say medium rare?" Joe asked.

"Medium well!"

"Okay then," Joe replied. "Medium rare it is!"

Mother and daughter dissolved into a fit of giggles, which drifted off the screened porch.

"I could take a nap," Mattie said softly a few seconds later, as she rocked on a barn red glider alongside her mother, sounds of boat motors and laughing children drifting along the lake breeze and onto the screened porch, along with the smell of charcoal.

"Sun will do that to you," Mary Ellen said. "This is heaven, isn't it?"

It had been a perfect summer day: eighty degrees, puffy white clouds bouncing overhead, and the water as flat as glass. Mary Ellen and Mattie had sunned on the beach and helped a neighbor's boy build a sand castle as "tall as the Gateway Arch," which had recently been completed in St. Louis and whose design fascinated everyone in the Midwest.

Joe and Don had searched the shore for stones, before taking everyone out on the old pontoon boat.

"Hey, Mom?" Mattie said. "I'm going to take a shower, clean up, and then get dinner started. You stay here and rest, okay?"

"That won't be a problem." Mary Ellen winked, before plucking a Kleenex from her sleeve to dab at her daughter's chin. "You have a little Grape Nehi right . . . there . . . that a shower just won't get off."

"You always have one on the ready, don't you?" Mattie laughed.

"A Kleenex is a woman's best friend," Mary Ellen said, chuckling. "Next to lipstick."

Mattie smiled and sat for a second more, before sneaking a look back at her mom, who was already beginning to nod off. Mattie stood, careful not to shake the glider, before sneaking off to the kitchen as Cher's "Gypsies, Tramps & Thieves" softly poured through the old radio on the deck, the music dying every few seconds as the reception faded in and out.

Mattie turned on the oven, then pulled a covered bowl out of the refrigerator. She had made cookies earlier when she told everyone she would bring a picnic basket down to the beach for lunch. Mattie placed scoops of dough onto a baking sheet and then slid them into the oven, before putting a kettle of water on the stove to boil.

While she waited, Mattie put another pot of water on the stove to boil for later, and then quickly shucked her father's favorite corn on the cob, "peaches and cream," which he purchased from Apple Blossom Farms. She nabbed a few plump ripe tomatoes, some green onions, some crisp radishes, and a few bell peppers and tossed them all into a colander to rinse, before chopping them up and adding them to the salad.

She peeked out the kitchen window at her father, who was beginning to spread the charcoals into the bottom of the grill and place the foiled potatoes on top.

"How much longer?" Mattie called to her father.

"A while," he said, sipping a Budweiser. "Coals still aren't hot enough. Maybe this beer's cooling them off too much."

Mattie laughed. "Take your time," she said, but thought to herself, *Pick up the pace.*

Mattie scurried into the dining room and eyed the empty dining room table.

This has to be perfect, she thought. *Just like this place. Just like this day.*

Mattie's eyes drifted out the double windows, which she had cranked wide open to let in some air and the stunning vista of the Lake Michigan shoreline. She walked over, scanning her gardens, which were in full bloom, the lake gleaming in the distance, and inhaled: The scent of cedar greeted her.

Yes, she thought, smiling at the tree she had planted long ago with her father. *You already know what I'm thinking.*

Mattie opened an antique buffet and scanned the linens, before selecting a white tablecloth. The square center and bottom edges were embroidered with pink and red flowers, a trail of green vine underlining them.

Perfect, she thought.

She nabbed some scissors and headed barefoot out the kitchen door to her gardens, where she cut some fragrant, puffy pink and white peonies. She zipped inside and slipped the heavenly smelling flowers into a beautiful McCoy vase and set it onto the center of the table.

Mattie stopped and listened.

All still quiet, she thought. *Hurry!*

Mattie ran all the way upstairs to the attic and moved the quilt that was covering her secret bounty. She opened the lid to her hope chest, which she had relocated to the cottage years earlier, after she and Don had married.

It belongs in this house, Mattie thought. She took a seat on her knees and rubbed her hand over the front of her hope chest, feeling the flowers her father had carved into it decades earlier. *My history. My family. My hopes and dreams.*

Up and down the stairs she went, as quietly as a mouse, slowing with each and every *clink* or *rattle*. By the fourth trip, however, Mattie was winded. She stopped and felt her stomach, until her breathing had slowed.

Mattie ran into the kitchen, pulled the cookies out of the oven just before the timer buzzed, and turned off the kettle just before it whistled. Up to the attic, she went once again.

Mattie caught her breath and then casually walked onto the screened porch and gently roused her napping mother. "Mom," she said, shaking her, making the glider move. "I need your help with dinner. Do you mind?"

"What on earth?" Mary Ellen asked, her suspicion growing as her daughter took her hand and led her to the attic instead of the kitchen.

The attic was filled with boxes and old furniture, but a pretty little silver tray sat perched in the middle of a hook rug on the floor in front of the hope chest. The tray held four cups of tea and a plate of cookies, and Raggedy Ann was already occupying a place of honor at one end.

"I thought we'd have a tea party," Mattie said, "just like we did when I was a little girl."

She continued, "Except, I made real tea this time."

Mary Ellen looked at her daughter with a quizzical expression. "Are you sure it's tea?" she laughed. "What's going on?"

"Have a seat," Mattie said, sitting on the floor, crossing her legs in front of her and lifting her cup of tea.

"Oh, my goodness," Mary Ellen said, taking a seat between her daughter and the doll. "Raggedy Ann? After all these years? Oh, and desert rose dishes! How sweet."

"Have a cookie," Mattie said. "Chocolate chip."

Mary Ellen took a bite of the warm cookie, chocolate sticking to her lips. She pulled a Kleenex from her sleeve and wiped her mouth.

"Where did you get these plate settings?" she asked.

"From you, remember?" Mattie asked.

Mary Ellen smiled. "Oh, my goodness. That was so long ago."

She looked around the attic, before her eyes finally locked in on the extra place setting. "Why are there four cups of tea?" Mary Ellen asked.

Mattie burst into tears. "I'm pregnant," she announced.

"Oh, honey!" her mother yelled, reaching over to hug her. "Congratulations! I knew something was up."

"And, Mom, I just have this feeling it's a girl," Mattie said. "I wanted to get all of this out of my hope chest as good luck. It's what I've dreamed of all these years. My own family. My own daughter. Now I can pass on these traditions."

Mary Ellen held her daughter, alternating between laughing and crying. "I'm so excited I don't know what to do."

"Steaks are ready!" Joe yelled. "Where is everyone?"

"Let's go tell Daddy," Mattie said. "Don has been itching to tell him all weekend."

Everyone came into the dining room at the same moment.

"Oh, honey," Mary Ellen gasped when she saw the table filled with a full setting of desert rose dishes. "Didn't I only give you a few starter pieces? Where did you get all these?"

"I just bought them," Mattie said. "I always told myself that when I had a family, I would have the full set."

"And now it's time," Mary Ellen said excitedly, picking up one of the plates and running her fingers over the beautifully painted design of pinkish-red flowers and green leaves that encircled it. "I can't believe you remembered after all these years."

"It's time to eat, is what time it is," Joe said, looking at his wife curiously. "I don't want my steaks to get cold."

As the food was passed, mother and daughter kept looking at one another. "You've always loved flowers, haven't you?" Joe asked, looking at his plate as he cut his steak.

"Thanks to you, Dad," Mattie said. "I just found out the flowers on these dishes—the desert rose—are designed for the *Rosa rugosa,* which is native to the Midwest and northern U.S."

"Just like us," Don said, finally realizing Joe had tricked him again. He held up a piece of red meat.

"Just the way you wanted it." Joe laughed.

"These plates make me happy," Mattie said. "They're about family."

Mattie looked around the dining room table, her face breaking into a smile as bright as the sun reflecting off the water. Don looked at his wife, and mouthed, "Go on."

"Dad," Mattie finally said, "I'm pregnant."

"What? When?" He stood excitedly and grabbed his daughter into a bear hug, before shaking Don's hand. Joe looked at his wife. "Why aren't you screaming?"

"I told her already, Dad," Mattie said. "We had a tea party earlier."

"Always the last to know," he replied.

"You've both been so good to us," Don said. "You'll make great grand-parents."

"We love you both," Joe said, his cheeks quivering. "More than any-thing."

"Oh, honey," Mary Ellen said, seeing her husband's emotion.

"I'm so proud of you both," Joe said. "This calls for a celebration. What have we got in there?"

Joe dashed into the kitchen, his heavy footsteps followed a few seconds later by a loud pop.

"Look what I found," he said, coming back in with a bottle of cham-pagne. "The beer man has a little class after all, doesn't he?"

Joe poured champagne into the desert rose cups for his wife and son-in-law and then raised his glass. "A toast," he said, "to happy days ahead!"

The family lifted their desert rose cups in return.

"To happy days ahead," they replied in unison.

Nine

"**M**rs. Tice, are you okay? Mrs. Tice?"
Rose's voice was escalating from questioning to concern.

For the last fifteen minutes, she had not been able to understand more than a handful of words—other than "Dad," "daughter," and "teacup"—that Mattie had said. To Rose, it was as if Mattie were watching a movie alone in her head.

"Mrs. Tice?"

Mattie's face appeared to Rose as if she had stumbled upon her nearly too late in an avalanche—still breathing, trapped against something more powerful than her, nearly frozen.

Finally, Rose saw Mattie's pupils narrow, and her eyes fixate on the plate in front of her.

"Mrs. Tice, are you okay?"

Mattie's hazel eyes slowly began to refocus on the room and then on Rose. She saw the cardinal out the kitchen window flutter in the tree, and she picked up her fork and unconsciously began to eat a piece of cantaloupe.

She is so out of sorts today, Rose thought.

Suddenly, Mattie began to choke, and Rose ran over to her, Mabel jumping out of Rose's lap with a start. Rose patted Mattie on the back, softly at first, but as Mattie continued to cough, unable to catch her breath, Rose began to panic.

Mattie's face turned pink, then red, before a small waterfall of drool ran out the edge of her mouth.

Mabel barked and began to circle Mattie's wheelchair.

Rose was about to give Mattie the Heimlich, but swatted her one more time, hard, across the back at the last second. Mattie coughed up a chunk of cantaloupe, and Rose, relieved, lifted her water, so she could take a drink.

"You scared me," Rose said. "No more cantaloupe, ever. I'm so, so sorry, Mrs. Tice."

Mattie looked at Rose, slowly putting the pieces of the present together in her mind.

"I'm okay," she said, before smiling at Rose and the dog, both watching her nervously. "It's okay, Mabel."

"I couldn't understand what you were trying to tell me, Mrs. Tice. I'm sorry."

"Few can anymore," Mattie said slowly. "I'm getting a little tired. Mind if I rest?"

"Not at all," Rose said, lifting Mattie's tray off her chair and setting it on the kitchen counter. Mattie moved toward the bedroom and stopped. "Could I get a cup of tea, too, please?"

"Of course," Rose said. "I'll be in with that and your medication in a moment, okay?"

Rose held it together until Mattie had left the room, and then she lowered her head and sobbed, shaken. Rose grabbed a kitchen towel and put it over her mouth to muffle her gasps until she had finally calmed herself.

Pull it together, she thought.

Rose dried her eyes with the towel and then lifted the sippy cup off of Mattie's tray, sitting on the counter. As she began to turn, she stopped, unable to divert her attention from the plastic dishes in front of her.

Rose shook her head and unlocked the kitchen cabinet containing Mattie's meds and retrieved her midmorning pills. When she relocked the cabinet, she again noticed the piece of masking tape on the lower cupboard. Rose rinsed Mattie's coffee cup, filled it with water, and placed it in the microwave. She pulled a tea bag from the pretty pink depression-glass jar on the kitchen counter.

Earl Grey, Rose thought, *for a grey day.*

Something fluttering out the kitchen window caught her eye: The bright cardinal sitting in the pine that Mattie had been watching earlier was staring directly at Rose. For a moment, their eyes locked, and they looked at one another, their heads slightly tilted. The cardinal chirped and then took flight, happily, cheerfully.

Rose grabbed Mattie's pills and her tea from the microwave and started for the bedroom, but stopped abruptly.

Pink and green are so pretty together, she could hear Mattie saying.

Rose then recalled the conversation she'd had with Mattie.

"Do you have children?" Rose had asked.

"No, I wanted them. Very much," Mattie had said.

Without warning, Rose returned and began to throw open the kitchen cabinets, one after another, leaving the doors wide open, until she found what she had been looking for.

"Here are your meds," Rose said a moment later, as she entered the bedroom.

When Mattie turned in her wheelchair and saw what Rose was holding, she smiled and cocked her head at her caregiver, just like the cardinal.

"I'm so sorry you lost your daughter," Rose said, her eyes filling with tears. "Did you lose others, too?"

Mattie nodded.

You understood every word I was thinking, Mattie thought, *even if you couldn't hear a single one.*

Rose put the first pill on Mattie's tongue, and then held the desert rose teacup up to her lips.

"I'll hold it," Rose said. "You sip. Tea is still hot."

Rose smiled at Mattie and continued. "I just thought that, no matter what happens—no matter how much life gets in the way of living—every day should be a special occasion, shouldn't it?"

Mattie took a small sip of tea, locked eyes with Rose, and nodded, nearly imperceptibly but proudly.

Then, at the very last second, she gave the little antique cup a kiss.

part four

The McCoy Vase

Ten

July 2016

Pop! Pop! Pop!

A round of firecrackers exploded down the block from the Tices' house, and Jeri screamed in excitement, dropping one end of the bunting she was holding to cover her ears, and jumping up and down.

"Fireworks!" she yelled, as Mabel scurried from the front yard—fluffy tail tucked between her legs—into the garage and underneath a table that still held moving boxes, to seek shelter from the racket. "Happy birthday, America!"

"You have to keep holding on to it," Don yelled from one side of the window box—overflowing with pansies, petunias, lobelia, geraniums, and sweet potato vine—that fronted the house. "It's bad luck to let it touch the ground."

"Sorry," Jeri said, quickly grabbing the red, white, and blue bunting off the grass and holding on to it with both hands until Don arrived.

"Good job," he said, thumbtacking the fabric to the side of the window box, the bunting draped across it instantly billowing in the breeze.

"Pretty!" Jeri yelled, before pointing at a flower in the window box. "Like those!"

"Those are angel wing begonias," Mattie said from the driveway.

"I love angels." Jeri smiled. "Like Grandma and Grandpa."

Just then, a bottle rocket screamed overhead. Mattie looked up and watched it streak across the blue sky before exploding in front of a puffy cloud. The rocket's white contrail looked like a white brushstroke of paint on an ethereal canvas.

"Angels," Jeri sang in the distance.

Mattie watched the little girl skip across the grass. She was wearing shorts that were as red as her hair and a T-shirt emblazoned with the American flag. Jeri pulled an unlit sparkler from the back pocket of her shorts and pointed it up at the sky, as if she were a conductor leading the fireworks symphony.

Another bottle rocket screamed into the air and popped, making Jeri giggle as if she had lit it herself.

"Angels," she said again.

Mattie looked up and watched the white contrail float in the heavens, the streak quickly dissipating, until it was no longer there, like a mirage.

We're all here just a brief time, Mattie thought. She shut her eyes and pictured her own angels in heaven, the ones who never had a chance to light up the world.

"Yes," Mattie finally said into her mic. "Angels are everywhere."

Firecrackers again popped in the distance.

"Ah, to be a kid again," Rose said, emerging from the front door carrying two glasses of sun tea, Mattie's in her favorite desert rose cup. "I used to love shooting off fireworks on the beach. Such great memories."

Rose saw Mattie's face wince. "I'm sorry," she said, placing her cup down on the driveway and holding Mattie's up so she could take a sip. "I know this is the first Fourth you've not spent at Hope Dunes."

"Nothing like watching fireworks over the lake." Mattie sighed, her eyes fluttering as if an old film reel were playing in her mind.

"Jeri was driving me so crazy for fireworks, I had to stop at a little stand on Blue Star and get her some sparklers, Black Cats, and a few other surprises," Rose said, trying to change the subject. "We both love the town's fireworks display, but we can't really see them from our house, and finding a spot downtown is nearly impossible. It's such a zoo now."

Nothing's the same, Mattie thought, her mind still blinking images of Hope

Dunes and the days they could meander through downtown Saugatuck and Douglas and always find a parking space, a seat in a restaurant, and a grassy space to watch the fireworks. *Those days are gone.*

"You didn't need to work today," Mattie said. "It's a holiday."

"Doesn't feel like work when I'm with you," Rose said easily. "I can't thank you enough for having us over today. Means the world. I hate to be alone on the holidays."

"Hey!" Jeri yelled. "These look just like fireworks."

"Hay is for horses," Rose said, peering around the front yard to locate her daughter. "You don't yell 'Hey,' remember?"

"Sorry," Jeri said.

It was then Rose saw her daughter standing in the middle of the Tices' front garden, her hair the same color as the blooms on a beautiful clump of flowers, already taller than Jeri, which appeared to rocket out of the garden—as if their roots were lit fuses—toward the sky.

Mattie moved her wheelchair closer to the front garden.

"I call those firecracker flowers," Mattie said to Jeri. "Real name is monarda, or bee balm."

She stopped, took a moment to swallow and catch her breath, and then continued. "They look like fancy fireworks, don't they?"

Jeri pulled one of the flowers close to her face to study it. Then she shook it gingerly, as if it were exploding, and said, "*Boom!* Pretty!"

"As pretty and fiery as you are," Mattie said.

"As what?" Jeri asked.

"Fiery means spunky," Rose said.

Full of life, Mattie thought.

"Honey, you shouldn't be tromping around in their garden," Rose said.

"It's okay," Mattie said, almost to herself. "I used to live in them . . ."

Her voice trailed off, and Mattie again shut her eyes and thought of the countless glorious days she spent in clients' gardens as well as her own. Mattie could hear the calming buzz of the bees, feel the wet earth in her hands, and smell the overpowering perfume of the blooming peonies.

I miss that, Mattie thought, a lone firecracker's pop in the distance serving as a sad exclamation point.

Rose watched Mattie's eyes flutter, before her daughter's voice broke the silence.

"These look like firecrackers, too," Jeri said, pointing at another beautiful plant whose extended arms looked as if they were filled with hundreds of tender bright red blooms exploding into the sky.

"Those really are called firecracker flowers." Mattie smiled.

"And these smell like candy," Jeri said, kneeling down to sniff a stargazer lily. "Can I eat them?"

Mattie's smile expanded until it filled her entire face. "No," she said. "But they do smell like heaven."

"I know these!" Jeri yelled. "Daisies!"

"Jeri," Rose warned. "Stop yelling. You're louder than the firecrackers."

"It's okay," Mattie said. "It's the Fourth. Like Christmas in summer."

"Yeah," Jeri agreed. "Like Christmas in summer."

"It's warm out," Rose said, lifting the teacup to Mattie's mouth. "You need to have a few more sips."

Mattie sipped her tea. Both Mattie and Rose watched Jeri dance with a four-foot-tall spike of pink phlox while Don sat nearby and weeded.

"You miss your family farm stand?" Mattie asked Rose out of the blue.

Rose shut her eyes and remembered busy Fourth of Julys past, people buying fresh produce for their big barbecues and flowers for their tables.

This time, it was Mattie watching the young woman's expression shift in front of her, a lifetime of emotion washing over her freckled face.

"I do," she said softly. "I miss being outside, too."

"Look what I made," Jeri said, running up to her mom and Mattie.

The two women turned to see Jeri sporting a long necklace of intertwined white daisies with yellow centers.

"It's a daisy chain," Jeri said proudly. "I learned how to make them in school."

She stopped and looked down at the flowers. " 'Cept ours were paper."

"Jeri," Rose started gently. "Those aren't your flowers. They're Mrs. Tice's."

Jeri squinched her little face—blotchy from the sun and activity—her hazel eyes growing big.

Her sweet eyes are as round as a hearty hibiscus and as pretty as her mother's, Mattie thought, before looking into her garden. *How ironic: Hearty hibiscus is also called rose mallow. More coincidence?*

"Sorry," Jeri said.

"It's okay," Mattie said, looking intently at the little girl. "My flowers are for sharing. Your necklace is beautiful."

Jeri smiled.

"Sharing makes a garden special," Mattie continued, suddenly remembering what her father used to tell her: *You can tell something deeper about a person's soul by the way he cares for his garden.*

Mattie stopped and took a deep breath. "Want to make an arrangement for our dinner table? You and your mom pick. Sound good?"

"Yeah!" Jeri said.

"I'll get a vase," Rose said, moving toward the house. "They're in the hutch in your dining room, right?"

Mattie nodded.

But as Rose neared the front door, Mattie said, "Wait."

Rose turned, alarmed. "Are you okay?"

Mattie nodded. "My hope chest," she started. "Aqua vase. Use that."

Her voice sounds more like a plea than a request, Rose thought. "Okay," Rose said instead. "I'll look for it."

As she entered the house, a bottle rocket zoomed over the roof and Jeri screamed her approval.

"Happy birthday, America!" Jeri yelled, jumping up and down, her curls bouncing just like the firecracker flowers in the summer breeze.

Eleven

July 1952

M y ears are still ringing!"

"You big baby. It missed you by a mile."

Mattie lifted her head off the beach and spit out a mouthful of sand. She kept her body still for a second, listening for the soft whoosh of Lake Michigan rolling onto shore, but the only thing she could hear was a deafening hum, as if a hundred ringing telephones had been stuffed into her ears. She laid her head back down onto the warm beach and dug her toes through the sand, as if to ground her body and calm her nerves.

Patty Dunkins held out her hand. Mattie grabbed it, and she helped pull her to her feet.

"It really did come close to your head," Patty whispered, as Mattie knocked sand off her knees and the front of her body. "My twin brother must have been adopted."

"What?" Mattie said, shaking her head to rid it of the hum, trying to remember how she'd even gotten here.

"You're fine," Perry Dunkins said, running up to Mattie. "Shake it off."

Perry had sneaked fireworks all the way from Chicago, a secret he had shared with Mattie a few days ago when the Dunkins family arrived to their cottage, which sat next to the Barnharts'.

"Hid 'em in my tackle box," Perry had told Mattie. "Bought 'em in a stand in the city. You in or out?"

Mattie had been standing on the screened porch of the Dunkins' knotty pine lake cottage, which was perched on a dune exactly 272 paces from Hope Dunes and 51 wooden steps from the beach. Perry Dunkins was actually a year younger than Mattie, but he seemed so big-city, with his ducktail hairstyle and Chicago accent.

"You're almost a teenager," he had pushed. "C'mon."

Mattie wasn't even friends with Perry. She was summer besties with Patty—*Mattie and Patty*, everyone sang—who couldn't have been more different than her brother. Patty was blond and bookish like Mattie, while Perry was dark and brooding. But Perry held an invisible power over his sister, too. When Mattie had looked to Patty for guidance that day, she had lifted her shoulders helplessly.

Mattie had instead turned and listened to the lake for advice, but it was still. She immediately wanted to say, "No, my parents will kill me," but instead she said, "I'm in!" with as much James Dean defiance as she could muster.

Everything had been fine at first: They had set off firecrackers on the beach, lighting the fuses and then running like the dickens in the opposite direction, the girls screaming and shutting their eyes, missing everything. They had lit jumbo magic black snakes on lake stones with lighters, watching them smoke and spew, and slither and coil just like a real snake. And Mattie had loved lighting smoke bombs and throwing them into the lake, watching them twirl in the water, a colorful curtain of smoke churning off the waves.

But then Perry had pushed the bottle rockets, and now here Mattie stood. Unable to hear a thing.

Perry was still standing in front of her as she continued to dust herself off and shake her head.

"See, you're fine," he said. "The reason you almost got hit is that the bottle rockets can't stay still in the sand. They spin around once they're lit. We need a soda bottle or something to hold them."

Perry's eyes then narrowed, and he took off his Cubs cap and scratched his head as if he needed more room to create the thought.

"Better yet, we need a big bottle," he said, replacing his cap and crossing his arms to stare down Mattie. "Like one of your mom's stupid flower vases. She has a gazillion. She won't miss one."

"But . . . ," Mattie started, turning to Patty, who just shrugged her shoulders yet again.

"Don't be a butt," Perry teased. "Hurry."

Mattie began to trudge through the sand, her ears still ringing, and up the warped wooden staircase that sidewinded up the dune. She stopped at the first landing and turned to inspect the scene: Perry was threatening to toss firecrackers at his sister's feet, while she hopped around the beach like a frightened bunny.

The wind tossed Mattie's blond hair, and she scanned the lake. The water was eerily flat today, and there was almost no distinction between the lake and the horizon, making it appear as if the world might, indeed, be flat. In the distance, her parents' pontoon eased along the shoreline, and to Mattie it looked like a seagull bobbing on the surface of Lake Michigan.

What would they think of what I'm doing? she thought. *I'm smarter than this.*

Her ears gave a deafening hum that made her shake her head like she did when a deer fly attacked. Finally, they began to ring just like her school bell, before the sounds of the wind and the water began to reappear.

"Hurry!" she then heard.

Perry stood on the beach, waving his arms.

"Go!"

Mattie turned and ran up the steps, through the screened porch, and into Hope Dunes. She slowed her pace as soon as she entered the dining room. She approached the old corner cabinet as cautiously as if it were a feral cat and stared through the wavy panes of glass.

Inside were her mother's beloved flower vases, the ones she called McCoys, in endless shapes and every shade of beautiful blue imaginable. There were vases that looked like hyacinths, hydrangeas, frogs and ferns, lilies and leaves, all in muted shades of aqua or mint green.

"You and your father grow beautiful flowers outside, and I have beautiful McCoy vases inside," her mother always said, humming like Doris Day as she made her arrangements. "This is the way I show how much I love and admire what you both do."

Her mother never let Mattie open the corner cabinet unless she was beside her.

"Pick your favorite," she would always say. "But be careful. They're fragile."

Mattie pulled on the cabinet door, but it refused to budge, as if it already knew what she had planned. Mattie tugged again, and the warped door—and its countless layers of white paint—finally gave way in the lake humidity with a great sigh.

Mattie nervously held her hands in front of the shelves, lined with contact paper dotted with daisies, and stared at the vases. She perched onto her sand-covered tiptoes and scanned the shelves. In the back, hidden away, was a beautiful vase she had never seen her mother use.

"Maybe she wouldn't notice that one missing," Mattie whispered to the cabinet.

Mattie carefully pulled it free. The vase looked like bluish-purple blooming hyacinths—one of her mother's favorite spring flowers—that seemed to be alive and floating high on their green stems. Without thinking, Mattie sniffed the vase.

Silly, Mattie thought, giggling at herself. *It looks so real.*

Her mother loved hyacinths, and her father grew a cotton candy–colored assortment of them, which smelled as sweet as candy.

Mattie stood frozen for a moment, hearing the dueling voices of her mother and Perry, voices of reason and risk. And then she heard the words "Hurry up!" drift into the cottage, and she turned and made her way back to the beach.

"What is that?" Perry asked.

"A vase," Mattie said. She held it out and nodded at its top. "See, it's filled with all kinds of crooks and crevices so we can shoot bottle rockets in a hundred different directions."

Perry narrowed his eyes. "Good job," he said, gruffly grabbing the vase from Mattie's hands.

Be careful, she wanted to scream, but she kept her words to herself.

Perry rushed over to a flat area of the beach, where the waves had made the sand hard like concrete. He set the vase down and began to dig.

To Mattie, Perry looked like a cantankerous terrier, his hair in his eyes, sand flying, mischievousness in his genes.

Perry settled the vase into the hole and then covered the base with sand, patting it until just the top of the vase popped out, like a turtle's head.

"Won't go anywhere now!" Perry said proudly, standing, before calling to his sister. "Bring me all the bottle rockets."

Seconds later, the beautiful blue vase was stuffed with bottle rockets, their wooden sticks like the stalks of dried hydrangeas. Perry produced a packet of matches from the front of his shorts and relit the punk he had stuffed in the back pocket.

He stopped and stared at Mattie and Patty. Mattie couldn't tell if it were a challenge or a plea to stop, but before the girls could say a word, Perry was on his front in the sand, arm stretched out, head low, holding the smoldering punk to every fuse. And then:

Screeeeeeeee! Wheeeee!

Bam! Bam! Bam! Bam!

Mattie's eyes were locked on Perry, who had turned over onto his back, a juxtaposed look of sheer wonder and horror etched on his face as bottle rockets screamed over his head.

Mattie looked up and watched bottle rockets looping crazily in the sky, like drunken birds, trails of smoke across the sky like in those war movies her dad always watched.

Pop! Pop! Pop! Pop!

Mattie jumped as the bottle rockets began to explode, seemingly all at once, the echoes off the lake even louder. The three of them stood, mouths open, watching the sky light up, a timpani of sound rousing the quiet coastline, as if God were a jazz musician playing a snare drum to get the world's attention.

Seagulls called out a panicked "caw," and Mattie lowered her head, watching them take flight for the open water.

And that's when she saw it: Her parents' pontoon was motoring quickly back to the dock.

"They heard!" Patty said, following Mattie's shocked gaze. "You're so dumb," she yelled at her brother.

Mattie sprinted over to the vase, sand flying as she ran, and her face dropped when she saw it. The top of the colorful vase was black from the smoke and residue of the bottle rockets. Mattie quickly began to rub her fingers over the edges of the vase, but they, too, became smudged from the soot. Mattie began to dig into the sand, just as Perry had done, going all the way around the vase as if she were unearthing a pirate chest filled with gold. When the vase was free, Mattie instinctively lifted it to her nose, as if pretend-smelling the hyacinths could return their beauty, but only the acrid stench from the exploding bottle rockets filled the air.

Mattie rushed toward the lake and submerged the vase into it, furiously scrubbing it with her fingers and then with sand, but the vase refused to come clean. "Did you have fun?"

The voice of Mattie's mother surprised her, and she yelped. She fell back into the surf on her rear, still holding the vase. She looked up at her mother, whose arms were crossed, and then back at Patty and Perry, who were rushing up the wooden stairs to their house, their parents on their heels, swatting their behinds.

"Not really," Mattie said, before bursting into tears and holding up the vase. "I'm so sorry, Mommy. I ruined your vase. I didn't mean to."

Mary Ellen angled the vase into the sun, turning it this way and that. "It's not ruined," she said. "I think we can scrub some of it away." She hesitated. "But it won't be the same, either."

Mary Ellen suddenly took a seat on the beach and patted the sand. Mattie scrambled backward out of the water on her hands and knees, like a lobster, and put her head on her mother's shoulder, again collapsing into tears.

"It was that mean Perry," she said. "He made me do it."

"Look at me, sweetie," Mary Ellen said, taking her daughter's face gently into her hands and looking deeply into her hazel eyes, now rimmed with red. "Remember what we talked about? You have to be strong enough to tell people no. You have to be able to stand up to peer pressure and do the right thing. You will never make everyone happy. True strength comes from believing in yourself."

Mary Ellen looked down at her vase. "And you can't borrow things that aren't yours, without asking."

"I'm so sorry." Mattie sobbed.

Mary Ellen sat the vase down in front of her, positioning it just so in the sand, and put her arm around her daughter. "Did I ever tell you the story behind this vase?" she asked.

Mattie shook her head.

"This is a McCoy vase, and McCoy makes beautiful pottery," Mary Ellen said. "Vases big and small, cookie jars . . ."

"You mean like that big elephant cookie jar we have?" asked Mattie, turning her big eyes toward her mom. "That's a McCoy?"

"Yes," said Mary Ellen. "And that little green planter with elephants that I put bulbs in during the winter is, too. Your father sent me flowers in this vase," Mary Ellen started, nodding at the one in the sand, "when you were born."

"What?" Mattie asked, her face suddenly as bright as the sun.

"When's your birthday?" Mary Ellen asked.

"March thirtieth!" Mattie said excitedly.

"You are my spring baby," Mary Ellen said, again putting her arm around her daughter and hugging her tightly. "That's why your birthday sometimes falls on Easter."

Mary Ellen stopped and picked up the vase. "Hyacinths, like Easter, are associated with spring and rebirth. They are signs, just like Easter, that everything is reborn, that all things are possible."

Mary Ellen set the vase down in the sand and stroked her daughter's blond hair. "That's why I love hyacinths so much, and why your father planted so many of them in our yard at home. They are proof spring is here, and that there is always hope."

"I didn't know, Mom. I'm so sorry."

"I just want you to be as resilient and yet as sweet as a hyacinth," Mary Ellen said. "Now you need to help me clean this vase and pick some flowers for it."

"Okay!" Mattie said, bolting into the air and then holding out her hand to help her mother up.

As the two walked hand in hand up the staircase to Hope Dunes, Mary

Ellen stopped—her free hand keeping a tight grip on the vase—and looked around suspiciously to ensure no one was in the vicinity.

"The next time that Perry asks you to do something you know is wrong," she whispered conspiratorially to her daughter, "you tell him what your father always says: 'I know better than to trust a Cubs fan.'"

"Mom!" Mattie gasped, doubling over in laughter and grabbing the railing, dune grass that had grown through the steps tickling her nose.

The duo then rushed into the kitchen, scrubbed the vase, picked an armful of firecracker flowers from the garden, placed them in the McCoy vase, and set it on the old wooden picnic table on the screened porch.

"I've never seen anything more beautiful," Mattie said to her mom as she stared at the vase.

"Me, either," Mary Ellen replied, staring at her daughter.

Twelve

I s this it?" Rose asked, emerging from the house holding Mattie's McCoy vase. "It's so beautiful. Hyacinths, right?"

Mattie nodded.

"It looks a little dirty," Rose said, holding the vase in front of Mattie and pointing at the rim, black smudge and lines encircling it. "I tried to give it a wash. Didn't help."

Mattie smiled. "Permanent." She hesitated. "My fault."

Rose laughed. "You have a lot of stories, I think. And you have so many wonderful things in your hope chest. I'd love for you to show them to me sometime. Reminds me of my mom."

Mattie's smile widened. "Deal. But one at a time . . . like my mom gave them to me. Okay?"

"Okay," Rose said, massaging her shoulders with her free hand. "Deal."

Jeri rushed over to Mattie and her mom, out of breath, her daisy necklace swinging. "I'm ready to flower rearrange."

Mattie smiled. "Have fun."

"But we need your help," Rose said, her face etched in concern.

"A flower garden is like a flower arrangement," Mattie said.

She stopped, before continuing very slowly. "Must be artfully designed but look natural . . . as if there were no effort."

Jeri cocked her head, trying to understand Mattie's words.

"Like your hair," Rose said, and laughed, tousling her red curls. "Artfully designed, but natural."

"Mommy!" Jeri said, poking her mom in the stomach. "You're funny."

"Pick what you like," Don said, walking over and placing his hands on his wife's shoulders, leaning down to kiss her head.

"Do you mind holding this?" Rose asked, handing the vase to Don before turning to her daughter. "Now, what flowers do you like? And what colors?"

"Red, white, and blue, of course!" Jeri said. "It's the Fourth of July, silly!"

As Jeri zoomed toward the front garden, Rose turned back to Mattie and Don. "Pick anything you want," he said, tightening his grip on his wife's shoulders. "This gives us more happiness than you can imagine."

"Hold on!" he suddenly yelled, pulling a pair of scissors from the front pocket of his gardener's tool belt. "You'll need these."

Mattie watched as mother and daughter stepped into the new garden— outlined with lake stones Don had hauled from Hope Dunes and Lake Michigan—and began to tiptoe amidst the flowers.

The garden was filled with new flowers that Don had purchased and planted to make it look more mature, as well as hundreds of precious plants and flowers that he had carefully dug up—under Mattie's watchful guidance—and replanted here. Some had taken off—the beauty of gardening in Michigan, where anything and everything seemed to grow quickly in the ideal summer temperatures—but it was still new, not the same.

It's not Hope Dunes, Mattie thought. *It's not what my dad and I started.*

Hopeless Dunes, Mattie couldn't help but think.

Don kissed his wife's head, as if he could feel her emotions.

"You smell like sunshine," he whispered. "I know they're not the same, but I tried to make your gardens look as if they had been here forever."

"I know," Mattie said.

They watched as Jeri zipped toward the white Shasta daisies—which comprised her daisy chain. Mattie smiled. She already knew the red, white, and blue flowers that the little girl would pick for the arrangement: bee balm for the red, daisies for the white, and catmint for the blue.

Jeri ran toward the red flowers and looked tentatively back at Mattie, who nodded, Don giving a big thumbs up. She did the same thing as she moved toward the catmint.

They're the same ones I picked every year for my Fourth of July arrangement, Mattie thought.

Jeri stopped in the middle of cutting flowers and whispered something to her mother while peeking back at Mattie dramatically.

Mattie's heart pinged: She could feel the bond—as clearly and loudly as the pop of errant firecrackers—between mother and daughter.

My life will end without knowing that bond, Mattie thought.

Mattie watched as Rose nodded and then kissed her little girl on the cheek, and Jeri proceeded to cut a tiny armload of the flowers.

"What do you think of our choices?" Rose asked, walking back to the couple.

"Yeah, how'd we do?" Jeri echoed.

"Perfection," Mattie said.

"It screams Fourth of July," Don said, before looking at all the flowers in the little girl's arms. "You picked lots of daisies."

Jeri looked up at her mom with a mortified expression. "Sorry."

"I didn't mean it that way," Don said, kneeling down to look Jeri in the face. "It's okay. Pick whatever you want, whenever you want, got it?"

Jeri smiled and nodded.

"You know," Don said, "you're as special and pretty as any flower here."

"You must love daisies," Mattie said. "Are they your favorites?"

"Yes." Jeri giggled, the daisies bouncing in her chubby arms. "They're happy!"

"Ready to arrange?" Mattie asked.

"Will you show me how?" Jeri asked.

Mattie beamed. "Of course."

The group headed inside to the kitchen, where Mattie instructed Jeri on how to make a beautiful floral arrangement—cutting the stems at an angle, varying the heights of the flowers for visual impact, and intertwining the colors for pop.

When they were done, Jeri stood back and gasped.

"It's beautiful," she said, her mouth wide open, unused blooms haphazardly stuck in her thick hair, giving her the look of a flower child.

"You're a natural," Mattie said, winking.

"Let me clean this mess up," Rose said.

"I have extra vases for those," Mattie said about the clump of extra daisies sitting on the counter.

"Okay," Rose said quickly, giving Jeri a wink. "I'll get one in a minute."

"Who wants to help me start dinner?" Don asked.

"I do! I do!" Jeri yelled, lifting her hand up high in the air, as if she were in class.

"I think I have a volunteer," Don said, scanning the entire kitchen before acting as if he had just seen Jeri. "How does salad, baked potatoes, corn on the cob, and barbecued chicken sound? A real Fourth of July dinner."

"Yummie," Jeri said. "Can I pluck the corn?"

"You sure can," Don said and laughed, before whispering, "although I think shucking it might be easier.

"And . . . drum roll," Don continued, imitating the sound and action, "blueberry crisp and vanilla ice cream for dessert."

"Yeah!" Jeri yelled, jumping, flowers coming loose from her hair. "My favorites!"

"We have lots to do," Don said. "Let's get started."

The two began to pull ingredients out of the refrigerator, while Rose cleaned up stems, leaves, and little pools of water.

Mattie smiled. *Lots of life in this kitchen. I never dreamed my first Fourth out of Hope Dunes would be so . . . nice.*

Mattie looked at the vase, and then at Don and Jeri shucking the corn, and an idea hit her.

"Rose," she started, before moving her wheelchair toward the open screen door as indication she wanted to talk.

Rose followed Mattie, until the two were in the backyard and alongside an emerging garden of rhubarb, asparagus, and strawberries, a trellised arbor over it, purple phlox and spotted tiger lilies brightening the border.

"I want you to take starts of these," Mattie said, her voice halting and filled with emotion. "Thought you could start your own garden again."

"I couldn't," Rose said. "I can't. I'm too busy. I don't have enough time or space."

"You only need enough time and space to let yourself remember," Mattie said slowly, looking into the kitchen to see Don and Jeri cooking, the McCoy vase—filled—on the counter.

The words hit Rose immediately. She thought of her parents and their farm stand, and—without warning—a tear reflecting Mattie's image rolled down her cheek.

"Looks like I have some work to do, then," Rose said, clearing her throat. "Let me get a spade from the garage and some little pots. I'll be right back."

Mattie shut her eyes. The air was thick with the smell and sounds of wood and water, family, flowers, and fireworks.

"Where should I start?" Rose asked upon her return, shaking Mattie from her memories.

"Rhubarb." Mattie smiled. "Strawberries. And tons of lily seeds."

Rose kneeled and began to dig, before turning to Mattie and saying, very softly, "Thank you."

"No," Mattie said. "Thank you. You can start a new tradition with Jeri."

"You're right," Rose said, digging up some rhubarb. "I can."

Rose dropped the spade and began to dig gingerly with her hands. "Found 'em," she said, exposing the little "feeders" that rooted the strawberries. "You know, my parents used to always say you can tell something deeper about a person's soul by the way he cares for his garden."

Rose turned to look at Mattie. "Or something like that. Ever hear that phrase?"

Mattie nodded. "Think so," she said, and smiled.

The smell of smoke began to billow through the backyard. Mattie rotated her chair and laughed, watching Don start his odd-shaped grill. "Don's big green egg."

"He loves that thing, doesn't he?" Rose asked.

"More than me, I think." Mattie laughed, before she returned to watching Rose in the garden and Don showing Jeri the magic of his grill.

We must plant something for it to take root, even if we'll never see it grow to its full beauty and maturity, Mattie thought.

The four ate dinner on the back patio—Jeri serving up big bowls of blueberry crisp, the ice cream melting over the crunchy brown sugar topping and fruit—and talked, until the first firefly of the evening blinked in the yard.

"The fireworks seem to get later every year," Don said of the massive display that Saugatuck-Douglas did every Fourth over Lake Michigan.

"Just getting old," Mattie joked, thinking of all the years they watched the show from Hope Dunes, where they had a front row seat to the spectacle.

I hope we can see some of it from here, she thought.

As Rose and Don cleaned the kitchen, dusk crept over the marsh, and the river faded from gold to black, while twinkling fireflies exploded like the emerging stars.

"I made this for you!"

Mattie jumped at the sound of Jeri's sweet voice, high-pitched and happy like the cicadas, and turned to find the little girl holding a ring of daisies.

"It's a halo!" she said, holding it out for Mattie to see. " 'Cause I think you're an angel."

She stopped and cocked her head, before continuing. "Just like your angel be-grow-nias."

Mattie's eyes filled with tears.

"It's a happy halo," Jeri said. "For protection."

Her words made Mattie remember the wreath that hung on the front door at Hope Dunes. *I'd made it out of happiness,* she thought, *and to protect my home.*

"Can I put it on you?"

Mattie nodded, and Jeri clambered into her lap without warning, putting the halo on her white-blond head.

"Pretty," Jeri said, giving her a kiss on the cheek.

"Mattie," Rose said, rushing outside. "Are you okay?"

Mattie nodded, her halo shifting.

"She's been planning that all day," Rose said. "She adores you."

An explosion of red lit the sky.

"It started!" Rose yelled excitedly to Don, who came rushing out with a dishtowel still in his hands.

Another burst lit the heavens, and Mattie could feel the reverberations rifle through her body along with the excitement of Jeri, who let out an "ooh" and "aah" with every explosion.

We do have a great view, Mattie thought, watching the fireworks high from their perch on the river's bluff.

Even though there was no reflection of the spectacular colors off the great lake, the river seemed to carry the colors downstream, as if it were on fire.

Another burst: this one red, white, and blue.

"Looks just like our flower rearrangement," Jeri gasped.

Mattie thought of watching the fireworks with her parents, perched on her father's lap.

For a moment, she was out of her body—free, soaring high in the sky amongst all of the colors, alongside her family.

She felt Jeri's breath hot on her neck, and when she turned, the little girl was staring at her, watching her intently, smiling.

"You're thinking of something from a long time ago, aren't you?" Jeri asked, surprising Mattie. She nodded.

"I can tell," Jeri continued, "because your mouth is open wide as mine when I watch the fireworks, too."

Jeri took her little hand and held it under Mattie's chin, closing her jaw as if she were shutting a drawer. "Now the lightning bugs can't get in and light up your stomach," she said, giggling. Jeri turned her gaze back to the sky. "Wow! I've never seen anything so pretty in my whole life."

"Me, either," Mattie replied, staring at Jeri.

Rose quietly watched the moment between Jeri and Mattie, then turned her head as if the fireworks had again transfixed her, secretly wiping away a tear.

part five

The Apron

Thirteen

August 2016

Don eased out of bed, an inch at a time so as to not wake Mattie, felt for his slippers in the dark, and tiptoed out of the bedroom like a cat burglar.

Sleep rarely came for Don, and when it did, he was haunted by a recurring dream: Mattie was gone, and he was alone.

Don flicked on the kitchen light and opened the cabinet to grab a filter for the coffee maker. He counted, stopped, and then—like always—put in a few extra scoops.

"You love your coffee as dark as the earth," Mattie would always tell him when he'd join her as she worked in her gardens. "Thick as mud."

"I do," he'd reply, handing her a cup of her preferred tea instead. "You like to work in the mud, I like to drink it."

She had been the early riser, waking at dawn to work and watch the sun rise. Don had always been in a hurry, preferring to shave the night before so he could sleep an extra twenty minutes and then rush off to work, his coffee on the go.

Don filled his favorite mug—the one featuring the Lake Effect Coffee logo on one side and "Do I Look Like a Morning Person?" on the other— that Mattie had gotten him long ago. He walked onto the screened porch and wiped the dew from an Adirondack chair with his free hand before wiping his hand on his flannel pajama bottoms.

Now I'm the morning person, he said, taking a seat. *Life is filled with surprises, isn't it?*

Don took a sip of steaming coffee and watched the sun rise over the marsh.

It looks like one of Mattie's paintings, Don thought. *Like a watercolor.*

The Kalamazoo River slowly meandered toward Lake Michigan, a rippling mirror of the sky: bright blue, heavenly gold, and a series of reds, yellows, greens, and oranges. The water flowed around stands of willows and cattails as well as bog plants, but it was the marsh hibiscus that stole the show: The flowers grew thick in the middle of the river, and their electric pink color reminded him of the bubblegum lipstick Mattie used to wear when they were first dating.

In the near distance, a hawk circled the marsh, its screeching cry echoing off the water. Don watched it float through the air, dipping and diving, like the paper airplanes he made as a kid.

Don and Mattie had long been members of the area's historical society and had even held a fancy fundraiser at Hope Dunes. Don had read many books about the Native Americans who had settled the area—the Potawatomi, Ojibwe, and Ottawa tribes—and he had heard even more history from the locals. Many of the town names and landmarks were rooted in Native American history, including Mount Baldhead, the six-hundred-foot dune that towered over the area and served as a sandy sentinel over Oval Beach, the town's stunning stretch of golden sand.

Don had heard from Mattie's father that the name Saugatuck was a Native American term meaning "river that pours out."

And here I now sit at that river, he thought.

Don watched the hawk circle lower to the water and remembered the times Mattie and he would watch hawks circle over Lake Michigan from Hope Dunes.

"Hawks are powerful omens for the Native Americans and are messengers of the spirit world," Mattie used to tell Don.

Don shook his head and closed his eyes, the image of the hawk seared in his mind.

The hawk represents the power to see clearly, to develop spiritual awareness, Don thought, remembering all the times he had laughed off Mattie's words.

And then Don's heart began to pound, and he remembered something else his wife had told him. *When the hawk is in your life, you know clearly what lies ahead and that you have the power within you to defy any obstacles in your way and soar even higher in life.*

The hawk cried, and when Don opened his eyes, it had landed high in a pine in his backyard and seemed to be staring at him. Don locked eyes with the hawk, and it stared intensely at him. The two didn't move a muscle for a long time, and Don could feel his emotions building up inside, before a lone tear trailed down his cheek. The hawk tilted its head at Don before sounding a heartbreaking cry. It then spread its wings and flew up, up, up.

Don stood on shaky legs and headed to the kitchen for another cup of coffee. He peeked in at Mattie. She was still sleeping, Mabel, Mattie's constant companion, nestled alongside her body.

Mattie's certainly not a morning person anymore, Don thought, tiptoeing toward the garage. Don opened the garage door, and a gust of summer air rushed in, along with the morning light. He walked over to a plastic storage bin, the words "PETOSKEY STONES" written in Magic Marker on a piece of masking tape adhered to the lid. He popped it open and began to peer at the Petoskeys.

Don picked out a stone and smiled.

The Petoskey stone was the official stone of Michigan, a fossilized coral with hexagonal chambers filled with the prehistoric remains of saltwater marine life from the sea, which used to cover Michigan. The stone is found in abundance on the coast of Michigan, especially north, but—with a careful eye—Don had found it along the beach at Hope Dunes.

Don loved the stone more than any other because it could be polished to a high shine that revealed the intricate beauty and history of the rock. To Don, each chamber, outlined in white and containing what resembled an eye of golden brown, was a work of art that Mother Nature had worked on for millions of years.

All I have to do is bring it to life, he thought.

Don suddenly thought of Mattie, and the words stung him, like the ground hornets that hatched in Michigan yards during the summer.

He rubbed the stone and remembered when he had found it.

I remember picking this one up on a beach walk with Mattie, he thought, studying the rock. *When she could walk. How long has it been?*

"You're a real Renaissance man."

Don jumped at the voice.

"Oh, my gosh," Rose said. "I didn't mean to startle you."

"I was in my own world," he said. "What are you doing here so early?"

"I couldn't sleep," she said. "Jeri stayed the night at a friend's house, and it was almost too quiet in the house."

Don contemplated her words and nodded. "I understand."

Rose walked over and studied the polished stones Don had sitting on a table. "These are so beautiful," she said. "I was right. You can do it all: cook, garden, polish stones . . ."

She stopped and looked at the turquoise T-bird. ". . . restore vintage cars . . ." She hesitated and continued. ". . . care for and love your wife with all your heart and soul."

Rose's kind words stunned Don, and he dropped the Petoskey, the stone rolling toward Rose, who picked it up. "You really do rock," she said, and laughed, handing it back to him.

"I just try to do my best," he said shyly.

"You are amazing," she said. "Don't ever forget that. And, Don?"

Again, Rose hesitated but continued. "Don't ever forget you are going to have to live after Mattie is gone."

Don stared at Rose. "What?"

"You are," she said. "I don't mean to be cruel by saying it out loud, but you need to know you are important to a lot of people, and your wife would want you to continue to have a wonderful life."

"Who?" Don suddenly asked. "Who am I important to anymore? We don't have any children or close family. Our friends don't come around anymore."

"You have friends," Rose said. "You have a community of support. They just don't know how to handle this very well."

She stopped, walked over to Don, and put her hand on his shoulder. "And you have me and Jeri."

Don slumped into Rose's arms, overcome by her words, and wept. Rose held on to him until his sobs had subsided. "There, there," she said. "You *need* to do that. You *have* to do that."

Don nabbed a clean towel from a stack he used to wipe his stones and dried his eyes. "Thank you," he said. "I think I needed to do that."

"Now, Mr. Renaissance Man," Rose said brightly, changing the subject, "would you mind showing me how to make that blueberry crisp you made on the Fourth? I thought I'd give you a break and learn a new recipe."

"We can't have that for breakfast," Don protested.

"Why not?" Rose asked.

Don stared at her.

"Well?" Rose asked again. "Jeri always poses questions like that to me, innocently, as if anything is possible and nothing is silly."

Rose continued. "When she asks, 'Why can't you go back to college?' and I say that I don't have enough money or time, she will still ask, 'Why not? They're everywhere!'"

Rose stopped and stared at Don's stones.

"I was so depressed after my mother died," Rose said, "but Jeri's innocence has taught me to see the world in a new way, in a way that makes everything seem possible. I try to remember that when I feel down. And that happens quite a bit."

Don smiled before turning back to nod at the house. "But not everything is possible," he said.

"I know," Rose said. "And that's exactly what I used to say to Jeri, and one day she just looked at me and said, 'Grown-ups just see it wrong.' When I asked her what she meant, she said, 'You see *im*possible, but it's really *I'm* possible.'"

"Wow," Don said. "That's amazing insight for such a little girl."

"That's what I thought," Rose started, "until I went to her classroom and saw a poster with that saying on the bulletin board."

Don laughed but then his face dropped.

"I know what you're thinking," Rose started tenderly. "Is it possible for your wife to recover? No, it's not, unfortunately. But it is possible for her life to still be filled with possibility. And it's just as important that your life after hers be filled with possibility, too."

Don thought of the hawk he had seen. He stared out the garage door, then at the stone in his hand.

Beauty remains even after all these years, he thought, studying the Petoskey.

"Let's bake some crisp, then," Don finally said, very softly. "But let me check on Mattie first."

The two walked into the bedroom, where Mattie and Mabel were just waking. "We have an audience this morning," Mattie said, laughing, to the mop-haired dog.

"We're going to make some blueberry crisp," Don said to his wife, walking over to give her a kiss on the cheek.

Mattie smiled. "Why not?" she laughed.

Rose laughed. "Do you want to get up now? Help us?"

"No," she said. "You two bake. I'll read."

Rose and Don set Mattie's voice-activated e-reader on the tray by her bed and positioned it in front of her face.

"What are you reading?" asked Rose.

"Anne Lamott," said Mattie. "Need a little faith right now."

"We all do," said Rose. "Especially if I'm baking."

Mattie chuckled. "Wait," she said suddenly as the two began to depart. "My apron."

"What?" Rose asked.

"My apron," she said. "In the hope chest, Don."

Don went to the end of the bed, opened the chest, and rifled through its contents, before producing a pretty apron outlined with delicate trim.

"Oh, my gosh," Don said. "I forgot about this." He stopped. "So many memories."

"It's so beautiful," Rose said. "Where did you get this?"

"My grandmother's," Mattie said. "Passed to Mom and then me in my hope chest."

She stopped, shut her eyes, and smiled. "Put it on."

"Oh, I can't!" Rose protested. "What if I get it dirty? What if I stain it with blueberries? It'll never come out."

"That's life," Mattie said, looking at the hope chest. "Show her, Don."

Don lifted the apron and pointed to a dark stain—faded over the years but still present, like a ghost—and said, "Blueberries. My fault."

Mattie smiled.

"If I'm reading my wife's mind, I think she wants me to tell you a story about this stain," he said. "And I also think she wants us to know these heirloom treasures in her hope chest need to be used. They need life . . . a new history . . . just like that McCoy vase."

"So?" Don asked Rose. "Ready to make that cobbler?"

She nodded.

"Here, let me tie this on you," he said, tying the apron around her waist with a little bow.

"Perfect." Mattie smiled after Don was done. Rose twirled in the apron and laughed.

"If you smell fire, I'm sorry," Rose said.

"Apron is good luck," Mattie said. "Shoo."

Rose and Don headed into the kitchen, where he began to pull out sugar, brown sugar, and flour from the cabinets, and butter and fresh blueberries from the refrigerator.

"Ready?" Don asked, pouring the blueberries into a bright red colander and washing them under the faucet.

"Ready to learn," Rose said, smiling, "and ready to listen."

Fourteen

August 1967

I'm ready to pick!"

The door slammed behind Don as he walked onto the screened porch, every inch of his body covered: long-sleeve flannel shirt, waders pulled up over the legs of his jeans, a hunter's cap with the flap pulled down over his neck and ears, his gloved hands holding two big buckets. His face was smeared white with suntan lotion, and an overpowering scent of mosquito repellant wafted from his body.

Mary Ellen and Joseph stared in silence at their new son-in-law for a few seconds, the only noise coming from the wings of the hummingbirds at the feeders.

"Your nose is still showing," Joseph said very seriously. "Might want to cover that up, too."

"Really?" Don said, panicked, raising his right hand to feel for his exposed nose and hitting himself in the face with the bucket. "Ouch."

Joseph doubled over in laughter, his hysterics causing the glider he and Mary Ellen were seated on to swing violently back and forth.

"They're only blueberries," Joseph said. "Not killer bees."

Mary Ellen had tried to remain poker-faced at Don's appearance, so as not to upset him, but she couldn't hold back after her husband's remark.

"Oh, my sides hurt," she said, tears running down her face.

"What's all the racket?" Mattie asked, rushing onto the porch. "Oh. I see."

She shot a sad look at her husband, tried to contain herself, but couldn't, and joined her parents in laughter.

"What?" Don asked. "I heard the mosquitos up here are like the state bird. And I've heard there are lots of hornets. And I burn easily. And . . ."

"Oh, sweetie," Mattie said, walking over and putting her hand around Don's waist. "It's eighty degrees outside."

She looked tenderly at him, waited a beat, and then continued. "I really like your look. Maybe you should wear this to work."

The Barnhart clan again busted out in laughter.

"Okay, that's enough," Don said, putting the buckets down on the wood-slatted floor with a thunk. "I've never picked blueberries in Michigan before. No one prepared me."

"Sorry, we're just teasing you, Don," Mary Ellen said. "Teasing is part of our family tradition. Just like Hope Dunes. Here's the scoop: We don't actually pick the berries anymore. We just go to Apple Blossom Farms over on Blue Star. They have the freshest blueberries around, and we still have the day free to go to the beach. Win-win."

Don shot a defeated look around the porch and then gave one of the buckets a little kick, just like a hurt kid.

"Just means you're one of the family now," Mattie whispered into his ear, giving him a peck on the cheek. "Means you're loved."

Don's face brightened and a mischievous smile curled his lips. "Let's go," he said.

"Don't you want to change first, son?" Joseph asked, standing.

"Nope," Don said, winking at his father-in-law. "I'm ready."

Don walked directly to the garage and got into the backseat of the car. When no one came out, he leaned forward and honked the horn—continuously—until his family appeared.

"This should be loads of fun," Don said, adjusting the flap on his hunter's cap.

Joseph steered the mint green Chevy—which he had named Ol' Betsy after an old, fat cow his father had owned growing up that Joseph believed could produce mint chocolate chip ice cream—toward Blue Star Highway and the farm stand.

"I think I'll stay in the car," Joseph said when they arrived.

"Oh, no," said Mattie, now playing along. "If you can embarrass me driving Ol' Betsy for so long, it's time someone return the favor."

She got out of the car, opened the driver's door, and pulled her father out by the arm.

"What are we getting today, BARNHART FAMILY?" Don yelled as they approached the farm stand, people turning to stare and point.

"Humiliated," Joseph deadpanned, before turning the tables. "This is my son-in-law," he said walking up, twirling his finger in a circle around his temple. "Just released from the loony bin. *Today*."

Summer shoppers in shorts tittered amongst the brightly colored flags—emblazoned with ASPARAGUS, CHERRIES, PEACHES—that dotted the rolling hillside.

APPLE BLOSSOM FARMS—the p's designed to look like shiny apples with stems and the o's like blossoms—had stood to mean summer had started in Saugatuck-Douglas seemingly forever.

A bright red 1950s Chevy pickup—slung low to the ground with white-wall tires, its flatbed filled with fresh flowers—stood alongside what looked like a tiny house whose front was comprised of two huge farm doors that had been flung all the way open to reveal an endless array of wooden carts and tables, overflowing with the season's latest produce.

"This used to be the old bus stop barn where local kids would gather and wait for the bus when it was snowing or too cold to be outside," Mary Ellen said to Don, picking up a basket and perusing the options. "Cute as a button, isn't it?"

"It is," Don said, removing his cap and looking around in awe. "It's so . . . Michigan."

Mary Ellen giggled. "It is," she said. "I think Michigan is a lot like heaven . . . in the summer, that is."

Don laughed and then watched mother, father, and daughter hold hands and walk among the wooden carts with a fondness and familiarity that made his heart ache.

They define family, he thought.

Don remembered his own parents and the small garden they had worked tirelessly. "The Garden of Eatin'," they both used to say with zero humor and complete seriousness.

Both were factory workers who labored long hours for not much money. They showed Don little affection growing up. "Children should be seen and not heard" was a constant refrain, along with, "Spare the rod, spoil the child." Both had died a few years earlier, and even their funerals had been unemotional events. Don knew they had loved him, in the only way they knew how, but there had been a lifelong emptiness and ache that had never eased until . . .

Don heard laughter. He smiled as he watched Mattie and her parents attempt to juggle apples, failing miserably, and then just tossing them to one another.

I am blessed, Don thought. *Surrounded by love.*

Don grabbed his own basket and began to peer at the produce when a pretty woman with auburn hair—a bright green silk scarf wrapped around her head—approached.

"Do you need any help?" she asked, smiling.

"No," Don said. "Well, actually, we're looking for blueberries."

"I thought maybe moose with the way you were dressed," she joked. "I'm Madge. I own this place with my husband, who's . . ."

Madge stopped and looked around, before pointing at a man in overalls and a bright plaid shirt. ". . . right over there."

"My first time here," Don said.

"Welcome," Madge said. "So, blueberries, huh? Got them this morning. Right this way."

Madge led Don to two carts overflowing with blueberries.

"They're so . . . *blue.*" Don laughed. "They look fake."

"Michigan blueberries," she said. "We grow the best. Lots of rain. Lots of cool springs."

"Do you grow them?" Don asked.

"No, sir," Madge said. "We're sort of a co-op. We sell the produce from all the local farmers. Farm to stand. Pick it up every day. I think it's going to be a big idea one day." Madge put her finger over her lips. "Just don't tell anyone."

Don chuckled. "My secret," he said, filling his basket with little cartons of berries.

"We're open through Christmas," Madge said. "We go from blueberries to apples, then from pumpkins to Christmas trees."

She stopped. "And then snow."

"I love Christmas! I love snow!"

A little girl with bright red curls came spinning up like a helicopter bud, the winged seeds that local sugar maples constantly dropped in late summer. She was holding an empty bottle of Grape Nehi soda, her lips, mouth, and T-shirt shimmering neon.

"This is Dora," Madge laughed. "My *purple* daughter."

Dora lifted her head up and giggled. "I'm just like Violet from *Charlie and the Chocolate Factory*!"

"You sure are," Don said. "But so much nicer."

"Thank you," Dora said, and laughed.

"How old are you?" Don asked.

"I'm five," she said excitedly. "And I start school this year."

"What do you want to be when you grow up?" Don asked.

"Happy!" she yelled, before extending her arms like an airplane and flying off across the hillside, a happy border of zinnias outlining her runway.

She's already figured out the key to life, Don thought.

"We have all of this fresh fruit, and she still prefers a Nehi." Madge laughed. "Do you need anything else?"

Don looked back at the girl running and then at his in-laws.

"I do," Don said, secretly making his purchase and slipping it in the car, before rounding up his wife and in-laws.

"Thank you for buying the berries," Mary Ellen said once they were back at Hope Dunes and Don had changed. "Are you ready to bake some blueberry crisp?"

"What?" Don asked, his smile turning into a frown. "I thought I was only the blueberry *buyer* not the blueberry baker."

"This is one of Mattie's favorite family recipes," Mary Ellen said, pouring the blueberries into a colander and setting them in the sink. "She always says this tastes like summer and smells like Hope Dunes."

Mary Ellen stopped and grabbed Don's hand. "My grandma taught me how to make it, and I want to teach you how to make it. You're part of the family now."

She stopped and looked out the kitchen window at Mattie and Joseph in the garden. "They say the way to a man's heart is through his stomach, but the way to a woman's heart is a teaspoon of kindness at a time. It's nice that a man know his way around a kitchen."

"But what if it's terrible?" Don asked.

"It's not about the outcome," Mary Ellen said. "It's about the effort."

She suddenly burst out laughing and continued. "And there's no way it can be bad. It's the best crisp in the world!"

"How do we get started?" Don asked, clapping his hands together.

"With this," Mary Ellen said, opening the door to the large cupboard and pulling an apron—delicate and trimmed with lace—from the back of the door.

"I can't wear that," Don protested.

"Oh, you can," she said, already tying it on him, "and you will."

She turned to face Don and a huge smile brightened her face. "A bit snug, but you look like a real Julia Child now."

"I think she's taller," he joked.

Mary Ellen pulled the cinnamon, nutmeg, and mace from the spice drawer and turned to look at Don, a serious expression now on her face. "My mother made that apron for me," she said. "Put in my hope chest, and I put it in Mattie's. It's like a living history. And it's helped us make so many great dinners, holiday meals, and desserts. My mom would be proud that you're wearing it."

"I have something for you," Don said, rushing out before returning with a bouquet of zinnias. "Thank you."

"For what?" Mary Ellen asked.

"For having me as a part of your family. I never had this."

"This what?"

"This . . . love," Don said softly.

"Oh, Don," Mary Ellen said, giving her son-in-law a big hug. "You are loved. Isn't happiness wonderful?"

Don thought of the little girl, Dora, and what she had said.

"It is," he said. "Now let's get to baking."

"Okay," Mary Ellen said excitedly. "But remember, this recipe can never get out to the public."

"My lips are sealed," Don said, gesturing as if he were locking his mouth. "Until dessert is ready, of course."

Fifteen

Silence engulfed the kitchen, before Rose began to sniffle.

"That was my mom," Rose said, her eyes misting with tears. "When she was a little girl. You used to make this crisp with blueberries from my family's farm stand."

"We did," Don said. "We're all connected in some way, even if we don't know it."

"I miss her and my grandparents," Rose said. "So much it hurts."

"I know," Don said softly. "I miss my family, too."

Don looked into Rose's eyes and held out his hands. "What connects us are these good memories, these pieces of history, like the apron and the crisp. Through them, we can remember and smile. We can make old traditions new again."

Rose nodded. "You need to remember that, too, you know."

"I know," Don said, turning to preheat the oven and nodding at a small plaque hanging over it. "See that? It was in Mattie's mom's hope chest, and she hung it in the kitchen at Hope Dunes. The poem is titled 'Recipe for Living,' and Mary Ellen told me it was the secret to making life sweeter than any dessert."

Rose leaned over the oven and read the poem aloud.

Take a cup of love
Add a dash of care
Mix with kindness
Add a bit of patience
Top it off with faith
Sprinkle liberally with understanding
Share with everyone you meet

"So true," Rose said. "Who wrote that?"

"I don't know," he said. "Always said anonymous. I wish I knew."

Rose turned to look at Don. She hesitated. "Can I ask you something?"

"Sounds ominous," Don said.

"Why are you selling Hope Dunes?"

Don blinked twice and tilted his head, confusion etched on his face. "What do you mean? You know why. It was too big, too old. Mattie couldn't navigate it any longer."

"But you can."

"Rose," Don started.

"I'm so sorry," Rose said. "I didn't mean to upset you or intrude. It's just that . . . you have to be happy, too, after your wife is gone. You just said what connects us are the good memories, these pieces of history, like the apron and the crisp, that through them, we can remember and smile. We have to make old traditions new again. Isn't that what Hope Dunes means to you? Will your true happiness be here, or there?"

Don stared at Rose, open-mouthed.

"I can't imagine living there without her," Don whispered, his lips quivering.

"Or have you never imagined living without her, period?" Rose asked cautiously, placing a hand on Don's arm.

Don again collapsed into tears, and Rose held him. "I'm so sorry," she said. "I didn't mean to upset you."

"No," Don said, calming himself. "I don't know what's gotten into me today." He continued, "I never thought about making myself happy *after*—" He stopped. "I've been so lost in the battle to keep her going, I lost all hope for myself. I've just been trying to get from one day to the next."

"I know," she said. "All caregivers do. But Mattie would want you to be happy and hopeful, right?"

Don nodded.

"A couple has been seriously looking at Hope Dunes now for a couple months," Don said. "I spied on them one day after you started here. They look very nice."

Don stopped. "They look like a very nice couple who don't belong in our house."

A surprise giggle popped out of Rose's mouth. "Have they made an offer yet?"

"Not yet," Don said. "Everyone waits until winter to make offers in Michigan. They know it's a long winter up here and a long way until spring . . . until anyone will look at homes again. You know how it goes. Buyers want you to sweat. They want the best deal they can get."

"Just make sure you're making the right decision," Rose said. "You can't undo regret."

"You're a wise, old soul trapped in a young body," Don said. "Are you ready to learn the secret family recipe now?" he asked.

"My lips are sealed," Rose said, pantomiming locking her mouth. "Until dessert is ready, of course."

"You're a good listener," Don said. "And a great caregiver and advisor."

"Thank you," Rose said. "Now let's get to baking."

She lifted the apron and gave it a little kiss. "I think I need a little luck."

"With me around?" Don said, smiling, quickly pulling out mixing bowls and ingredients, whispering each step of the recipe to Rose as if he were afraid someone might secretly be recording their conversation.

"So how did you stain the apron?" Rose asked.

"Well, it remained unscathed until I actually tried to sneak a taste of the crisp when no one was looking," he said. "It was so hot, I spit it out without thinking, and it dribbled onto the apron. Bakers can't be clean, I've learned. Or maybe I'm just a sloppy eater."

An hour later, the kitchen was filled with the smell of bubbling blueberries and cinnamon sugar.

"Smells so good," Mattie said when Rose brought her into the kitchen. "Let's eat outside. So pretty today."

The three sipped coffee and watched Mabel chase squirrels around the backyard.

"Looks like she had a lot of sugar today." Rose laughed.

"Better than I remembered," Mattie said, slowly chewing the crisp, her eyes shut. "Thank you, Don."

"Thank your family," Don said, standing and giving his wife a kiss on the head.

"*Your* family," Mattie corrected. "Did the apron help?"

Rose beamed. "It did."

Mabel suddenly began to bark, and the trio looked up to see a hawk circling the yard, just as it had earlier in the morning.

"A messenger," Mattie said.

Don watched his wife watch the hawk.

I'm almost ready, she thought, as the hawk floated and dipped across the sky. *Just need a little more time.*

Mabel came running up and jumped into Mattie's lap.

"What do you have?" Mattie asked her dog.

In Mabel's mouth was a hawk feather.

Don plucked the feather from Mabel's mouth. "I'll take it," Rose said, "and clean up the kitchen. Thank you for teaching me this recipe. I hope it's okay I make it for my family now."

"Of course," Mattie said.

Rose began to clear the plates, but stopped and tucked the feather into the top of the apron. "It's not dirty," she said as Mattie and Don stared at her. "I promise. My mom always said it was supposed to be good luck, a harbinger of the future."

Mattie smiled as she watched Rose walk away.

A messenger indeed, Mattie thought.

part six

The Scrapbook

Sixteen

September 2016

September was Mattie's favorite month in Michigan.

Mattie called it the "not quite" month: It was not quite summer and not quite fall. It was not quite hot and not quite cold. Even her gardens, still beautiful, were not quite at full peak but not quite ready to be cut down, either.

The summer crowds had dissipated—parents returning to work and children to school—and yet summer remained. The temperatures held steady in the seventies, the beaches were quiet, and—in the past—Mattie could walk right in and get a latte or a seat in any restaurant.

But as a painter, Mattie knew the light was not quite the same, either. It was signaling a change in seasons, a change in the life cycle of Mother Nature.

Lower angle, Mattie thought, analyzing the light. *Less intense, getting weaker.*

Mattie was sitting in her wheelchair reading on the back porch, basking in sunlight alongside Mabel. The dog had earlier been on guard for any squirrel, rabbit, or chipmunk, but the sun was winning now, and Mabel's eyes were blink, blink, blinking until she was sound asleep.

Mattie smiled at her dog, mentally stroking her black fur with her hands.

I miss petting you, she thought. *Throwing the ball for you, rolling around on the floor, and playing with you.*

She looked up and out onto her gardens and the marsh beyond, and sighed.

And I miss painting in September because of this light, she thought.

Again, she could feel her hands moving, her fingers gripping her brushes, the feel of her watercolors against the canvas. Mattie pictured herself setting up her easel. She scanned the scenery.

What will I paint today? she thought, lost in her mind.

Her hazel eyes peered left and right, up and down, and then—there—she saw it: an arm of red waving in the breeze.

One branch of an ancient sugar maple was turning crimson, its soft leaves the color of fire, while the rest of the tree was still iridescent green.

Not quite, Mattie thought.

"I have to see this, Mabel," Mattie said to her dog. "Sorry to wake you."

Mabel slowly stood and stretched—*Now that's a downward dog,* Mattie thought, admiring the dog's flexibility—before moving alongside her mistress's wheelchair as Mattie navigated down the wooden labyrinth to the fence.

Wow, Mattie thought, staring into the branches of the tree and then through the slats of the fence. *How have I not noticed this beauty before?*

The sugar maple was big by Michigan standards, tall and wide, and it had somehow miraculously managed to expand to that size despite growing at a thirty-degree angle out of the steep bluff that descended to the Kalamazoo River and marsh below.

Tough old bird, Mattie thought. *Continues to go on despite all odds. A real survivor.*

She chuckled at the irony. *Just like me.*

Mattie shut her eyes and could picture herself painting this branch. She imagined she felt her arms move her brushes over the canvas, her hands in sync with the movement of the limb.

Mattie kept her eyes shut and listened to the sugar maple talk to her. It sighed in the sunlight, it giggled in the warm breeze, its old body creaked.

Mattie inhaled. She could smell its spirit, its soul, its being.

"Look what I got!"

A girlish shriek pierced the silence, and Jeri came running out, leaping off the patio in a big bound, Mabel running over to greet her.

"Mrs. White, my new second-grade teacher, gave me an iPad!" Jeri yelled, jumping up and down. "We get to use it for one night."

Jeri stopped and inhaled sharply, trying to calm herself and catch her breath, but she was too excited: Words kept rushing forth, her pink cheeks puffed. "Mrs. White said she trusted us. But I still had to check it out. My mom had to sign for it. She has to hold it and help me."

Jeri stopped and turned. She put her hands on her hips impatiently. "Mom!" she yelled, Mabel barking along with her. "Where are you?"

Rose came onto the screened porch, Don following. "Jeri. Stop yelling."

Rose walked over to Mattie, holding the iPad. "You're giving the entire world a headache," she said to her daughter. "I'm so sorry I had to run out, Mattie."

"No problem," she said into her mic. "Nice to be on the run."

Rose smiled softly at Mattie.

"Can I show Mrs. Tice my 'puter?" Jeri asked, tugging at her mother's shirt. "Pleeeease."

"Let me open it for you," she said. "And then you can show her."

"It's just like the one you have," Jeri said proudly. "Like the one you read on."

"It is," Mattie said. "Tell me about the assignment."

"And your new teacher," Don added.

"Well," Jeri started excitedly, "I love her! She's so nice. She wants us to take a picture of something outside that's really fall-y, then write about it and Photo drop it."

"Photo*shop*, Jeri." Rose laughed. "The teacher wants her to do an art project about something that represents the beginning of autumn."

"Things have changed," Don said, nodding at the iPad, before kneeling down to talk to Jeri. "In my day, we had stone tablets and a chisel."

Her eyes grew big. "Really?" she asked.

"He's teasing you," Rose said. "Although, you're sort of right. I mean, we still used crayons when I was in school."

"Good and bad," Mattie said slowly. "Technology's changed my life. But simple's nice."

Just then, a red leaf from the sugar maple overhead released its grip on the branch, and, as if on cue, floated down on the current to where the group was gathered.

"I should take a picture of that," Jeri said, picking up the leaf with great care and studying its color and veins. "It's so pretty."

"First fall leaf," Don said. "Everything's about to change."

Her husband's words resonated deeply within Mattie, who immediately thought of a first fall leaf she had gathered with her mother long ago.

A leaf I still have, Mattie thought. *A memory kept and not deleted on a computer.*

"Yep," Don said again quietly, watching Jeri hold the crimson leaf, "everything's going to change quickly now."

Not quite, Mattie thought, smiling.

"My scrapbook please," Mattie said out of the blue. "Red. In my hope chest."

Seventeen

September 1953

"I can't believe you were snooping in my room!"

Mattie stomped around the kitchen and pulled the milk out of the refrigerator. She took a dramatically wide turn around her mother and headed toward the pantry. She pulled a box of Sugar Frosted Flakes from the shelf, a smiling, kerchiefed Tony the Tiger juxtaposing Mattie's mood.

"Don't take that tone with me, young lady," Mary Ellen said. "And I wasn't snooping. I was cleaning. And your scrapbook just happened to be sticking out from underneath your bed."

Mary Ellen smoothed her sleeveless polka-dot dress and then her blond bob. "And remember we put that scrapbook in your hope chest. It should be in there."

"Stupid hope chest," Mattie said, her mouth full of Frosted Flakes. "And you know where the stupid key is to it, anyway. I can't hide anything from you!"

"Get changed," Mary Ellen said abruptly. "Put on some shorts. We're going for a walk."

"I don't want to go for a walk with you," Mattie said.

"Young lady," her mother said, "you don't have a choice. Now, go change."

When Mattie returned, Mary Ellen headed to the garage instead of the front door and the neighborhood street beyond. Mattie stopped. "I thought you said we were going for a walk," she said.

"We are," Mary Ellen said blankly. "But we have to drive to get there."

When Mary Ellen pulled into a parking lot at Forest Park, Mattie's confusion grew. "I thought the Muny was closed for the season," she said, referring to the park's outdoor theatre. The Barnharts attended every live musical production at the Muny when they weren't in Michigan and had just taken Mattie to see the premiere of *Annie Get Your Gun*.

"It is," her mother replied, turning off the Chevy, grabbing her purse, and getting out of the car. "We're going for a walk," she said, opening the big trunk and locking her purse inside. "Ready?"

Mattie sat inside the car for a second, her arms folded. But with the windows up and her mother walking away, she began to feel stuffy, scared, and claustrophobic.

"Wait for me!" she finally yelled, locking her door and scrambling after her mother.

The two walked in silence along a path that led into the historic park, over an ornate bridge and small lake.

Forest Park was known as the "heart of St. Louis" and featured a variety of attractions, including the St. Louis Zoo, the Saint Louis Art Museum, the Missouri History Museum, and the Muny.

The two climbed up Government Hill across an expanse of green grass and walked through an archway into a beautiful open-air pavilion.

"Do you know what this is?" Mary Ellen asked, taking a seat at a table. Mattie shook her head.

"It's the World's Fair Pavilion," she said, noting the stunning red-roofed, yellow structure that was bookmarked by twin towers. "It was constructed to help restore the park after the 1904 World's Fair."

Mattie looked at her mom and then scanned the expanse: From their seat in the pavilion at the top of the hill, they could see not only a historic fountain reflected into a pond below them but also the entire expanse of Forest Park.

"It's pretty," Mattie said.

"Did you know the 1904 World's Fair was in St. Louis?" Mary Ellen asked. "Right here. It changed the city. And the world."

"How?" Mattie asked.

"It brought people from all over the world to St. Louis, of all races and cultures," she said. "And you know what else?"

Mattie shook her head.

"The ice cream cone was invented and sold for the first time at the Fair."

"Wow," Mattie said, her mood breaking and her eyes growing large. "I thought ice cream had been around forever."

Mary Ellen scooted over on the concrete bench closer to her daughter. "I'm sorry I snooped," she said quietly. "I didn't mean to. It's just that . . . well, we don't talk as much as we once did. You have more friends. You keep secrets. We don't even add anything to your hope chest anymore."

Her mother stopped. "You're getting so grown up," she said, her voice shaky. "I just wanted to be a part of your life again."

This time, Mattie scooted a bit closer to her mother. "It's okay," she said. "I understand. But I do need some privacy."

"I know," Mary Ellen said. "But you can still share things with me. You know, memories—even the ones you keep in your scrapbook, like Valentines from boys and notes from friends—aren't meant to be kept to yourself. Memories are meant to be shared, passed along, just like the items in your hope chest.

"Memories aren't just scraps in a book, they're alive," Mary Ellen continued. "Of course, your scrapbook is yours, and I should have respected that. But I still want to be a part of your life. You're still my baby."

A little girl screamed as she ran down the hill, her mother scurrying after her. Mattie watched the mom grab the girl, lift her in the air, and twirl her in the beautiful September afternoon.

"I do love you, Mom," Mattie finally said. "But I'm not a baby anymore."

"I love you, too, sweetheart," Mary Ellen said. "More than anything in this world. And I know you're not a baby. But you're still *my* baby."

She grabbed her daughter's hand, and the two stood and continued their walk. As they approached the Jewel Box—an art deco conservatory with cantilevered vertical glass walls that rose majestically fifty feet high—they stopped.

"I want to get married here," Mattie said. "It's so beautiful."

Mary Ellen's eyes filled with tears, and she turned her head.

Why can't I stop time? she thought.

"Are you okay, Mom?" Mattie asked.

Mary Ellen nodded and looked down at her daughter. "Promise me you will only marry a man who treats you like a queen," she said, very seriously. "He doesn't have to be the richest man, or the handsomest, but promise me he will be the sweetest and nicest."

"I will," Mattie said with a smile. "Just like Daddy."

As the two passed by the Jewel Box, the path continued under an arbor of old oaks, which choked out the late day sun. It grew dark, and the two grabbed hands again as the path led into a forested area.

"Look," Mary Ellen said. "We already have some fall color."

A few branches on some maples, devoid of sun, had turned crimson, while clumps of sumac, which grew low and wild along each side of the path, was turning fire engine red.

As the two stopped to take in the glorious color, a lone maple leaf flitted and fluttered down and landed at their feet.

Mattie picked it up. "So pretty," she said. "I think it's the first one of the fall."

"Can we add it to your scrapbook?" Mary Ellen asked softly, taking the leaf, her head down.

Mattie looked at her mom.

"If we don't save this leaf, this memory, it will fade away, lose its color," Mary Ellen said. "You won't remember this day after I'm gone."

"How do we do it?" Mattie asked.

Mary Ellen lifted her head to look at her daughter, her face beaming. "I'll show you!"

When they got home, Mary Ellen put the leaf between two sheets of wax paper, set an old cotton cloth over it on her ironing board, and then turned on her iron.

"We need to seal it with heat," she said, her hand on Mattie's, the two ironing in unison. "There. Now it's preserved forever."

Mary Ellen followed her daughter to her bedroom. Mattie kneeled to the floor and pulled out her scrapbook from underneath the bed.

"As if you didn't know where it was," she laughed. "I just need a little privacy, Mom."

"And I just need a little daughter time," Mary Ellen said. "Deal?"

"Deal," Mattie said.

She opened the thick, red leather cover—the word "Scrapbook" embossed in a dramatic scroll—and turned to an empty page in the middle.

"You do the honors," Mattie said to her mom, handing her a tube of Elmer's glue.

Mary Ellen drew a rectangle of glue on the black construction paper and then pressed the waxed leaf down, holding it for a few seconds.

"Your turn," Mary Ellen said, handing her daughter a red marker.

Mattie tilted her head, thinking, and then began to write:

First Fall Leaf, Forest Park, September 1953
Me & Mom
"Memories Aren't Just Scraps"

"I love it," Mary Ellen said.

"Now can you *leaf* me alone." Mattie giggled.

"One day you will open your hope chest, pull out this scrapbook, and remember today," Mary Ellen said. "The leaf won't look like it does now. You won't look like you do now. But the memory will be as colorful as this leaf is right now."

Mattie smiled, hugged her mom, and then shut her scrapbook and slid it back under her bed. As she started to stand, she stopped, pulled the scrapbook out once again, and opened it to the very first page.

"This is a Valentine's Day card Bobby Bradley gave me," Mattie said, holding out a Cupid cutout shooting an arrow into a heart. "We have sort of been going steady since then."

Mary Ellen took a seat on the floor next to her daughter.

"Thank you," she said softly, running her fingers over the Valentine before grabbing her daughter's hand. "Thank you.

"Now," her mother said, and giggled, "tell me everything!"

Eighteen

Don walked into the backyard holding the old scrapbook, its cover as crimson as the leaf Jeri was holding. He opened the scrapbook to the first page, and a worn, torn Valentine greeted Mattie, her heart jumping as if it, too, had been pierced by that old Cupid's arrow.

"Keep turning," Mattie said. "There!"

A single red leaf, its edges crumbled but still red and preserved, shimmered in its wax home under the sun.

"Wow," Jeri said, her mouth wide open. "That's an old leaf."

"It is," Mattie said. "Found it with my mom. On a day like this."

"Neat," Jeri said. "Can I look through it?"

"I'd love it," Mattie said.

Jeri began to turn the pages, oohing and aahing over old postcards, report cards, and photographs, asking questions in rapid succession.

She stopped about halfway through the scrapbook and shot Mattie a concerned expression.

"Why are all of the rest of these pages still empty?" she asked. "Why did you stop adding stuff?"

Mattie looked at the girl and then up at the sugar maple jutting toward the sky.

"I grew up," she said. "I stopped."

Mattie hesitated. "And I wanted to give this to someone . . . my daughter . . . to continue the memories."

Don put his hands on his wife's shoulders and gave them a tender squeeze.

"Is this why you started keeping scrapbooks of every start and every flower anyone ever gave you?" Don asked. "And why you filled them with watercolors and they became your signature gifts to clients?"

Mattie nodded.

Jeri threw her arms around Mattie. "No one should ever grow up." She stopped and looked back at the sugar maple reaching for the sky. "Or stop trying to grow."

Mattie's heart again felt as if it had been pierced with love, and she could feel herself hug the little girl, squeezing her back.

Jeri flipped the scrapbook open to the page with the leaf and lifted it into the sky. She began to fly the scrapbook back and forth, making it seem as if the old leaf were alive again, and was floating down for the first time.

"Got it!" Rose said.

Everyone jumped, and Rose came from behind them, holding the iPad.

"I took a picture of that," she said. "It was just too beautiful to pass up. Look!"

Don looked at his wife, and he could immediately sense she was uncomfortable. Since Mattie's diagnosis, she hated photos of herself, feeling as if she were like that leaf, trapped beneath a layer that kept her face frozen, expressionless, haunting, like a wax figure.

Rose held the iPad in front of the group's faces, angling the screen just so to avoid the glare of the sun.

"My goodness," Mattie said with a quivering voice.

Jeri was giggling, her little arms a blur as she floated the scrapbook, the red leaf appearing alive in the wax paper, her curls looking as if they were ablaze. Mattie's hair was even lighter in the sun, her entire body ringed by white, as if an angel were hugging her.

"My face," Mattie said, her voice now even shakier. "It's not . . . frozen."

Mattie's face was lit, from outside and from within, her cheeks rosy, her hazel eyes piercing, a smile of pure happiness pulsating from the screen.

Don smiled. "You're beautiful," he said.

Mattie looked at Jeri and then at the sugar maple. "I'm alive," she whispered, as if she were someone who had just survived a horrible accident and never expected to see the world again.

"I've got an idea," Rose said. "Mattie, would you mind teaching Jeri how you and your mom saved the leaf in your scrapbook? And we could videotape it. It might be fun to show Jeri's classmates a fall project they could do with their parents and grandparents that doesn't revolve around technology."

"Yes," Mattie said.

"Something old-fashioned captured with new-fangled technology," Don said with a smile. "You're smart."

"I wouldn't go that far," Rose protested.

"I would," Mattie said, staring closely at Rose.

Mattie continued. "I'll show you, if you . . ."

Mattie stopped suddenly as if the batteries on a tape recorder had run out. She then began to have labored breathing.

"Are you okay, sweetheart?" Don asked.

Rose immediately handed Jeri the iPad and sprinted into the house, returning in seconds with a glass of water in one hand.

"It's okay, Mattie," Rose said. "Just short of breath. You've just overdone it today. It's called air hunger. Just relax. Breathe. You're okay."

Slowly, Mattie's breathing eased.

"I'm okay," she said, looking over at her husband, who was holding Jeri, scared looks etched on both of their faces. "I'm okay," she said again.

Jeri wiggled out of Don's arms and gave Mattie a big hug and kiss. "What were you going to say?" Jeri asked with a sense of urgency. "You never finished."

Her eyes were wide.

Mattie smiled at the little girl and began to speak, one word coming out at a time. "I'll show you if you make that picture your mom took my screensaver."

"Deal!" Jeri screamed.

It was then Mattie noticed that tears were running down the little girl's cheeks.

"I'm okay," she reassured her.

Jeri looked at Mattie and nodded bravely. "I know," she started, before asking the question everyone was thinking but only could be posed by the honesty of a child: "But for how long?"

Jeri handed her mom the iPad and began to run toward the house and into the kitchen. "Where's your wax paper?" she yelled back. "Hurry!"

Mattie began to move her wheelchair toward the house, but Don grabbed it. "You're tired," he said. "You need to rest."

"I know," she said, parroting Jeri's words, "but for how long?"

Don bit the inside of his cheek and looked at his wife.

"We have a school project to finish," he said, before turning to Rose. "Let's get busy."

part seven

The Embroidered Pillowcase

Nineteen

October 2016

T he doctor said you don't always have to try so hard, you know."

Don wished he could take back the words as soon as he'd said them, but it was too late. They hung in the air like the autumn fog.

"I'm sorry," Don said, pulling a blanket over his wife's legs. "You know I didn't mean to say that."

Mattie glared at her husband. "Yes, you did."

It had been two days since Mattie's checkup at the Cleveland Clinic, and both she and Don were still exhausted from the trip.

"You're such a fighter," Mattie's specialist had told her before revealing test results that showed her growing ever weaker.

I've never been a quitter, she thought. *Ever.*

Her fighting instinct took over, and Mattie literally blew the specialist and Don away with a score that was too strong to qualify her for any additional care.

"Well done," the doctor had said.

Don had given his wife a sad but knowing wink and then taken the doctor outside. Still, Mattie could make out some of what they discussed.

Future feeding tube. Future ventilator.

When Don and the doctor returned to the room, Mattie used the last reserves of her strength to yell, "No! More! Machines!"

"I'm sorry, sweetheart," Don said, bringing Mattie back into the present moment.

"I don't need hospice," Mattie said defiantly, turning her eyes to look at the spreading fog that seemed to gobble up everything in its path.

I feel like that fog, Mattie thought. *Here, but not here, like a ghost walking among the living.*

"The doctor said it wasn't hospice for end-of-life care," Don said. "He explained that if your breathing was at a certain level, you would qualify for additional care that hospice provides."

Don hesitated. "A little extra help might be welcome," he said, "to give me and Rose a little break."

He turned to look at his wife. "I know you were trying to pass that test," he said. "Trying really hard. But it's okay to admit you need help. That you're not sleeping. That you're choking more."

Mattie's glare only intensified, her eyes penetrating the thick mist as if they were a flashlight. "What would *you* do?" she asked, her voice filled with emotion and determination. "I know damned well you'd try till your last breath."

She paused and looked hard at Don. "I'm not ready to give up yet."

Don's heart leapt into his throat, and he bit the inside of his cheek— hard—to keep himself from crying, to pretend he was as strong as his wife.

"Me, either," he whispered, kissing Mattie softly on the cheek. "I'm sorry. Forgive me."

Rose stood outside the bedroom door, listening, waiting for the right moment to enter. Listening to their talk caused Rose's hands to tremble, and the desert rose teacups on the tray she was holding quaked briefly, tinkling like a wind chime.

Sssssshhh, Rose, the caregiver thought. *Stop it.*

She waited a second longer, took a deep breath, and walked in with a broad smile, as if she hadn't heard a word.

"That fog is terrible today," she said. "Look what it's done to my hair."

Mattie looked at Rose.

"You're a terrible actress," Mattie deadpanned. "Too shaky to be on stage."

Rose shook her head at Mattie's honesty and chuckled. "I am," she admitted. "That's why I was always assigned to paint the sets instead of perform on them."

Don and Mattie laughed. "We needed to break the tension," Don said. "Thank you."

"I know you haven't been sleeping well," Rose started, picking her words as carefully as she set down the tray of teacups. "I think it's tied to your increased breathing difficulties."

"No," Mattie said, turning her piercing glare at Rose. "Breathing is fine."

"I heard," Rose tried to joke. "But I have some ideas. There's a machine called a . . ."

"No!" Mattie said, thinking of her doctor before looking over at the ever-present BiPAP machine, the noninvasive ventilator she used at night to help her breathe more easily. "No trachs. No tubes. No more machines."

"Okay," Rose said slowly. "Okay. Then I have some exercises I want you to try."

Mattie eyed Rose warily.

"They only take a few minutes every day," Rose said, lifting the teacup so Mattie could take a sip. "Easy, breezy, I promise."

Mattie's gaze softened, and she nodded.

"And I also brought this sleep aid," Rose added.

"No," Mattie protested yet again.

Rose reached into the front pocket of the family apron she now wore nearly every day since she had baked with Don, and pulled out an embroidered pillowcase.

"What's that?" Mattie asked.

Rose winked. "A *natural* sleep aid."

She stopped and pulled a chair up to Mattie's bedside. "I had trouble sleeping as a little girl," Rose said, "and my mom made this for me."

Rose spread the antique pillowcase out on Mattie's mattress, unveiling a delicate embroidery of a young woman in a pink gown with a purple bow being tied by birds, the flowing bottom of the girl's gown making up the pink ruffle of the pillowcase. She was carrying a bouquet of pink and purple flowers, her curled hair bound by the same flowers, which also trailed down overhead and alongside her, as if she were walking under an arbor of flowering trees at a spring wedding.

"'Beautiful dreams for a beautiful girl,' my mom told me when she gave it to me," Rose said.

"Pretty," Mattie said, her eyes touching every stitch. "Pretty as you."

"What does it represent?" Don asked, moving closer to take a look.

Rose looked at Don. Her lips were quivering. She turned to hide the emotions breaking through despite her efforts and stared out the window at the fog. The mist seemed to be eating all of Michigan with its ghostly maw, the window frames dripping, the trees gone.

I've chosen to make my memories foggy, Rose thought, *in order to survive.*

Rose burst into tears, wet drops falling onto the pillowcase like a sudden spring shower.

"There, there," Don said. "It's okay. It's all going to be okay. We'll all be okay."

Rose lifted her head, a pained expression on her face. "Is it really?" she asked. "Will we?"

Mattie's heart ached, and she wished she could reach out and hold Rose, comfort her. She looked down at the pillowcase, the happy girl, happy flowers, and happy birds belying the scene in front of her.

"*Hope is the thing with feathers that perches in the soul and sings the tune without the words and never stops . . . at all,*" Mattie said slowly.

Rose's expression changed, and she tilted her head at Mattie.

"Emily Dickinson," she said. "My favorite."

Rose ran her finger over the embroidered pillowcase and a tiny smile replaced the shadows. "Thank you," she said to Mattie.

"Tell me a story," Mattie said, her face suddenly weary, her words coming out more garbled. "Bedtime story."

"It's only ten a.m.," Don said.

"I'm tired," Mattie said. "Please."

Rose reached out and grabbed Mattie's hand.

"This is the story of two girls," she started. "Let's call one Rose, and the other . . ." Rose stopped and stared at Mattie. ". . . Hope."

Twenty

October 1994

There you are!

    Dora Hoffs stopped on a dime, took a deep breath to calm her racing pulse, and wiped away the tears of relief that suddenly flooded her eyes. She looked at her sleeping daughter and let out a relieved giggle.

Rose was sound asleep in the middle of a replicated pumpkin patch at the family farm stand. Her chubby body was nestled in the hay, her head propped atop a small pumpkin, and hay was strewn throughout her hair. She held her beloved cloth doll tightly in her arms along with a tiny gourd that she had painted to resemble a smiling gnome.

In her tiny overalls and flannel shirt, cheeks flushed, Dora thought her five-year-old daughter resembled one of the adorably friendly scarecrows they had placed throughout Apple Blossom Farms to attract customers and frighten away the birds.

"Mommy?"

Rose rustled in the hay and rubbed her eyes, dropping her doll and the gourd.

"I was so worried about you," Dora said, taking a seat on a giant pumpkin and lifting her daughter onto her lap. "You didn't tell me where you were going."

"I got so sleepy, Mommy," Rose said. "I couldn't keep my eyes open any longer."

It was a surprisingly mild October Saturday, the leaves still holding on to the trees, and the sun had made Rose's body as warm as the basking pumpkins.

Rose yawned. "I'm sleepy all the time."

My beautiful, sensitive daughter, Dora thought, caressing Rose's hair. *Kindergarten was supposed to be a magical first year of school for kids, wasn't it?*

It had been a rough couple of months for Rose: Kids at school—even the ones she had grown up playing with on the beach—had teased her about everything, from the color of her hair to the fact that her family owned a farm stand. It wasn't that everyone was mean to Rose, it was just that no one was standing up for her.

Cliques start in kindergarten? Dora thought, her heart breaking.

Dora had talked to her teacher, a wonderfully kind woman who had taught in the public schools forever. She said Rose was always included in projects and games, but she wasn't a leader.

"Rose is always going to be the people-pleaser," the teacher had told her. "She's going to be the one who's behind the scenes."

"How can a five-year-old already be typecast?" Dora had asked, angry and confused.

As a result, Rose had trouble sleeping. Dora took her to the doctor, who said she was anxious and nervous, a "worrywart." When he suggested Rose take a sleeping aid or anxiety medication, Dora had walked out of the office.

"What can I do to help you sleep better, baby girl?" Dora asked her daughter.

Rose wriggled out of her mother's arms, retrieved her doll and the painted gourd, and placed them side by side on a pumpkin—their bodies dangling over the rounded edge—as if they were talking.

"What do you need to sleep better?" the gourd asked the doll.

"A new school?" the doll asked in a higher-pitched voice than Rose's.

The little girl stopped and skewed her eyes at her mother.

"That's not possible, Ann," Dora said to the doll. "I'm so sorry."

Rose looked up at the sun, squinting her eyes, silent for a second. Then she leaned the gourd's happy, painted face toward the rag doll, as if it were whispering a secret into the doll's ear. Rose bounced the doll on the pumpkin, as if it had just heard the most exciting news in the world.

"*Better dreams,*" the doll said. "*Beautiful princesses have beautiful dreams!*"

Dora smiled, choking back tears, and again lifted her daughter into her lap. "No one is perfect," Dora said softly. "You know that, right? And even the most beautiful princesses have trouble sleeping sometimes. I just want you to know that I love you more than anything in this world."

"I know that, Mommy," Rose said. "But it's nice to dream. 'Specially at night."

"Stitch in time saves nine!"

Dora jumped at the sound of her own mother's voice.

"We have a long line of folks buying apples and pumpkins," Madge said, her silver hair giving off a hint of blue that matched the cloudless sky.

Stitch, Dora thought, looking up at her mom and then down at her daughter. *Sleep.*

"Why isn't anyone moving?" Madge asked, sticking her hands into the front pocket of her University of Michigan hoodie and producing a honey crisp apple as shiny as the day. She took a big bite and shrugged her shoulders. "Are you okay?"

"Mom, I have a favor to ask of you," Dora said.

For the next month—as the days grew shorter, the produce dwindled, and the resorters stopped coming for the autumn art walks and produce—Madge and Dora sat side by side on a wooden bench in the little farm stand and stitched every day, Madge teaching Dora the beautiful art of embroidery.

"The simplest, least expensive things—needles, fabric, a hoop, embroidery floss, scissors—result in works of art that will last forever," Madge said, as she showed Dora how to make an array of beautiful stitches, split stitch, back stitch, satin stitch, French knot, chain stitch. "Like this farm stand, my tablecloths and runners will be yours one day. And you will remember our life together every time you pull one out."

The week before Halloween, Madge and Dora presented a pillowcase of a young woman wearing a pink gown—the ruffle of the pillowcase made from the flowing bottom of the dress—spring flowers in her hair and arms, walking through an arbor of flowering trees.

"A princess!" Rose yelled. "How pretty!"

"Your grandma and I made this pillowcase specially for you," Dora said, leading her daughter into her bedroom and placing the case over Rose's pillow. "I think it will help you sleep."

Dora fluffed her daughter's pillow and patted the bed. Rose jumped onto it and bounced excitedly before placing her head on the pillowcase.

"Remember, you are just as special as anybody in this world. Dream big," Dora said, stroking her daughter's curls. "Don't ever let anyone hurt your feelings. Don't let anyone keep you awake at night."

Rose's eyes immediately began to flutter, and she blinked—once, twice, three times—to fight off sleep.

She turned her head and stared at the embroidered girl. "I want to be a princess for Halloween," she said, sighing. "Just like her."

"Okay," Dora said. "We'll make an outfit just like this one. But first, you need to be Sleeping Beauty."

Dora pulled the covers over her daughter and kissed her cheek. "Beautiful dreams for a beautiful girl," she whispered.

Before she could make it to the doorway and turn off the light, Rose was sound asleep.

"This is now Jeri's pillowcase," Rose began.

"I can't take it," Mattie protested.

"She wanted you to have it," said Rose. "*We* wanted you to have it."

Rose tightened her grip on Mattie's hand and smiled. "She sleeps like a log anyway," Rose said. "Opposite of me. I'm still not a good sleeper."

"Why not?" Mattie asked.

Rose stopped and looked at the embroidered girl and again became emotional. "I've never been that girl," she said. "The pretty princess, the homecoming queen, the . . ."

Rose's eyes filled with tears. ". . . perfect bride."

She stopped and wiped her eyes with the hem of the heirloom apron. "I've always been the girl in the stands watching everyone else celebrate. I just feel like I let my parents and grandparents down. I couldn't keep the farm stand going. It stopped when my mom got sick. I only wanted to be with her."

Rose stared at the pillowcase and continued. "I didn't marry the right guy. I don't even know where he is. I can barely pay the taxes on the family cottage. I'm a failure."

"Stop," Mattie said. "Stop."

"I'm sorry," Rose said.

"You . . . have . . . *everything*," Mattie said slowly, forcefully.

Mattie looked at her husband, her eyes narrowed. Don knew she wanted him to speak for her. "We all make mistakes, but the beauty is in acknowledging that we have made them—like I did earlier," Don said with a wink at his wife, "and moving forward with confidence.

"And you do have everything," Don continued. "Yes, you've lost your parents and a husband. You're struggling to make ends meet. But you're doing a terrific job raising a wonderful daughter. You're doing an outstanding job here. You have your whole life ahead of you. Never forget that."

"This," Mattie added, her eyes locked on the pillowcase, "can still come true."

"You are not the same little girl you were then," Don said.

"Thank you," Rose said softly. "Thank you both."

She stood and gently eased Mattie's pillow from behind her head, while Don held his wife. She put the embroidered pillowcase on and then placed it back behind her head.

"Smells like Jeri," Mattie said with a smile. "Hopeful."

"This was going to go in Jeri's hope chest one day," Rose said, smoothing the covers over Mattie's legs. "Along with a lot of other special things from my mom and grandma. But I never got around to it. Where does the time go?"

Mattie watched Rose tidy up the room in the family apron, talking to Don as if she'd known him her whole life.

"Time for those breathing exercises," Rose said to Mattie. "No machines. Just me and you, okay?"

Mattie nodded.

"I want you to take deep breaths—fully expanding your lungs," Rose said. "We're going to take five to ten deep breaths, with a short rest in between, and we're going to be doing this several times a day. This will help you maintain good lung function. Ready?"

Mattie and Rose inhaled in unison, exhaled, and then waited a beat before starting again.

"Nine," Rose counted. "Almost there. Ten! Good job."

"That was great, sweetheart," Don said, kissing his wife on the top of her head.

A phone chirped, and Rose pulled her cell from her pocket. "Sorry," she said, before giggling. "It's a photo of Jeri in her costume at the school Halloween parade."

Rose held the phone in front of Mattie's face.

"She looks just like the pillowcase," Don said. "And she's holding a bouquet."

"Always a princess," laughed Rose. "She's calling herself Princess Hope today. Always sparkly. Remember what she wore the first day you met her?"

Don laughed at the memory. Mattie's face beamed.

"Is it okay if I bring her by tonight?" Rose asked. "She wants to show you her costume before we go trick-or-treating."

"Of course," Don said. "We'd love it."

Mattie's eyes darted to the hope chest at the end of her bed and she thought of the spring flowers—like the ones embroidered on the pillowcase—that her father had carved, just for her.

She looked over at Rose, who was laughing at one of her husband's bad jokes.

"What happens when a ghost gets lost in the fog?" Don was asking Rose, gesturing toward the window.

"I don't know," she said.

"He is mist," Don laughed, turning to smile at his wife. "Speaking of which . . . looks like the fog is dissipating. Will be a good night for ghosts and trick-or-treaters. Hey, I better run out and get some candy, if there's any left. I'll be right back."

As Don scooted out the door, Rose fluffed the pillow underneath Mattie's head, her hair looking as if it were outlined in flowers, a pink ruffle extending behind her.

"Thank you," Mattie said.

"Of course," Rose said. "It means the world to me. I just hoped it might help, even a little. Let me get your medication before you take a nap."

Mattie watched Rose leave, and again her eyes focused on the hope chest.

Have I found someone who loves Don and family as much as I do? Mattie thought.

Suddenly, her eyes drooped, and she pictured Rose as a young girl asleep on a pumpkin.

Cinderella should have her pumpkin carriage, Mattie thought. *We all should have our wishes come true.*

The soft pillowcase and worn embroidery made Mattie feel as if she were home, happy, a child again. Out of the corner of her eye, Mattie watched bluebirds tie the sash of the young woman.

Hope is the thing with feathers that perches in the soul and sings the tune without the words and never stops . . . at all, Mattie thought. *Don't stop fighting yet, Mattie.*

"I have your meds . . ."

Rose stopped at the door and smiled.

Mattie was sound asleep, a smile on her face, her cheeks as pretty and pink as those of the pillowcase princess.

"Beautiful dreams," Rose whispered, pulling the covers up over Mattie, "for a beautiful girl."

part eight

The Family Picture Frame

Twenty-one

November 2016

Mattie's wheelchair was perched in front of the patio doors overlooking the backyard. Mabel was lying on the hook rug, her head tilted, her long, floppy ears nearly horizontal to her head, like the wings on a plane.

The black-haired mutt was royally confused: The old rug, which Don and Mattie brought out every Thanksgiving, featured an image of a wild turkey that looked as realistic as the one strutting by in the Tices' backyard.

Mabel was confounded: She didn't know which was real.

After a few seconds of fogging up the patio door, Mabel turned her sights on the rug, barking and pawing at it, until she had the rug rolled into the shape of a giant Tootsie Roll, and scooted into the kitchen.

You fierce hunter, you, Mattie thought, giggling at her dog.

Mattie's beloved grandfather clock—which she had bought with Don in Switzerland while working on the gardens of a successful banker—chimed. She shut her eyes and counted the chimes, her mind transported back to the Swiss shop and the beautiful music of the clocks—grandfathers, regulators, cuckoos—ticking, chirping, dinging, chiming.

Mattie had painted that shop filled with clocks and given the finished artwork to her client.

Time was boundless then, Mattie thought.

The final chime echoed throughout the living room and kitchen.

Nine o'clock. Rose will be here any second, Mattie thought.

Even though it was barely fifty degrees, Mattie had asked Don to crack the door a sliver after he'd helped her get ready for the day.

I need to listen, she thought.

November on the coast of Michigan brought quiet, a momentary lull before the winter wind and snow.

If you still yourself and listen, Mattie thought, *you can hear the world pull up the covers, tuck itself in, and begin to hibernate.*

She shut her eyes and let her mind go blank. Through the crack in the patio door, Mattie could hear the trunk of an old spindly pine creak in the wind, its aged body sounding like her husband's knees in the morning; a cardinal's wake-up whistle, one of morning's first sounds; the whir of line, as fishermen patrolled the marsh; the voice of Matt Lauer on *Today* coming from a neighbor's TV.

In all of its horror, ALS had provided Mattie with one gift as her body betrayed her: She could still her mind and find a semblance of peace, even if only for a few moments a day.

Just enough to survive, Mattie thought. *Forget time is working against me.*

Mattie opened her eyes and looked out at her winter garden: Her beautiful flowers had been deadheaded, stalks cut, as if Rapunzel had gotten a bob.

And yet Mattie saw an undeniable beauty to her garden in this season as well as an undeniable parallel to her body with ALS.

It is dying, but not dead, she thought. *It, too, will be reborn come spring.*

Mattie could feel her hands move, as if she were clutching a brush and easel, painting her garden. Mattie had been a perfectionist as a child, a student, and a landscape architect. Painting had taught her to be still, to calm herself, to slow her mind and body, to be present, when she was a flurry of emotion and busyness.

Painting had taught her to see the beauty in the now, to stop and focus on what was in front of her, without looking ahead, and to simply be.

After years of denial, of medication, of tortured nightmares that had come with ALS, Mattie had finally reminded herself of those same things.

No matter how much time I have left, I must try to be present in the moment, she told herself. *Not only for Don, but for myself.*

The Fourth of July and Halloween, Rose and Jeri . . . they've all kept me in the present, despite my weakening body, Mattie thought. *I'm thankful for that.*

Mattie shut her eyes again. The cry of the ever-present hawk pierced the Michigan sky. The dull roar of Lake Michigan in the near distance called to her.

And then Mattie could detect the whispers of her husband coming from the bedroom. She tilted her head, just as Mabel had earlier, to listen.

"Can I think about it?" Don said. "Yes, I know that's a great offer. Yes, Mattie knows about their interest."

Silence.

"You did a great job, Jane," he continued. "I just need a little time. Yes, the house needs new memories. Very exciting. Yes. Very exciting news. I'll get back to you."

Silence.

"I need to run out for a little while after Rose gets here," Don said, startling Mattie, whose eyes were still shut. "I'm sorry. Were you napping?"

"A little," Mattie fibbed. "It's the weather."

"Did you need anything from the store?" Don asked. "I'm going to try and beat some of the Thanksgiving madness and get a few things."

"No big Thanksgiving," Mattie said. "Just the two of us."

"I know," he said. "But I still want it to be special."

Because it might be the last one, Mattie thought.

"And you still haven't told me what you want for our anniversary," Don said. "New Year's Eve. Fifty years. Can you believe it?"

Mattie shut her eyes, remembering their wedding. Her eyes fluttered, and she could feel her body dancing with her new husband.

Don put his hands on his wife's shoulders, looking out at the backyard.

"I remember our first dance, too," he said, reading her mind.

"So long ago," Mattie said softly.

"I wouldn't change a single second," he said. "A single second. We've had one beautiful dance, haven't we?"

Mattie smiled. "Yes."

"I love you," Don said. "More than anything."

"Me, too," Mattie said.

"Me, three!"

Jeri came sprinting into the house, her rag doll bouncing in her hand, and threw her arms around Don and Mattie.

"Surprise," Rose said, sarcasm and apology folded into the single word. "I'm sorry we're late. And I'm sorry for the surprise."

She stopped in the kitchen and dropped her bag. "I forgot Jeri didn't have school today. Teachers have in-service," Rose said, her red curls like mini-tornados all over her head, as if she hadn't even had time to run a comb through her hair. "And don't look at me!"

"I forgot to give her the note," Jeri said, her face drooping.

"And I didn't read the ten emails they sent," Rose said, walking over to tousle her daughter's own unruly locks. "Not your fault."

She stopped and looked at Don, Mattie, and her daughter intertwined like a pretzel. "Now that's a photograph," she said. "Don't move."

Rose ran back to her purse and grabbed her cell, before snapping a photo.

"You're a regular Annie Leibovitz," Don said.

"I can't pass up these pictures," she said. "They're so good."

"Who's Annie Llamawhich?" Jeri asked.

"Famous photographer," Mattie said with a chuckle. "Takes pictures."

"Oh," Jeri said. "Did she do this?"

The little girl walked into the living room and pointed at a beautiful painting of a summer garden, the flowers seemingly lit with an internal light, their colorful blooms dancing in an invisible breeze, the lake in the background an ethereal blue like the sky.

"I did that," Mattie said. "It's a watercolor."

"You?" Jeri asked, eyes wide. "How?"

"Jeri!" Rose admonished.

"It's okay," Mattie said. "I used to paint."

"Wow," Jeri said, eyes even wider. "It looks like a picture. So pretty."

"Thank you," Mattie said, her eyes narrowing. "I've got an idea."

She stopped and looked up at Don. Again, it was as if her husband could read his wife's mind.

"I think Mattie might like to teach you to paint, Jeri," he said, looking at his wife and nodding, before looking at the little girl. "How does that sound?"

Jeri squealed, jumping up and down. "Ann, would you like to learn how to paint?" she asked the doll.

"Don?" Mattie asked.

"I'll get your paints, pastels, and easel and set them up on the back patio," he said. "Then I'll head out and leave you two to create a masterpiece."

"Thank you," Mattie said.

As Don began to walk to the garage, Mattie looked over at Rose, who was still admiring the photo she had just taken. "Wait."

"Yes?" Don asked, stopping in his tracks.

"Picture frame," Mattie said. "Hope chest. Please."

"Picture frame?" Don asked.

Mattie nodded.

"I never knew this was in there," Don said, returning seconds later with an old, empty frame and holding it in front of Mattie.

Mattie looked at the frame and smiled sadly. "Was meant for our first child."

"Oh, sweetheart," Don said. "I didn't know."

Rose walked over and pulled her daughter into her arms, still holding her cell.

"I want Jeri to paint a picture on it," Mattie said slowly, smiling at the little girl before looking at her husband. "New memories, right?"

Don's eyes widened and he tilted his head at a comic angle, just as she and Mabel had done earlier. He stared at his wife.

"I'll get your paints and your pastels," he said, "and then I'll be back in a little while. Have fun."

Twenty-two

November 1977

Mr. Chance will be with you shortly. Please, have a seat."

Mattie nervously smoothed her skirt and then her hair, before turning and asking, "Where?"

The stone-faced butler—as starched as his uniform—had been taught never to show emotion, but he couldn't help it. A small smile ebbed across his face, as if a match were being held to an ice cube.

"Anywhere you'd like, ma'am," he said, gesturing dramatically to a marble living room overlooking the Pacific Ocean, which was filled with Hollywood Regency furniture and seemingly enough chairs and sofas to seat much of Los Angeles. "Would you like something to drink?"

Yes, Mattie thought. *Whiskey.*

"Water would be nice," she said, her throat dry and hoarse.

"Of course, ma'am."

He disappeared without a sound.

Mattie walked into the living room, her heels echoing throughout the enormous, empty space. Sunlight glinted off the shiny floors and reflected off the gilded, mirrored furniture. Mattie felt as if she were in an expensive fun house, and she steadied herself, took a seat in a stiff, high-backed upholstered chair, placed her portfolio against the chair, and then took a deep breath.

Calm down, she thought. *Be in the moment. This is your time.*

A few months back, a garden design Mattie had done for a famed New York chef who summered in Michigan had been featured prominently—and unexpectedly—in the *Times* Home section. Gorgeous flowers intermingled with herbs, chives, and garlic; the *Times* had termed Mattie "the hip, new Mother Earth," saying her designs perfectly balanced beauty with practicality.

Her phone had not stopped ringing, prompting Don to beg her to hire a full-time assistant and a full-time general contractor.

But out of all the calls, one message left on her answering machine had stopped her cold, prompting her to play it over and over, to ensure it was real:

"Good morning, this is Elise Elliott, the personal assistant for Dandy Chance. Mr. Chance would like to speak to you about designing the gardens at his new home in L.A. Give me a call at your earliest convenience. Thank you."

"I can practically hear the sunshine," Mattie had said to her assistant in her attic office at Hope Dunes, replaying the recording once more while staring at Lake Michigan, but instead seeing the ocean.

"I can practically hear the cash register," her assistant had said, laughing. "Want me to start researching Mr. Chance?"

Mattie laughed. "No need," she said to her youthful assistant.

Dandy Chance *was* Hollywood, especially to anyone born and raised on TV.

He got his start in the movies—singing, dancing, playing the funny friend or the nice guy who got jilted for the handsome fellow—but he soared on television. His variety show, *Take a Chance on Me*—filled with music and comedy—had made him a household name. He parlayed that into *Chance Encounter*, a show about a divorced man with three boys and three dogs who marries a divorced woman with three girls and three cats, who he meets in therapy. It ran for nearly fifteen years—America adopting the family's children as its own—and, ironically, the show mirrored his personal life times a hundred. Dandy, it seemed, was a bit randy, and he had been divorced more times than Elizabeth Taylor. As Dandy grew older, his wives grew younger.

But Dandy was an icon in Hollywood and in Michigan. He had grown up on the northern coast of Michigan and still loved the state. He had purchased an old fishing compound on Lake Michigan that he loved, but—according to rumors and the press—his new wife hated it. He had recently purchased a new estate on the ocean for his new bride.

"Your water, ma'am."

Mattie jumped, her mind racing back to the present.

He's like a cat, Mattie thought.

"Thank you," she said instead.

"Of course," the butler replied. "Mr. Chance is still tied up but will be with you as quickly as possible."

Mattie sipped her glass of water and stared at the expanse of water in front of her: The Pacific was turquoise green today, and surfers dotted the distant waves. Peeks of mansions—towers and turrets—rose above and through the tree lines, their grandeur hidden but still clear. The beach stretched out as far as Mattie's eyes could see. She shut her eyes: In the distance, she could hear the dull roar of the ocean.

Sounds just like Lake Michigan, she thought, centering herself. *I deserve to be here. I've worked so hard.*

Nearly a decade after launching her own company—of sinking her and Don's money, as well as some of her parents', into the business—it was finally taking off, like the gulls she watched flying over the coast.

Mattie stood, picked up her portfolio, and walked toward the floor-to-ceiling windows that engulfed the space. Although expensive paintings were hung on the walls, the view was truly the only art necessary.

She took a few echoing steps toward a set of massive French doors and pulled on one. It didn't budge.

How heavy are these, she thought.

This time, Mattie set down her portfolio and the glass of water and yanked again with all her might. The door opened with a silent whoosh, the warm, salty air infiltrating the chilled perfection of the house. Mattie gathered her things, walked outside, and slid the door shut with an *oomph*. Her eyes widened.

Stunning, she thought.

Colors immediately overwhelmed Mattie's visual senses: The home was white, sleek, almost an homage to an ancient Greek structure, and it sat against a towering hill lined with cypress and old grape vines. The outdoor patio was a world unto itself: Green-grey flagstones surrounded a blue-black lagoon heated pool, spa, and waterfall, and a glass-enclosed pool house reflected the blue ocean and sky, the green linear cypress, the white clouds, and house.

There was a large area on the far side of the patio that butted against another hill. The grass was brown and uncared for, and an old outdoor kitchen and wine-tasting room had seen better days. There was no flow, no garden, no connection between the spaces.

Mattie set down her water and portfolio on a small outdoor table. Her mind whirred. *This is it,* she thought. *I need a dandy design.*

"Ms. Price?"

"It's Tice."

Mattie heard a cacophony of clacks and jangles. She turned, and standing before her was Dandy's new wife, Cherry Chance.

"My apologies," Cherry said, extending her left hand slowly and gracefully. A series of thick, brightly colored, jewel-encrusted bracelets slid down her tan arm and collided loudly at her wrist like a drum roll, leading up to the introduction of her wedding ring, which was so big Mattie wondered how Cherry could even lift her thin arm.

That ring's as big as a peony bulb, Mattie thought.

For a moment, Mattie stood confounded. Between the size of Cherry's ring and the extension of her left hand rather than her right, Mattie helicoptered both arms a few times before forcing her left one to stop in midair.

Cherry shook her hand and then dropped it, eyeing Mattie closely.

Mattie self-consciously touched her hair and again smoothed her conservative skirt.

To Mattie, Cherry looked a lot like Jane Fonda in *Barbarella*: tousled, long blond hair that looked as if she had just gotten out of bed and shaken her head; cat-eye makeup giving her big blue eyes a vampish quality; dark brows and bubblegum pink lips; tan skin as golden as the Pacific's sand. Cherry was wearing a skintight pantsuit with high boots over the legs.

Mattie immediately wanted to weed Cherry's fashion choices—much like she did a garden—in order to get to the root of what really lay underneath all the clutter.

"You must be exhausted from the trip," Cherry said as if she didn't mean it. "So I'll just get to the point: Dandy only called you here because you're from Michigan."

Cherry stopped and let out a small yawn and then held out her left hand. Mattie didn't know if she was supposed to shake it again, or kneel and kiss her ring, but, before she embarrassed herself, the butler appeared—as if Cherry knew he would—and put a glass of rosé into it before disappearing.

"Dandy has very strong ties to the state, which I'll never understand," she said, shrugging her shoulders, her hair moving as one piece, and taking a generous sip of the pink wine. "I can't go back to that summer house. It's a former *fishing* compound. And Michigan is in the middle of nowhere."

Cherry looked directly at Mattie, her blue eyes growing even bluer. They reminded Mattie of the color of the ice caves that often formed on Lake Michigan in harsh winters. "Let's call this meeting a formality, shall we? Dandy is very loyal. And your little piece in the *Times* was sweet, but it was in the wrong *Times*. This is L.A., not New York. Different coast."

Mattie's heart, which had been racing, felt as if it had suddenly stopped. "Michigan has a beautiful coast," she said, trying to pick words from space. "Longest coastline in America."

"Interesting," Cherry said, again as if she didn't mean it. "I already have a designer chosen. He's hip and all the rage in California. He wants to put a lot of pots everywhere: philodendron and trailing plants. Macramé everywhere."

No! Mattie screamed in her head. *No!*

"And a lawn of green grass, just like they have on Dandy's TV show," Cherry continued, sipping her rose, lost in her own words. "Suburbia is very trendy right now, did you know?"

Yes, I get suburbia, Mattie wanted to say. *I read Erma Bombeck. And she'd have a lot to write about if she were here.*

"Lovely to meet you," Cherry said, shutting down the conversation without giving Mattie an opportunity to respond or discuss her work or thoughts. "I have a charity luncheon to attend. Someone will see you out."

Before Mattie could open her mouth, Cherry was gone, her bracelets signaling her exit.

Mattie was dumbfounded, crushed.

Don't cry, Mattie told herself. *Be strong.*

She took a few shaky steps, picked up her portfolio, and then downed her glass of water. Suddenly, Mattie began to cry.

"I think you might need something stronger."

Mattie jumped.

Standing beside her, with a small tumbler filled with amber liquid, was the butler.

"You're like a ghost," Mattie said before she could stop herself. "I'm sorry."

The butler laughed. "It's all in the shoes," he said, winking, and whispered, "No squeaks, no slides."

He stopped and looked around. "No bracelets."

Mattie giggled. "Is this whiskey?"

The butler nodded.

Mattie looked around, like he had just done, took the tumbler, and downed it.

" 'Atta girl." He laughed.

The whiskey instantly warmed Mattie—even though it was already eighty degrees outside—and her face flushed. Seconds later, Mattie felt lightheaded but relaxed.

"What's your name?" she asked without hesitation.

The butler smiled. "No one has ever asked me before," he said, before extending his hand. "George. George Lane."

"George, I'm Mattie Tice. It's nice to meet you. Even if for just a moment." She stopped and gathered her portfolio. "It seems a decision has already been made. I best be going. Sorry to waste everyone's time."

"So soon?" George asked. "Mr. Chance says people from Michigan never give up. He said it's the reason he's a success: 'Everyone will tell you no,' he always tells me, 'but it's up to you not to believe them.' "

Mattie smiled. "I don't give up," Mattie said. "But it seems as though, well . . . I don't stand a chance with Mrs. Chance."

"She's gone," George said, a twinkle in his eyes, his moustache twitching. "And Mr. Chance is still in a meeting about a big movie he wants to star in and direct. But—" George stopped. "You're the last designer that was called in for a meeting. Why don't you sit for a while and see if inspiration strikes out here. I'll bring you another drink—just to coax the muse— and I'll try to get Mr. Chance out of his meeting before Cherry returns. How's that sound?"

Mattie began to move toward the door but then stopped and did a full pirouette, her body and eyes circling around the property.

"Very Mary Tyler Moore of you," George said with a laugh. "I'll get that drink."

As he departed, George began to sing, *"You're gonna make it after all."*

Mattie laughed and took a seat. She opened her portfolio and pulled out the sketchpad and set of soft pastels she always carried.

Okay, Dandy, Mattie thought, pulling out a green pastel. *Here's to Michigan.*

Mattie shut her eyes and held the stubby pastel over the paper. When she drew, a calm came over her body, as if she were weightless, floating over the world, her mind the pastel, her soul the canvas.

You can do and be anything when you create. Just be still. Be in the moment. It's in that quiet that wonder begins.

Mattie smiled to herself, recalling the words her mother said to her when she first taught her to paint at Hope Dunes, on their beach, the dunes and the endless lake their inspiration.

Mattie had shut her eyes that day and began to paint. She had never stopped.

For the longest time, the only sounds were the ocean, Mattie's pastel dragging along the paper, and two hummingbirds chasing one another around the patio. Mattie opened her eyes, and furiously continued to draw, fusing Dandy's love of Michigan—peonies, white birch, clematis, irises— with the natural setting of the California coast: gardenias, poppies, agave, sage.

"It's beautiful."

Mattie stopped drawing and looked up at George. He was holding out another small tumbler of whiskey.

"Thank you," Mattie said. "I wanted Mr. Chance to be surrounded by inspiration, *home*. I wanted to mix the coast of California and the coast of Michigan, and it can be done. Different planting zones, but some plants overlap and can do so beautifully."

She stopped and scanned her eyes around the outdoor area. "This space should be inviting, timeless. It should complement the setting, not overpower it. And I was thinking—since he rarely gets to Michigan—I would go to his cottage and dig up some of those plants he has and bring them here. My own garden in Michigan is filled with starts from family and friends from around the country."

"Mr. Chance loves that idea," a familiar voice said. "And your design."

Mattie quickly stood, dropping her pastel, and reached out her hand. "It's a pleasure to meet you, sir," she said.

The actor smiled his famed dimpled smile, and the world seemed to stop for Mattie, who felt as if she were watching him on TV. He extended his hand and took a seat.

"Please, no *sir*," he said. "Just Dandy. Have a seat."

Dandy Chance was wearing a short-sleeved polo shirt and bright red pants, his dark hair slicked to one side, his teeth whiter than any Michigan blizzard. "May I?" he asked, reaching out his hands for Mattie's sketchbook. He studied it for a second, his dimples growing even deeper. "I knew there was a reason I invited you here. You're hired. When can you start?"

"But your wife . . . ," Mattie started.

"Cherry," Dandy said, his hair ruffling slightly in the ocean breeze, "is like the wind. She'll end up loving what you do. And take credit for discovering you."

Mattie laughed. "What do you have in mind," she asked, "you know, budget wise?"

This time Dandy laughed. "You can't put a price on beauty," he said, handing Mattie back her pad. "You are quite the talent."

He smiled his megawatt smile again, the one that millions of Americans saw every week, and stood.

"I'm sorry, but I have another meeting," he said. "It was lovely to meet you. Let me know when your design plans are finalized, and we'll get started. You can mail my assistant a contract."

Mattie stood, and he shook her hand again before lifting it up into the air. "The state of Michigan," he laughed, showing Mattie's palm to George as if it were a map, "is called 'the Mitten'. It's shaped just like a hand."

He stopped and looked Mattie deeply in the eyes. "I trust your hands with my home," he said before sauntering away.

Mattie felt woozy and took a seat. "Did that just happen?" she asked.

"It did," George said, handing her the tumbler. "Aren't you happy you stayed?"

"Yes," Mattie said, downing the drink in one gulp. "And I'm even happier I took a cab."

Mattie's landscape design—and enduring working relationship with Dandy—outlasted his marriage to Cherry.

As well as his next two relationships.

Twenty-three

Mattie watched her beloved pastels roll over the paper, her smile widening across her face.

"What should I paint on the frame?" Jeri asked Mattie, shaking her from her memories.

"Up to you," Mattie said into her mic, toggling her wheelchair closer to view what Jeri had been sketching: the sun and some clouds. "Pretty."

"Pretty boring," Jeri said, her face serious as she scanned the yard and horizon. "Everything is dead now."

"Not in your mind," Mattie said slowly. "Shut your eyes."

Jeri considered Mattie's advice for a second and then clamped her eyelids together quickly, scrunching her entire face as if to shut out the world.

Mattie stifled a chuckle. "Be still. It's in quiet that wonder begins."

Jeri kept her eyes shut. For a moment, there was complete silence, before the warbling, rolling cries of sandhill cranes filled the sky.

Suddenly, Jeri popped her eyes back open and watched the lanky, gray-bodied, crimson-capped birds head toward nearby wetlands and fields to eat and rest.

"I've got it!" she said, setting down her pastels and picking up a paintbrush. "How do I hold it? What do I do?"

Mattie explained, step by step, how to hold the brush, dip it into the water and the paints, and build a scene.

"Don't look," Jeri said, setting the old picture frame onto the outdoor table and using her body as a barrier to shield her work from Mattie.

"Promise," Mattie said.

Jeri hummed as she painted, taking a step back to consider her work every so often and reminding Mattie not to look. After a few minutes, Jeri stopped and turned to Mattie.

"Is painting what it's like to be you?"

Mattie looked at the little girl and raised her eyebrows.

"Well, you can't move your body, but you can move it around in your mind, right?" Jeri said, gesturing the whole time with the paintbrush.

Tears rushed to Mattie's eyes, but she swallowed hard to stop their rise. "Yes," she said, her voice breaking. "Yes."

Mattie steadied herself and continued. "You're exactly right. It's like I'm stuck in place—like my body is in quicksand—but my mind is flying and full of wonder. I can go anywhere and do anything and be anyone I want in my head, even though I can't move."

"That's art," Jeri said, nodding decisively. She was still for a moment. "It's good to be quiet sometimes. Good things happen."

She turned on her heels and began to paint again in earnest.

"All done," Jeri finally said.

She held out the frame for Mattie to inspect, her posture rigid and a proud look on her face. "What do you think?"

Mattie's eyes widened. On the frame, Jeri had painted a birch arching over the window where a photo would go, its bark white. Instead of leaves dangling from the tender branches, Jeri had painted faces: Mattie's, Don's, Rose's, her own, even Mabel's. At the bottom, roots painted in Technicolor supported the photo and the tree. On the right side of the frame, she had painted FAMILY TREE in pink.

The tree and faces were painted amateurishly and were depicted in a very childlike way, Mattie noted, but the thought behind it was very mature and deeply sensitive.

Again, Mattie swallowed hard to squelch the tears.

"Beautiful," she said. "You're a true artist."

"Thank you," Jeri said, taking a dramatic bow. She considered her own work, before looking at Mattie and asking, "Life is like flowers . . . and art . . . and quiet, isn't it?"

Mattie looked at the little girl.

"Hard but pretty," she explained. "And no one thinks about all that stuff enough."

"I'm proud of you," Mattie said.

"I'm proud of me, too." Jeri giggled, before studying Mattie closely. "I'm proud of you, too. You never give up."

This time, Mattie couldn't hold back her tears, and they poured out. "Thank you," she said.

Jeri used her sleeve to wipe Mattie's face.

"I made cookies," Rose said, walking out with a tray and a few glasses of milk. "Chocolate chip."

Jeri immediately reached for a cookie and shoved it in her mouth, warm chocolate smearing all over her fingers, lips, and face. "Mmmm," she mumbled.

"What do you say, young lady?" Rose asked.

"Thank you," Jeri said, her mouth full.

Mattie laughed. "Look," she said to Rose, gesturing to Jeri's frame.

"Jeri, this is so pretty," Rose said to her daughter. "You really have talent."

"Thank you, Mommy," Jeri said. "Mrs. Tice taught me everything. I was quiet, too."

"She was?" asked Rose.

"She was," said Mattie.

"Well, I think that deserves another cookie," Rose said.

As Jeri plucked another cookie from the tray, she noticed something sitting underneath the plate. "What's that?" she asked.

"Mr. Tice and I printed this off before he left, while you two were out here creating," Rose said. She held up a shiny photo: It was the one she had taken earlier of Jeri, Don, and Mattie hugging, all intertwined like a pretzel. "I thought it would be perfect for this frame."

Rose nabbed a pair of scissors off the tray. "Do you mind?" she asked.

Mattie shook her head, and Rose trimmed the photo until it fit snugly into the newly painted frame.

"You're not in it," Mattie said when Rose presented the frame to her.

"I am," she said, pointing to her painted face dangling from a branch.

Mattie nodded and smiled, staring at the birch, thinking of Dandy, stillness, art, and courage.

She looked over at Jeri, who was sneaking another cookie off the plate while her mother threw the paper scraps into the trash.

Jeri put her finger over her mouth, quietly entrusting Mattie with her secret.

Mattie winked and Jeri giggled.

Mattie looked at the frame, the words "Family Tree" in neon pink flashing in her eyes.

I never thought I'd be able to teach someone to paint, Mattie thought. *I never thought I'd have a child in my life.*

Her mind whirred back in time, and Dandy's dimples—still seen in late night reruns, although he was long gone from this earth—danced in her head.

There are no chance encounters in this world, are there, Dandy? Mattie thought.

part nine

The Antique Christmas Ornament

Twenty-four

December 2016

D on shook the front page of the *Saugatuck-Douglas Daily* in Mattie's face, his finger thumping the top of the page.

"Only Twenty Shopping Days Till Christmas," read a calendar held by a jovial Santa Claus in front of his belly.

"I need your list," Don said, sipping a toffee latte as he lay in bed beside his wife and their dog. "Even Mabel has given me her list," he continued, patting the dog. "She wants more treats."

Silence.

"And Mabel doesn't want to have to wear the velvet reindeer antlers like the dog from *How the Grinch Stole Christmas*," he tried to joke.

"No list," Mattie said.

Don acted as if he didn't hear her, but the paper trembled in his hands, an unsettling rattling in the quiet.

The snow had begun in earnest just after Thanksgiving, and it hadn't let up yet. It likely wouldn't until March. The western coast of Michigan—particularly Saugatuck-Douglas—was in what was termed the snowbelt. Every year, as colder winter air moved across the warmer waters of Lake Michigan, a phenomenon known as lake-effect snow occurred. For residents who stayed year-round in the resort towns, the result was akin to living on the wrong end of a snow blower.

The Tices had once loved winter in the resort towns: Whereas Missouri had a relatively mild winter—where it would "snow and go"—there was still lots of ice and weather in the heart of the Midwest that resembled a roller coaster. Michigan truly had four seasons, albeit many would joke in March that winter had too much of the share.

Don and Mattie used to snowshoe and cross-country ski. They used to decorate Hope Dunes, which was once part of the town's Holiday Home Tour. But once Mattie got ill, it all became too much.

I'm a shut-in, Mattie thought, looking out the window, the snow falling steadily. *I can't even decorate, make my wreaths, shop.*

Mattie's eyes studied the pines that were flocked in white, and the frost that had created an intricate pattern in the edges of the window, a frozen stencil of lace.

I used to love Christmas, Mattie thought, before a question popped into her head. *Is this my last one?*

Don flipped the paper open, and something else on the front page caught Mattie's eye: There was a feature and many pictures about the towns, which were in the midst of decorating for the holidays.

A smile lit Mattie's face.

So beautiful, she thought. *Nobody does the holidays better than Saugatuck-Douglas.*

Every year, the neighboring towns decorated as if Santa himself were coming to personally inspect the decorations. Everyone—*everyone*—turned out like elves to hang lights and wreaths and, quite literally, bedazzle and douse the town in holiday cheer.

But tradition ruled the towns' decorating: Saugatuck always put up a million white lights, while Douglas always hung a million colored lights. Both towns were draped in pine boughs and red velvet bows. Every shop window gave Macy's a run for its money, and during the holidays carolers sang on street corners, horse-drawn carriages pulled families up and down the snow-covered streets that paralleled the channel, and performers acted out *A Christmas Carol* at the local theatre. Giant, lit snowflakes and holiday wreaths—along with holiday flags—were hung from the bridge that connected the two towns, and a huge, lit tree was placed in the middle of the bay between Saugatuck and Douglas.

A beacon of hope, Mattie thought. *That's what the tree represented to me. Hope that the next year would be even better.*

Don rustled the paper again, which rustled Mattie from her thoughts. Her attention was drawn to the back page of the paper, where the local real estate companies listed the houses for sale.

There, at the top, under the headline, "One-of-a-Kind-Properties" was Hope Dunes, a photo of the house in all its stunning glory, the lake glimmering and spread out behind it.

It looks like a beautiful bride waiting for her husband to return from sea, Mattie thought.

Her heart began to race, as she remembered overhearing Don on the phone a few weeks back.

She is *waiting,* Mattie thought, looking at the photo of the cottage. *For my husband to return.*

"I know what I want for Christmas," Mattie said out of the blue.

"You do?"

Don dropped the newspaper into his lap and leaned toward his wife, his face lit with a smile. "Really?"

Mattie nodded. "I want Mabel to wear the antlers," she joked.

Don rolled his eyes and rubbed the dog's belly. Mabel was upside down between the two of them, legs toward the ceiling, snoring.

"I want to attend the holiday parade," Mattie said slowly. "The Parade of Lights."

A sad smile replaced his happy one, and he reached out and grabbed his wife's hand. "You really shouldn't be out in the cold, or around too many people, sweetheart," he said, his voice low. "You know what the doctor says: The chance of getting sick is too great. You can't risk getting pneumonia."

"Don't care," Mattie said. "I want to see it. Before . . ."

Mattie's voice trailed off with a heartbreaking squeak, and Don moved Mabel and scooted over in bed, until his arms were around his wife. "Okay," he said.

"And I want to decorate for Christmas," she said. "A tree. Presents. Everything."

"Okay," Don said, a new smile making his freckles dance.

Mattie stopped and looked her husband directly in the eyes. "At Hope Dunes," she said.

"Honey, we can't do that," he said. "You know that. The house is for sale. People may be looking at it over the holidays."

"Don't care," Mattie said again. "I want to do it before . . ."

She stopped again, the unsaid words dangling in the air.

"And I want to dance in front of the tree," she continued, very slowly, "for our anniversary. Like we used to. . . . One last time."

Don bit the inside of his cheek, but the pain couldn't prevent his eyes from filling with tears.

"Don't say that," he whispered.

"True," she said, before mimicking her husband's previous words. "You know that."

Don let his wife's strength flood into his body. He gave her a gentle kiss on the cheek and said with enthusiasm, "Well, then, I've got a lot of work to do. I'm glad I know what to get you finally. But, first, I'm finishing my morning paper."

Mattie smiled as Don returned to reading the paper. A sense of peace, purpose, and routine—as gentle and beautiful as the snow falling outside—came over Mattie.

And I'm glad I know what I'm getting you, too, she thought.

"Pretty!" Jeri yelled, running up to pet the horse—dressed in a red velvet bow and top hat with red feather plume. "Can we go on a ride?"

Snow was lightly falling, and it looked as if Jeri's red curls had been flocked like a Christmas tree.

"Go," Mattie urged. "All of you. I'll wait."

The four had arrived very early to the annual Parade of Lights, so that Don could find parking for the van and get Mattie's wheelchair situated at the starting point—the corner of Main and Water—before the crowds arrived.

Even though the parade was still over an hour away—and it was bone-chillingly cold—revelers had already begun descending on Saugatuck, and the parade lineup snaked around the block: bands, shop owners in antique cars, revelers dressed as elves and the Grinch, and, of course, Santa.

"Are you sure?" Don asked.

"Where am I going?" Mattie asked.

Don laughed and wrapped Mattie's scarf a bit more snugly around her neck. He buttoned the top of her coat and then checked her mittens.

"Go!" she said.

Don looked back at her hesitantly.

"Go!" she said again.

"Can I sit by you?" Jeri asked the carriage driver, her eyes wide.

"Of course, m' lady," he said, adjusting his bow tie and leaning over to help her into the front seat.

Rose and Don scrambled into the backseat, and with a flourish of the reins, the horse began to trot down the street, the bells draped across its neck jangling with every step.

Mattie could feel herself waving to them as they took off, the scene like one from a storybook: a horse-drawn carriage jingling in the snow down a throwback street lined with luminaries.

Mattie smiled to herself. The carriage—with its large, thin wheels and top draped in boughs and ribbons—was exactly the same as what Mattie used to ride on when she was just a bit older than Jeri was now.

The horses for the carriage were still rescues, and they lived a glorious life on the Smith Farm outside of town. Besides grazing and frolicking, this was their one job of the year—almost like equine Santas—and the towns-folk coddled them royally. It was still only a dollar per ride, money that went to the rescue organization.

"Mattie," a woman said. "Oh, my goodness. Is that you?"

A singsong voice chirped behind Mattie's shoulder. Between the syrupy tone and the buckets of perfume, Mattie immediately knew who it was: Fern Reynolds.

"Yes," Mattie said. "Hi, Fern."

"You must have eyes in the back of your head," Fern said, coming into view. "Guess who I am?"

Fern was dressed as Mrs. Claus and, to Mattie, it was typecasting: Fern really did look like Santa's better half, even without the round glasses, cap, long red dress with fur cuffs, and apron.

"Mrs. Claus," Mattie said, playing along. "Perfect."

"Ho, ho, ho," Fern said, her hands on her stomach like her husband, but the signature laugh coming out more like the squeak of one of Mabel's dog toys rather than a boom of happiness.

Fern smiled and, without thinking, began to reach for Mattie. But she stopped, midair, snow twirling around her still body, before retracting. Her face fell as she really looked at Mattie for the first time.

"You look well," Fern said, her happy chirp escalating into a nervous shout. "We've all missed you. The clubs just aren't the same without your drive and energy."

I look well? Mattie thought. *You've missed me? Then why has no one even bothered to visit me? I'm five minutes away. I thought you all were my friends.*

Fern looked up and down the street, as if she had somewhere to be, right now. Mattie watched her squirm, and her stomach dropped. ALS may have crippled her body, but people's reactions to her illness crippled her spirit.

Does it spread? Can I catch it? Will I break you if I touch you? How are you alive? Mattie knew people were thinking by their reactions and whispers. To her face, people just shouted at Mattie, as if she were aged, infirmed, and hard of hearing.

But mostly, Mattie thought, *the sad truth is my terminal illness reminds others that their lives are not infinite, that sickness can intrude, that—at any time—the fragile beauty and perfection of their health and lives can be shattered like a holiday ornament.*

And, Mattie concluded, *the best way to continue with that façade is simply to avoid those who are ill. Out of sight, out of mind.*

"I have to run," Fern said, waving at an invisible person in the crowd. "The women's club is selling holiday ornaments again this year in front of the Christmas store, and Mrs. Claus is a main attraction. You know, your ornaments were still the best sellers we've ever had."

Fern's lip quivered for a second, and she looked closely at Mattie as if for the first time, reality seeming to settle into her consciousness. "I'll try and stop by and see you soon. You moved, right? So busy with the holidays, though. And then Bill and I are off to Florida."

Fern suddenly stopped talking, turned, and strode off, disappearing into character once again, Mrs. Claus happily chirping, "Ho, ho, ho!" to parade-goers.

My ornaments, Mattie thought, watching Fern scamper away.

For decades, Mattie had designed and hand-painted the holiday orna-ments that the women's club sold. The proceeds were used for the Parade of Lights and all of the other town holidays, from the St. Patrick's Day Pub Crawl to the Memorial Day Race, the Labor Day Bridge Walk and Pan-cake Breakfast to the Halloween parade.

As soon as every Christmas ended, Mattie would immediately begin to brainstorm ideas for next year's ornament. She would spend months sketch-ing designs and then months hand-painting each ornament. Her designs had focused on town landmarks—from the lit tree in the bay to the last hand-cranked chain ferry in America that carried tourists from one side of the channel to the other every summer to climb Mount Baldhead. But Mat-tie's specialty—and most beloved ornament designs—was of local plants and flowers: trillium, ferns, May apples, hydrangea, white birch.

I miss doing that, she thought.

Mattie thought of all the years she had decorated for Christmas with Don and her parents—in St. Louis and Michigan—the memories flashing through her mind, like antique ornaments twinkling under the flickering lights on a decorated tree.

Each ornament is a memory, Mattie's mother had told her every single year as they decorated the tree with boxes of unique, antique ornaments. *Beau-tiful, special.*

Every ornament is fragile, like life, and must be handled with care, her mother would always continue. *But when we hang it, we remember the beauty and blessings of life.*

"That was fun!"

Jeri came sprinting up to Mattie, her excitement coming out in a rush of words.

"The horse was so pretty, and he jangled the whole way, and I got to feed him a carrot at the end, and then Mommy took my picture kissing him, and then . . ."

Mattie laughed.

Without warning, a drum crashed and the high school band began to march, playing "Jingle Bell Rock," signaling the start of the parade. Jeri mimicked playing the trombones, acting as if she were moving the long slide, and then high-stepped like the band members in their uniforms and white spats.

A big truck—decorated to look like Santa's workshop and filled with elves busily making toys—slowly moved by, followed by another that appeared to have penguins skating on ice.

"One, two, three, the snow is coming, Whee!" chanted a group of men in Santa hats and T-shirts that read "The Shovel Brigade."

Mattie felt herself clapping. The Shovel Brigade was a parade mainstay, comprised of local men carrying snow shovels and dressed in flannel pajamas who stopped to perform a precision routine—not with batons or flags, but with shovels, which they twirled and tossed, before dancing with them, as if the shovels were their dance partners. The brigade had been performing for decades, the tradition passed down from father to son, grandfathers to grandchildren.

"Yeah," Jeri yelled. "I love the shovel guys!"

A fire truck honked as it slowly drove past, the firemen tossing candy to the kids. Jeri dropped her mother's hand and scurried for some candy in the street.

"Jeri, be careful," Rose said.

"It's not for me," Jeri said. "It's for Mrs. Tice."

She smiled innocently and popped a couple of chocolate kisses into her mouth, before unwrapping a hard candy and holding it out for Mattie, who grinned and stuck out her tongue.

"Be careful," Don said.

Mattie shot him a look and then closed her eyes, snowflakes falling off her lashes.

"Mmm," she said. "Butterscotch."

Jeri clapped, nestled closely into Mattie's side, and the two watched the parade. Finally, Santa arrived in his sleigh, and Jeri's eyes widened.

"Is that . . . ?" she asked.

"Who's been naughty, and who's been nice?" Santa said into his mic, his voice rumbling throughout the downtown streets.

"Nice!" Jeri yelled, jumping up and down to get Santa's attention. "I've been nice."

"Well, I've got a present, since the whole town has been nice." Santa laughed, flicking a big, fake switch in the sleigh. "Ho! Ho! Ho!"

And with that, the entire town lit up with a million lights, the winter world draped in white: buildings, rooftops, trees, pine boughs lining shop windows, even the small town park and its ornate fence.

"Wow," Jeri said. "Pretty."

"Look," Mattie said.

Jeri followed Mattie's gaze to the top of Mount Baldhead, the highest dune in the area, overlooking the lake and the little resorts. A star—as big and bright as a full moon—twinkled atop the mighty dune.

"Wow," Jeri said again.

She blinked, mesmerized by the light, and then turned to her mom, Mattie, and Don.

"Is that for the wise men?" Jeri asked. "To follow?"

"Yes," Mattie said with a smile, the snow falling at a quickening pace.

"They knew stuff we didn't," Jeri said, a sound of conviction in her voice.

Mattie watched the parade-goers take pictures of the star and then rush into the street to get photos of Santa and Mrs. Claus. Fern was smiling, her head tilted against that of her jovial faux husband. She turned, and—for a second—she and Mattie locked eyes. Then Fern turned away.

I sure hope they knew stuff we didn't, Mattie thought, silently answering Jeri's question. *I sure hope so.*

"Who wants hot chocolate?" Don asked.

"I do, I do," Jeri said.

"Will you help me?" Don asked, and Jeri nodded. "We'll run to Lake Effect Coffee and be right back. I think I need a toffee latte to ward off this cold. Back in a jiffy."

"I think she had a good time," Rose said, her cheeks red, as Don and Jeri walked away holding hands.

"Me, too," Mattie said.

"Thanks for including us," Rose said. "I used to come with my parents."

"Me, too," Mattie repeated.

The two watched as people began to scramble into the local restaurants and shops. A man in an elf costume scurried past, yelling toward some similarly dressed friends heading into the Sand Bar Saloon.

"This elf needs a drink," he yelled.

Mattie and Rose laughed, and then Mattie looked at Rose with a serious expression.

"Speaking of elves," Mattie said. "I need your help."

Twenty-five

I think it's colder inside than out," Don said, pushing Mattie's wheelchair into the family room of Hope Dunes, Mabel trailing alongside. He walked over to the thermostat and turned it up. "I better build a fire, too. But first . . ."

". . . you better turn on some lights," Mattie added, her words spoken into the mic sounding robotic in the empty house.

"Voila!" Don yelled.

A smile lit up Mattie's entire face, even more than the twinkling lights on a Christmas tree that came to life in the corner of the room.

"Don," she said.

"Merry Christmas, my love," he said. "Your Christmas wish is my command."

"How?" she asked. "When?"

"I sneaked over the day after the parade to our woods and cut it down," he said. "We still own the place for now, right?"

"Right," Mattie said, still smiling.

"Fraser fir," he said. "Your favorite."

"Smells like heaven," Mattie said, toggling her wheelchair toward the tree, onto which Don had already woven twinkling lights through the branches and hung an assortment of vintage bulbs—the big ones—in red, green, and blue. "Merry Christmas."

The lights twinkled off Mattie's face. Don watched his wife—her face rapt, a dreamy look shadowing her eyes—and, for a second, Don could see the young girl who had decorated her first tree here so long ago with her parents and, then, for decades, with him.

"Oh, Don," Mattie said, her eyes fixed on the base of the tree. "Too many."

Beautifully wrapped gifts were stacked underneath the tree, and Mabel was inspecting each and every one.

"Stick-on bows?" Mattie asked.

Don reared his head back and laughed harder than he had in a long time.

"Caught me again," he said. "Velvet-handed."

While Mattie may have spent her career designing elaborate gardens, Don was a perfectionist and artist as well, not only in his work in the furniture industry but also in his stone polishing. But his gift-wrapping skills—which he had learned from Mattie's mother—were as magnificent as Martha Stewart's.

When Mattie was in the midst of too many jobs one Christmas—and constantly on the road—she had had very little time to shop for the holidays. She ran into the basement, where her mother had created a wrapping station years ago, to hurriedly wrap her presents, but could not find a single stick-on bow to expedite the process. Instead, she found drawers filled with stunning ribbon and rolls of velvet.

"Are you kidding me?" she had yelled.

When Don had rushed down to see if she were okay, she had yelled, "Not a single stick-on bow?"

"Would you stick a plastic plant in one of your designs?" Don had asked with a straight face.

"No." Mattie had sighed with a chuckle. "Teach me."

"Gifts should be as beautiful as the one receiving them," Don said to his wife, knocking her from the memory.

Mattie smiled at her husband and then noticed the pretty round tree skirt—embroidered with tiny Santas coming down miniature chimneys and

decorated with snow-covered pine trees, gifts stacked underneath—that encircled the trunk.

"Is that . . . ?" Mattie started.

"Yes," he said. "From your hope chest. And I brought the Nativity scene,
too. It was still boxed in the garage."

"And I brought these!"

Rose scurried into Hope Dunes, Jeri and a curtain of snow following.

"Merry Christmas," Rose said, setting down an armload of bags and
then knocking the snow off her coat.

"What are you doing here?" asked Don. "It's Christmas. You should be
at home."

Jeri came running over to him, still in her coat, and threw her arms
around him. "We are at home, silly," she said, her face buried in his leg.

"What a lovely surprise," Don said.

"We're elves!" Jeri yelled, which brought an immediate, "Jeri! Hush!"
from her mother.

"You're not the only one who can still do all the surprising," Mattie said
slowly, a sly smile emerging on her face, still twinkling in the lights.

Rose walked over with the bags. "Jeri's right," she said, giving Mattie a
kiss and Don a hug. "We are elves."

"Mommy said Santa was so busy this year, he needed extra special help,"
Jeri said. "So he asked us!"

Mattie laughed, and Rose leaned in to whisper into her ear. "I brought
everything you asked."

"Envelopes in tree," Mattie said softly, turning her head away from the
mic. "Ornaments in front."

"What's going on?" Don asked.

Mattie, Rose, and Jeri all looked at one another, heads moving back and
forth, like gophers in the old arcade game, whack-a-mole.

"Okay, Stooges, I get it," Don said. "I'm not in on this secret. I'll go
gather some wood and start a fire, so we can warm up and I can give you
a little time to talk in quiet. I think we still have some wood stacked out
back from last winter."

"Oh, Don," Mattie said, finally noticing what was hanging from the log mantel above the fireplace: four fuzzy stockings, with the names Mattie, Don, Mary Ellen, and Joseph written in glitter glue at the top of each one.

Don winked at his wife, tightened the scarf around his neck, pulled on his gloves, and grabbed a worn canvas firewood carrier that still sat draped over the iron log holder. "C'mon, Mabel," he called to the dog, as he opened the front door and disappeared into a swirl of snow.

"Thank you," Mattie said. "For everything."

Rose set down the bags and reached into one, pulling out two envelopes— *Don* written in cursive in beautiful gold ink on the outside of both—which she placed between branches on opposite sides of the tree. She then carefully eased out a few old, worn boxes from the bags. Around the lid of each box was written *Shiny Brite Christmas Tree Ornaments,* a plastic window in the middle that provided a peek at twelve colorful, frosted vintage ornaments.

Jeri rushed over to look at the boxes and study the ornaments. "Look! Each one has its own bed."

Rose carefully opened one of the boxes. "My grandma had ornaments like this," she said, her voice tinged with wistfulness. "I think we sold them all."

"These were my grandmother's, too," Mattie said. "They *are* Christmas."

"Can I look?" Jeri asked.

Mattie nodded.

"Be careful," Rose warned. "They're old and very fragile."

"Like me," Mattie said with a smile.

Jeri slowly lifted a yellowed top off another old box of ornaments and ran her finger over each one.

"Pretty," she said, her eyes wide. "Every one is different."

"Like people," Mattie said.

One at a time, Jeri gingerly lifted each ornament from its little bed. Some were all gold, some all red, a few pink, and a few aqua. Some of the ornaments were ringed with colorful paint and glitter, while others featured dainty designs in white and silver of candles that read *Greetings,* or sacks of toys, snowmen, or cardinals on branches. A few of the ornaments looked like bells while others were shaped like pinecones, and some featured beautiful, shiny starburst cutouts in the center.

The ornaments were crackled and the glitter dulled. Some of the paint had worn off the others.

"Put the first one on the tree," Mattie said to Jeri.

"I can't," she said. "What if I break one?"

"You won't," Mattie said. "Please."

Jeri nodded, her red curls bouncing. "Which one?"

"Up to you," Mattie said.

Jeri slowly opened every box, leaning over each ornament, as if it were the biggest decision of her life. She finally picked one that looked like a little top, red and green with frosted glass between the colors.

"Let me help you," Rose said.

She grabbed the hanger that was attached to the end of the ornament. "Pick the perfect spot," Rose said.

Jeri walked around the tree, eyeing it up and down, before stopping and pointing. "Right here," she said excitedly, her finger directing her mother to a tiny opening between green branches that was at her eye level.

Rose hung the ornament in the small space, and it twirled there, just like a top, twinkling in the lights.

"So we both can see it," Jeri said with conviction, looking at Mattie and smiling.

"Perfect spot," Mattie said.

Jeri's face exploded into a bright smile.

"Keep going," Mattie urged.

"Really?" Jeri asked. "Will you help me, Mommy?"

Together, the two began to pick perfect spots for every ornament that Rose had smuggled from the Tices' new garage, leaving room to later layer the tree in shiny garland and tinsel.

"Who wants a fire?" Don asked, breathing heavily and bursting through the door, a big load of wet firewood making the carrier sag under the weight. Mabel rushed in and shook a pile of snow onto Jeri.

"Mabel," she said, giggling. "No!"

Don muscled the wood over to the rack, set it down with a thump, and gasped for air. Finally, he looked up. "Someone's been busy," he said, walking over and pulling from Jeri's hair a piece of tinsel—a remnant of a long-ago Christmas—which was clinging to her red curls thanks to the static electricity in the cottage.

She giggled. "Isn't it pretty?" Jeri asked. "Our tree at home isn't very big."

"I'm sure it's beautiful," Don said. "What did Santa bring you this morning?"

"This," Jeri said, spinning in a pretty pink princess dress. "And this," she continued, running over to pull her rag doll from one of her mother's bags, which was wearing a matching dress.

"And a new coat, and a new game, and a new Taylor Swift CD!"

"And one more thing," Mattie said, looking at Rose, who pulled a big present from another bag.

"I thought Santa brought this for them," Jeri said.

"Open it," Mattie said, her eyes big as she looked at Don, who shrugged, clueless that any of this had secretly been planned.

Jeri tore off the ribbon and pretty paper. "Paints!" she yelled, running over to hug Mattie and then Don. "Thank you."

Mattie beamed.

"Now I can be just like you," Jeri said, staring at the picture of a painting on the front of the box.

"Okay," Don said, picking up the wrapping paper and rolling it into a ball. "Now we can have a real fire."

He knelt on an old hooked rug—a giant circle of richly colored coiled fabric—and placed the paper in the middle of the huge fireplace, whose lake stones of greens, red, and greys were aged by smoke. Don then built a small pyramid of sticks and kindling over the paper, before standing to retrieve a long lighter and setting it ablaze.

"What kind?" Mattie asked as Don reached for a log.

Don laughed. "It's not sassafras," he said to his wife, sarcasm dripping off the words. He turned to Rose, still breathing heavily. "We have a genetic tendency in this family to set chimney fires in Hope Dunes. Her father did it when he bought the house, and I used to do it nearly every fall when we'd build the first fire.

"How did that old saying go?" Don continued, nodding at the ghostly square that still appeared over the fireplace. "'The Firewood Poem'? It used to be on a plaque that sat right there in that spot forever. I can even remember the poet's name. It sounded so royal for the poem and this old cottage."

Don stopped, bowed, and said in his best English accent, "Lady Celia Congreve."

Mattie shut her eyes and could remember her father hanging it there the very first day he'd bought Hope Dunes. She opened her eyes and stared at the square over the fireplace, an empty spot there just like in her heart.

"*Birch and fir logs burn too fast . . . ,*" Mattie started.

"That's it, that's it," Don said excitedly to both Mattie and the fire, which had started to take off. "Let me see if I can finish it . . ."

> *Blaze up bright and do not last . . .*
> *But ash green or ash brown*
> *Is fit for a queen with golden crown*
> *Poplar gives a bitter smoke*
> *Fills your eyes and makes you choke*
> *Apple wood will scent your room*
> *Pear wood smells like flowers in bloom*
> *Oaken logs, if dry and old*
> *Keep away the winter's cold*
> *But ash wet or ash dry*
> *A king shall warm his slippers by.*

"Was that right?" Don asked, standing and looking at his wife. "I didn't make an ash of myself, did I?"

"Yes and no," Mattie said with a smile. "In that order."

"What a fire," Jeri said, taking a seat on the rug next to Mattie's wheel-chair, patting the floor for Mabel to join her. "Warm."

Mattie looked at Rose, her eyes glowing in the fire. "Ready?" she asked her.

Rose nodded and walked over to the bags still sitting by the tree. She pulled one last box from a bag. "From your hope chest," she said, "as you asked."

"For the top of the tree," Mattie said.

"An angel, I bet," Jeri said excitedly, walking over on her hands and knees. "Or a star."

She opened the box, and a strange look came over her face as she pulled out a misshapen globe comprised of mismatched pieces of all different colors and shapes—a sort of junkyard collage-cum-mosaic.

"What is this?"

"Tree topper," Mattie said.

"It's . . . ," Jeri started, "ugly."

"Jeri," Rose said. "That's not nice."

"No, it isn't perfect," Mattie said, staring at the topper Jeri was holding. "All of us are broken, but that doesn't mean we're not beautiful. Tells a story."

Mattie looked at her husband, who walked over and put his hands on his wife's shoulders, the meaning moving him. "You've seen Rudolph, haven't you?" Don asked Jeri, taking a seat on the rug and patting a place next to him. Jeri scooted over, still holding the ornament from the hope chest, and tilted her head up at Don.

"Just this week," Jeri said, as her mom took a seat beside her and Mabel.

"Well, this could be from the Island of Misfit Toys," Don said. "This ornament tells a story of a Christmas ruined and renewed. It's a story of hope."

Twenty-six

Christmas 2002

E ggnog?"
Mattie shook her head no and looked up at the empty Christmas tree. Red and green crates filled with lights, tinsel, and ornaments surrounded the base. The little Nativity scene sat off to one side, unassembled, the wise men facing opposite directions, looking as if they were lost and in need of a map, while sheep lay on their sides.

Don sat the eggnog down on the mantel over the fireplace and took a seat on the floor on a hooked rug next to his wife. He gently put his arm around her back.

"I know it's hard this year, my love," he said softly.

Mattie didn't look at him. Instead, she looked out the doors leading to the porch, where snow was filtering through the screens like sifted flour.

She turned and looked toward the quiet kitchen, and then focused again on the empty tree.

My mom would have trees in every room of the house by now, she thought. *My dad would be playing Dean Martin and Rosemary Clooney Christmas songs.*

Mattie leaned her head onto her husband's shoulder and began to weep.

"Christmas will never be the same," she said, her words coming out in big, heaving gasps.

Don pulled his wife close and held her until she stopped crying, until only the sound of the howling wind roaring across the water remained.

"You're right," he said. "Christmas will never be the same now that both of your parents are gone."

Don stopped and put his hand under his wife's chin, forcing her to look him in the eyes.

"But that doesn't mean Christmas will never be beautiful again."

Mattie smiled weakly at her husband.

"I think I'll take that eggnog now," she said.

Don stood and offered Mattie his hand. He pulled her to her feet and then handed her the eggnog.

Mattie took a sip and sighed.

I love eggnog, she thought.

She set her sights on the crates before her, took another sip, and then looked at Don. "I don't know if I can put the antique ornaments on this year, though," she said.

"That's okay," Don said. "I'm going to go cut a little Charlie Brown pine for your kitchen tree and then find a sturdy blue spruce for the screened porch. If I'm not back in a half hour, send a Saint Bernard with whiskey."

Mattie tried to smile as Don walked outside into the snow.

She opened the first crate, marked *Family Tree,* and without warning a flood of memories rushed into her head along with new tears.

On top sat four stockings—names written in cursive with glue and glitter—for Mattie and Don, and for her mother and father. Underneath were small boxes filled with family ornaments: cookie ornaments Mattie had baked and shellacked with her mother in St. Louis; crocheted ornaments of angels, wreaths, snowflakes, and Santa faces that her grandmother had made; little dog bones with the names of beloved pets; souvenir ornaments—sand dollars and a silhouette of the New York City skyline, with the Rockefeller skating rink and holiday tree—as well as handmade ornaments Mattie had made in school.

I miss you, Mattie thought, touching each ornament.

Mattie's eyes scanned the remaining crates, all marked on top with her mother's looping cursive, each one designating a specific tree's decorations.

The *Kitchen Tree* crate was filled with adorable ornaments in the shapes of utensils and blenders, coffee cups and cookie cutters, gingerbread men and women. The *Garden Tree*—always wrapped in raffia on the screened porch—crate contained beautiful birdhouse ornaments, ornate ornaments that resembled beloved flowers, birds, and gardening Santas as well as antique garden implements and mini-garden gates. The *Michigan Tree* crate was overflowing, of course, with "Mitten" ornaments as well as needlepoint lighthouses and beach scenes, tanning Santas and elves, and a little flocked tree sitting in a birch basket. The *Cottage Tree* crate contained all things nostalgic: ornaments of canoes and fishing poles, lit log cabins and glittering pinecones, dancing deer and snowshoes.

Every year, Mattie's mother had put up ten trees, one in nearly every room. It took the four of them nearly a week to finish decorating, inside and out, a labor of love Mattie didn't know if she had the energy to complete this year.

She looked at the electric Christmas candles her mother had put in nearly every window and dormer to greet guests and tell passersby, "Happy holidays."

My holiday flame has been extinguished, Mattie thought.

Mattie took a sip of eggnog and eyed the tree before her, halfheartedly beginning to intertwine the garland throughout its limbs. She gave a heavy sigh and then slowly began to hang some of the beloved antique family ornaments, standing on her tippy toes, starting at the top of the tree.

"I'm dreaming of a White Christmas . . ."

"How can you decorate without holiday music?" Don's voice asked from the kitchen as music flowed from the speakers. Don started to sing Bing again. "It's like eggnog and snow. You *have* to have it at the holidays."

Don poked a tiny tree through the doorframe and into the family room, making it appear as if it were dancing to the music. He eased his head through the frame and saw his wife's shoulders sag even more as Bing continued to sing. He set down the little pine and walked into the family room.

"Your mother would want you to have a merry Christmas," Don said, pulling Mattie in for a hug.

"I hate platitudes like that," she said. "How would you know?"

Don held his wife at arm's length. "I do know that," he said. "Look at all the effort she went to her whole life to make the holidays special for you . . . for all of us."

Don stopped, and his face became filled with emotion. "Do you know how much I miss your mother and father?" he asked, his voice shaking. "I didn't have this growing up. They treated me like their son. I want to continue all of their traditions because that means they will forever be with us."

"I forgot you were hurting, too," Mattie said. "I'm sorry."

As they hugged, they heard a twinkling, a shudder, and they pulled back to look at one another.

"Must be the wind," Don said.

The twinkling continued, this time louder, and the two turned toward the tree, whose branches were shaking.

"Earthquake?" Mattie asked.

"In Michigan?" Don said, his eyes drifting toward the base of the tree. "Oh, no! You didn't secure—"

Before he could finish his sentence, the tree tilted and then toppled, as if it were being chopped down by a lumberjack. Don and Mattie scurried like church mice away from the tree as it gained momentum, turning just in time to see the tree crash onto the floor.

"Our ornaments!" Mattie cried, rushing over—her shoes crunching on the shattered glass.

She stooped and picked up a piece of a glittery aqua ornament that had once showcased a scene of kids building a snowman in the very center of it. "This was one of my favorites!"

Mattie rushed from shattered ornament to shattered ornament, her hysteria growing.

"Be careful, honey," Don said. "Don't cut yourself."

"I knew we shouldn't have decorated this year," she cried. "I knew it."

Mattie rushed out of the family room and returned with a broom, pail, and trash bag. "I'm cleaning this mess up and putting everything away."

Don watched his wife sweep, tears plopping into the pail along with her memories.

Mattie didn't notice as Don slipped away and returned a few minutes later.

"Instead of ending a tradition," Don said, "why don't we start a new one?"

"What?" Mattie asked, dropping a pail filled with glitter and glass into the trash bag. "This Christmas is over. It's filled with sadness and bad luck."

"Bring that trash bag to me," Don said, taking a seat on the rug in front of the fireplace. He lay some newspaper down and set a glue gun in front of him.

"What are you doing?" Mattie asked, her face a mix of anger and confusion.

"We're starting a new tradition," he said. "Bring me that bag."

Mattie handed her husband the bag. He went deep inside it, as if he were dumpster diving, and came out with the base of a large bulb-shaped ornament that was still intact. He then began to pull out broken pieces of nearly every shattered ornament and arrange them on the newspaper.

"New tree topper," he said, focused on his work.

"That's silly," Mattie said. "That will be ugly. I told you, Christmas is over."

"Christmas is not over!" Don suddenly yelled, his voice high. He lowered his head and took a deep breath to contain his emotions, and when he spoke again, his voice was low. "Your parents lost their parents, we lost children, and still—somehow—we went on as a family. Christmas is a time when we must be surrounded by love, when we must be able to forgive, when we must, somehow, rediscover the joy and spirit we lose as adults."

Don looked up at his wife. "If we stop this year, will we do it next year? Probably not. I *need* this Christmas. You need this Christmas. Our hearts can't remain dark. There is no bad luck. There is only life, and it's heartbreaking and awful sometimes, but it's still beautiful and . . ."

Don stopped and picked up a shattered piece of glass. ". . . as precious as one of these ornaments."

Mattie took a seat next to her husband and put her hand on his arm. "You are amazing," she said. "And beautiful . . . and precious."

She looked down at the ornaments. "And crazy sometimes," she added with a small laugh. "Okay. I hear you. Let's start a new tradition."

And together Mattie and Don salvaged a segment of every broken ornament—and every family memory—and pieced it back together and placed it atop the tree where it would always remind them of what was most important.

"Are you okay, Mommy?" Jeri asked.

Rose was sobbing as she stared at the tree topper.

"Yes, sweetie. This is a happy cry," she said to her daughter before turning to Mattie. "No wonder you keep it in your hope chest."

"One of the last things she added," Don said.

"New traditions," Mattie said, her eyes moving from the tree topper sitting in Jeri's hands to the radiant face of the little girl. "New hope."

Rose stood and walked over to caress Mattie's shoulders. "Well, you two still have Christmas presents to open," she said. "We best be going. Thank you for letting us be a part of this new—and old—tradition."

Rose held out her arms for Jeri. "There's an iced Santa Christmas cookie with your name on it at home," she said.

"Yeah," Jeri said. "And eggnog?"

"Of course," Rose said.

"Bye," Rose said, giving Mattie and Don a hug and a kiss. "We'll see you tomorrow."

"Bye," Jeri said, giving the Tices a hug. "Merry Christmas, Mabel," she added. As she pulled on her coat and opened the front door, snow swirled inside, and she began to sing:

"Dashing through the snow . . . "

"She's still hung up on the one-horse open sleigh since the parade," Rose laughed, buttoning her coat. "I'm hoping she can paint a horse instead of wanting one now. Bye."

Silence engulfed Hope Dunes, and Mattie and Don watched the lights of Rose's car brighten the cottage before disappearing into the night.

Mattie shut her eyes and sniffed the air, a mix of pine needles and firewood.

"Nice to be home," she said.

"Even for a night," Don added. "It's time for presents."

Don walked over to the tree and looked over the wrapped presents. "First

things first," he said, picking up a glittery bag and pulling out a pair of antlers. "Mabel, merry Christmas."

Don walked over and put the antlers on the dog. "Oh, Mabel." Mattie
laughed. "You look just like Max from *How the Grinch Stole Christmas.*"

The dog sat patiently for a few seconds, her golden eyes searching the
top of her head at what lie atop, before she stood and shook, the antlers
flying across the room.

Don laughed and reached inside the bag for a treat. "Sorry, girl," he
said. "I had to, for old time's sake." Mabel sat and Don gave her the treat,
before she again settled on the rug in front of the fire.

"Hmmm," Don said, returning his attention to the tree. "Which one
should you start with?"

"No," Mattie said. "You first."

Don looked at his wife. "Please," she added. "Left envelope first."

Don plucked the envelope from the tree.

"Gift wrap is lacking," Mattie said.

Don smiled at his wife and opened the envelope.

"Read it out loud," she said.

"Okay," Don said, shooting his wife a bemused look. "Looks like a formal invitation.

"*You are invited,*" Don read on the front of the card, opening it to continue,
"*To a fiftieth golden wedding anniversary celebration for Don and Mattie Tice. When:
New Year's Eve. Time: 7 p.m. Where: Hope Dunes. Attire: Black tie. Gifts: Gold (of
course). Dinner: Created and served by chefs Rose and Jeri Hoffs.*"

Don looked up at Mattie, a huge smile on his face.

"Surprise," she said.

"Oh, honey, this is beyond amazing," he said. "But what if the agent
has showings. We shouldn't really even be here right now."

"Open the other envelope," Mattie said.

Don pulled the second envelope from the tree and opened it. He pulled
out a large sheath of paper, a note paper-clipped to the front. As he read,
his face changed quickly from confusion to surprise to shock.

"*Hope Dunes isn't just my home, it's your home,*" Don read. "*It should remain in
our family. When I am gone, this house should be filled with love, hope, and new memories. You should piece your life together and remember, as you taught me, that we must*

somehow rediscover the joy and spirit we lose as adults, that our hearts can't remain dark. There is no bad luck. There is only life, and it's heartbreaking and awful sometimes, but it's still beautiful and precious . . ."

Don stopped and looked at the tree topper sitting on the rug. *". . . as precious as one of our family ornaments."*

Don's eyes filled with tears. He lifted the letter and continued. *"I contacted the real estate agent and asked her to pull Hope Dunes off the market. I want you to keep the house, because it is our home, and will be forever. I wish you only love and happiness, and pray this home surrounds you with peace and happiness as well as a new beginning after I'm gone. I love you."*

The papers shook in Don's hand. He pulled the note free and finally realized he was holding the agent agreement.

"Burn it," Mattie said. "Right now."

"Honey, I can't," he said, crying. "I can't live here without you. I can't go on without you."

"You don't have a choice," she said. "Burn it."

Don walked over to the fireplace and stood in front of it, his hands trembling. He looked at Mattie, and the two locked eyes seemingly forever, before he dropped the contract into the flames, and the fire burst higher in delight.

"How did you . . . ," Don started.

"Rose helped me," Mattie said.

"I don't know what to say. I'm overwhelmed," he said. "We need to talk about so many things."

"Not tonight," Mattie said in a sweet tone that belied the determination in her face. "I have gifts to open. Or rather," she continued, "you have gifts to open for me. But first . . ."

Mattie swept her eyes down to the rug, where the tree topper still sat.

"Do the honors," Mattie said.

Don stood on his tippy toes and positioned the tree topper until it stood as straight as a sentinel. He then put his hands on his wife's shoulders, and the two admired the tree, the lights dancing across their faces and driving away the darkness just like the North Star.

part ten

The Wedding-Cake Cutter

Twenty-seven

New Year's Eve 2016

Rose sat in her little living room and stared out the windows at the holiday lights that seemed to encircle her: Lights twinkled on Christmas trees in the huge homes that surrounded her cottage, bulbs blinked on the snow-covered branches of pines, window box boughs, and wreaths. Over the tops of shrubs and fences, Rose could see a peek of Saugatuck's holiday lights swaying on the tree branches in the stiff breeze.

Rose nervously sipped a cup of coffee with one hand while fidgeting with the white piping on her blue sofa—the one she had chosen after her mother had passed, in order to honor her favorite color—enjoying a momentary window of silence while Jeri and the world slept, avoiding the task at hand.

I'm a tiny raft in a sea of cruise ships, Rose thought, staring at the huge homes that surrounded her.

Rose's hand drifted from the piping to the stack of bills that sat beside her on the couch.

And the sharks are beginning to circle, she thought.

Rose sighed and set her coffee cup down on a tray perched on an ottoman. She turned to pick up the bills, and a pillow her mother had made stared back at her.

A House Is Made of Bricks & Beams,
A Home Is Made of Hopes & Dreams

Rose ran her fingers over her mother's embroidery and then inhaled deeply. She smiled. The pillow was pine scented and smelled like heaven. Rose lifted the pillow to her nose and inhaled again.

Smells like Mattie's hope chest, she thought.

Rose let her fingers trail over the word "house" and then "hopes," before setting it down and picking up the stack of bills. She ran her nail underneath the back flap of the first envelope.

"Pine Ridge Home Mortgage. Payment due."

"How's that for irony, Mom?" Rose whispered to the pillow, giving the bill a flick with her finger. "Only five years left until it's mine. . . . If I can hold on that long."

She continued with the stack of bills—utilities, cell, credit card, cable—but her heart dropped when she opened her winter tax bill, which had quadrupled in the last few years.

It's Christmas, Rose thought. *They don't even give you time to make it through the holidays.*

Rose lifted her eyes to the mini-mansion that blocked the water view she had once enjoyed years ago and thought of the Tices and of Mattie's brave decision to have her husband keep their cottage.

Home is *hope*, Rose thought.

Rose reached for the cell in the pocket of her fuzzy robe and pulled up her online bank account.

Balance: $1,731.28

She then typed in the name of her financial advisor and pulled up the account that contained the small inheritance from her parents: *$44,965.*

Rose glanced out the wavy glass of her old house, a few big flakes beginning to drift from the sky. She leaned back and closed her eyes, dollar signs replacing the falling flakes. Although the regular hours with the Tices had allowed Rose more financial flexibility, the home health company only paid her $12.50 an hour, $26,000 a year *before* taxes.

Okay, I have enough to pay my bills, Rose thought, *but not enough for the taxes. I can tap my inheritance again . . .*

Rose clamped her eyes tightly, as if they were a leaky faucet she didn't want to drip.

. . . Or I can sell this house and property, move somewhere else, and have a more solid financial foundation, Rose thought.

KA-ZOOOO!!!!

Rose jumped and screamed, a big yelp releasing from her mouth, the shocking sound causing her to toss her cell across the living room.

Jeri was standing in front of her, a party horn fully extended from her mouth like a dragon's tongue.

"Sorry, Mommy," Jeri mumbled, her eyes wide.

"You scared me to death," Rose said. "Where did you get that?"

"Mr. Tice," Jeri said, her face falling as the extended horn withered and then retracted.

"It's okay," Rose said, patting the couch. "Come here."

Jeri padded over in pajamas and socks and jumped onto the couch, pulling a blanket over her. "Mr. Tice said New Year's was for fun," Jeri said. "He said that's when they got married, and that New Year's means new hope."

Rose smiled at her daughter and leaned over to tousle her red curls, before instinctively grabbing the pillow beside her and giving it a big hug.

"I sure hope so, sweetheart," she said. "I sure hope so."

KA-ZOOOO!!!!

Don entered the bedroom wearing a New Year's party hat, blowing a party horn, and carrying a tray.

Mattie's face brightened at the raucous sound. Mabel began to bark furiously.

"Happy fiftieth anniversary, my love," Don said, the horn dangling from his mouth, before tooting it a few more times as if he were a car in a passing parade. Mabel lunged at the horn every time it extended.

"Oh, Don," Mattie said, smiling.

He set down the silver tray. Mattie's favorite breakfast sat on top. Don removed the horn from his mouth and plucked a red rose from the tray. He put the rose stem in his mouth and snapped his fingers.

"Tango?" he asked.

"Later." Mattie laughed.

He held the rose to her nose.

"Sweet, like you," Don said, before snapping off the long stem of the flower and sliding the rose behind her ear. "And no thorns, like you."

"I'm plenty thorny," Mattie said slowly.

Don pulled a white napkin from the pocket of the apron he was wearing and gave it a dramatic flip before laying it across his wife's lap.

"Madame," he said, pouring her a cup of tea in her favorite desert rose cup. He held it up for her to take a sip.

Don pulled up a chair and began to pour syrup over a stack of pancakes.

"Blueberry," he said. "Picked and frozen from last summer. Your favorite."

He cut a small bite of pancake, dragged it through a pool of maple syrup, and lifted it to his wife's lips.

"Mmmm," she said.

"Same breakfast for fifty years," Don said, before considering his choice of words. "These are some old pancakes."

Mattie's hazel eyes focused on her husband. "Couldn't have asked for a better husband," she said.

Don smiled at his wife.

"You're my best friend," she continued slowly. "I'll miss you."

"Honey," Don started, his voice cracking. "No."

"I will," she said. "Fifty years. Long time."

Don nodded, his heart in his throat, and he took a big bite of pancake to hide his emotions.

Not long enough, Don thought.

"What do you think the girls are making us for dinner tonight?" Don asked.

"Our favorites," Mattie said. "Like the last fifty years."

Don's mouth watered—thinking of the meal the couple had shared since they were first married on New Year's Eve in 1966: standing rib roast, twice-baked potatoes, roasted asparagus, homemade bread, pecan pie, and champagne.

Don smiled and lifted another forkful of blueberry pancake to his wife's lips. She took the bite and then began to choke. Mabel began to bark. Don stood quickly and leaned his wife forward, patting her back with force, the bite of pancake flying onto the napkin along with the rose from behind her ear.

Don lifted a cup of water to his wife's lips and she took a long, steady drink from the straw.

"Sticking to soft foods tonight," Mattie tried to joke, her eyes watering. "And champagne."

Don couldn't help but look at the photo of him and Mattie on the bedroom wall, the one of them on the beach smiling before a Lake Michigan sunset, in that twilight before ALS, before death became a guest at the breakfast table, when nightfall was a time to celebrate and rest, rather than agonize and worry.

"We were young," Mattie said, following her husband's eyes. "Didn't know."

Don grabbed his wife's hand. "In sickness and in health," he said.

Mattie smiled, but neither completed the vow, or the other's thought.

'Til death do us part.

"This is how you separate the white from the yolk," Rose said to her daughter as they stood in the kitchen, the old preheating oven sending out enough heat to steam up the tiny window in the narrow space.

Rose cracked an egg on the side of a mixing bowl and split the shell in half, carefully cupping the yolk in one half of the shell and using the other half to hold it in place while allowing the white to drain into the bowl.

"See, there's a little left," Rose said, her eyes still focused on the egg. "It's attached to the yolk. So, you have to do this."

Rose transferred the yolk from one half of the shell to the other and gave it a soft jiggle, the remaining white coming loose from the yolk.

"Now you just carefully pour the white into the bowl," Rose said. "The egg whites will make the batter fluffier and lighter."

"You're like a magician," Jeri said, clapping.

Rose smiled and finally looked at her daughter. "And you look like a ghost," she said as she took in her daughter's typically rosy cheeks and red hair, which were dusted in flour.

"Of Christmas past?" Jeri asked, referencing Charles Dickens's *A Christmas Carol*, which they had seen at the local theatre over the holidays.

"Of New Year's now," Rose joked, wetting down a kitchen towel and giving her daughter's face a few swipes.

"I like to cook," Jeri said, her face contorting as the towel moved across her cheeks.

"Me, too," Rose said. "Okay, what's the recipe say next?"

Jeri picked up the recipe card, her eyes growing wide. "Can I ask you a question, Mommy?"

"Of course," Rose said. "Anything."

"This isn't a pie like Mr. and Mrs. Tice wanted," Jeri said, looking at the recipe card. "This says it's a one, two, three, four cake. And you keep calling it a white wedding cake. I'm confused."

Rose smiled. "Well, they did ask for a pecan pie, but I wanted to surprise them. It's their fiftieth wedding anniversary. It's a big day."

Rose hesitated. Her lip quivered, and she looked out the steamy window.

How do I tell my daughter it's probably their last one? Rose thought.

"Let me put it this way," Rose continued, her voice sounding upbeat. "You're seven years old. Mr. and Mrs. Tice have been married over seven times longer than you've been alive."

"Wow," Jeri said.

"And this is the wedding cake my grandmother made for my mom's wedding," Rose said.

"Did Grandma make it for your wedding?" Jeri asked.

Rose's heart leapt into her throat. She ignored the question. "I just wanted to do something extra special for them. It's a big day," she replied instead. "My grandma called this a one, two, three, four cake because it was easier to remember the ingredients that way—one cup butter, two cups sugar, three cups flour, four eggs—and because it was fairly easy to make."

"And eat," Jeri said with a big giggle.

Her eyes grew wide again as she stared at the recipe card, whose edges were bent and yellowed, the ink dulled and smeared, the paper flecked with stains of past cakes and icings. "Can I ask you another question?"

Rose nodded.

"Why is the recipe on this card," she asked, "and not on a computer?"

Rose moved a few bowls into the sink, leaned down, picked up her daughter, and set her on the counter, legs dangling off the edge.

"Well, your grandmother and great-grandmother didn't have computers growing up," Rose said. "They only had pens, pencils, and paper. So, they wrote everything down."

She reached over and picked up her old recipe box. "And this was like their computer," Rose said. "This is where they stored everything."

Jeri dragged her finger through the thick, white frosting sitting in a bowl that was waiting to top the baked cake, and then angled her head dramatically at her mother. Rose thought her daughter resembled a finch on a feeder trying to take in everything that was going on around it in the world.

"Can I ask you *another* question?" Jeri asked. "Why is the writing on the card so weird?"

"What do you mean, sweetie?" Rose asked.

"Well, some of the words are printed, like when I write," Jeri said, "but some of the words look like the water. They're all wavy."

This time, Rose's eyes grew wide.

I forgot she doesn't know what cursive is, Rose thought. *They're not teaching it anymore in school. Just printing and keyboarding.*

"Let me show you something," Rose said, opening the junk drawer in the kitchen and extracting a pen and pad of paper from a jangle of phone chargers, letter openers, scissors, and pizza coupons.

Rose wrote her name in print, and then in cursive, as well as a few words from the recipe card.

"See?" Rose said to Jeri, holding up the paper. "Cursive has its own personality. Like the way you draw, no one else in the world draws the exact same way."

"Really?" Jeri asked.

"Really. And see my writing compared to the recipe card?" she asked, holding the pad next to it. "I write like your grandmother. She's the one who taught me. Just like she taught me to make this cake, like I'm teaching you now."

"That's so neat," Jeri said. "And so pretty. You should write like that on top of Mr. and Mrs. Tice's cake."

Rose leaned in and hugged her daughter, lifting her into the air and setting her gently back down on the floor. "You're brilliant," she said.

"I know." Jeri giggled.

"And your great idea just made me think of another one," Rose said.

She walked over to a corner cabinet in the dining room, yanked open the warped glass doors, and reached in to pull out a pair of silver utensils.

"These were used at my grandparents' wedding," Rose said. "They're a wedding-cake cutter set. Aren't they pretty?"

Jeri ran her finger over the worn silver handles.

"I need to polish them before tonight," Rose said, before looking carefully at the set. "You know, I was going to put this in your hope chest, like the one Mrs. Tice has."

"Why didn't you?" Jeri asked.

"Time," Rose said, thinking of her family history and her own wedding. "Mistakes."

"Maybe it's time for no more mistakes," Jeri said.

"Maybe you're right," Rose said, setting down the set and giving her daughter a kiss on the head. "Let's get this cake in the oven."

Rose and Jeri finished mixing the batter, poured it into a pan, and then slid it into the oven.

"Now, I want you to try your hand at writing cursive," Rose said, grabbing her daughter's hand, a pen, and a pad of paper, and heading toward the living room couch. "I want you to write 'Happy Fiftieth Anniversary' on the top of the cake."

"Oh, Mommy, I can't," Jeri said, her voice rising. "I don't wanna mess it up."

"You won't," Rose said. "I'll be right beside you. Let me show you."

The two practiced writing cursive until the cake was ready.

"Smells good," Jeri said.

"It has to cool before we ice it and write on it," Rose said.

She stopped and looked at the wedding-cake cutter sitting on the counter.

"But, first, I need to call my friend Grace," Rose said. "Remember her? She runs the jewelry shop downtown. She never closes."

Rose ran her finger over the silver set. "And she knows calligraphy and engraving."

"You look beautiful," Don said. "Just like the day we met."

He walked over to Mattie, whose wheelchair was perched in front of the fireplace at Hope Dunes, and gave her a kiss on the head.

"You smell like sunshine," he said. "Even in the middle of winter."

"Handsome devil," Mattie said with a wink, admiring her husband's tuxedo.

"Happy anniversary, my dear," Don said. "I love you."

"Me, too," Mattie said.

Don watched his wife by the fire. She was wearing a light blue dress that set off her eyes just so and matched the beach glass pendant from her hope chest.

"This dress," Mattie had said earlier, as Don helped her get ready for the evening. "Finally."

Mattie had picked out the dress while on a trip to Chicago. She had planned to wear it on a German river cruise with her husband, but that trip had never taken place: She had been diagnosed with ALS.

The dress hung on Mattie's withering frame, almost like a sheet that had been tossed over a stick chair in a cottage that was being closed up for the winter, but Don could still see his wife's illuminating spirit and soul filling the dress and the cottage.

She glows from the inside out, Don thought.

Don watched his wife in the flicker of the fire. Her face was lit from the front, light dancing in the growing shadows on her face, but her chin was strong, her features proud, her eyes and mind the same as they had always been. The lighting made Mattie seem as if she were in a 1950s movie— dramatically backlit, a halo around her hair.

"I can't believe it's not snowing this year," Don said, walking toward the windows. "I can't remember an anniversary on New Year's Eve when it hasn't been a near whiteout."

Mattie moved her wheelchair over to the windows, and the night sky took her breath away. The sky was clear, the stars piercingly bright, and the moon reflected off Lake Michigan, casting the water and shoreline in an ethereal glow.

"Looks like my wedding ring," Mattie said, staring at the bright white circle on the water.

"Our adventure began right there," Don said, nodding to a place on the beach and grabbing his wife's hand. "Fifty years ago today."

Twenty-eight

New Year's Eve 1966

"Y ou're both nuts! No one gets married in a blizzard!"

Mary Ellen Barnhart waved her arms crazily, like a wet bee trying to take flight: One hand scurried to keep her hat secured on her head, one hand spun to keep her mother-of-the-bride dress from flying skyward, while both arms simultaneously tried to block the snow from her face and keep her body warm.

Lake-effect snow swirled around her body, engulfing her in a white tornado, as she stood on the back patio of Hope Dunes, her heels sinking in the snow.

"We're young and in love," Mattie yelled into the wind, taking each snow-covered step down to the beach with great caution, Don holding her hand. "And we're already married!"

Mattie turned back to her mother, her hair whipping in the wind, a heavy coat over her wedding dress, snow boots having replaced her heels, mittens instead of white gloves. "I love you. Back in a jiffy."

"I love you, too," Mary Ellen said, before yelling, "but the 'something blue' is going to be your frostbite. Kids today."

Mattie laughed as the door slammed shut.

All of the guests who had attended the "first" wedding at the church on the hill were standing at the windows of Hope Dunes, their faces pressed to the panes, their collective breath steaming the glass so quickly, fingers constantly had to wipe away the condensation.

Mattie's bridesmaid, Patty Dunkins, stood in the window, her index finger circling around her temple to indicate Mattie was crazy, her teeth faux chattering like one of those gag gifts to reinforce the fact that Mattie might, indeed, suffer frostbite.

Mattie had waved at Patty and blew her a kiss before grabbing Don's hand and making her way down the steep, slick steps.

"Are we crazy?" Mattie asked Don over the wind.

"Yes," he said. "But that's why I love you. Our life will always be an adventure."

As Mattie slowly made her way down the steps, she smiled, remembering the first kiss she and Don had shared: at a college New Year's Eve party. The party had been organized by the college's interfraternity council at a local country club. Don had picked Mattie up wearing a tux. She had picked out a blue dress to match the beach glass pendant she had worn the day they first met, fittingly at a wedding.

Students had danced while a big band played Chubby Checker and Ricky Nelson. Mattie had expected Don to kiss her when they slow-danced to "Crying" by Roy Orbison. But Don was a real gentleman, more so than the drunken college boys who were trying to scale the pillars in the ballroom as if they were trees in order to unleash the netting of confetti, balloons, and streamers that trembled overhead.

Mattie's nerves had gotten the best of her that night as she waited for the first kiss—Don had told her he wanted their first kiss, like their lengthy courtship, to be perfect—and she quickly drank three glasses of champagne to calm them.

"Thirsty?" Don asked, smiling, an eyebrow raised.

"Parched," Mattie replied, downing another.

When Patsy Cline's "I Fall to Pieces" began to play, Mattie grabbed Don by the arm, dragged him into the middle of the floor, wrapped her arms around his body, and looked him in the eye. "Let's get this over with already," she said, kissing him.

Don was taken by surprise at first, but he quickly melted in to her, and they danced and kissed the entire song.

"That was certainly worth the wait," Don said. "I like you, Mattie Barnhart. I like you a lot."

Mattie had felt fuzzy and light-headed from the champagne, the kiss, and Don's admission. "I like you a lot, too," she said. "A whole lot."

Before Mattie could stop herself, she was saying in a breathless stream of words, "I want to get married on New Year's Eve. I want to get married on the beach in Michigan. It's my happy place. I want to have two children. I want my own career as a landscape architect. I want to travel—"

Don leaned in and kissed her. "I want you to have all of that, and more," he said. "Hopefully, with me. But, first, I wanted you to put a period on that sentence."

Mattie laughed, and she leaned into Don's body, and the two swayed to the music, soft lights flashing across their young faces.

"New Year's means new hope, the start of a new chapter, just like a wedding," Mattie whispered into Don's chest. "I want to see every new year of my life moving forward as one filled with possibility. And New Year's seems like a perfect time to marry: Everyone is already wanting to dress up and have a big party. And black and white go so beautifully together: black tuxes, white wedding dresses, black bow ties, and white wedding cake—"

Don suddenly leaned in and kissed Mattie, the surprise and passion knocking her back on her heels. "I think you needed another period to end the sentence," Don said. He hesitated and then pulled Mattie close. "And I think I more than like you, Mattie Barnhart. I think I love you."

Mattie's eyes had filled with tears and again her head became dizzy. "I think I love you, too, Don Tice," she said, as the band began to play "Auld Lang Syne," balloons began to drop from the ceiling and people yelled, "Happy 1963!"

"You made it!"

A voice knocked Mattie from her memories. Through the blur of white, she could barely make out a figure, a mirage, Lawrence of Arabia but in the snow. Mattie crunched through the snow, which had become hard and ice packed on the shore. As she neared, she could finally make out Minister Flanagan, Bible in hand, perched on cross-country skis.

"Beautiful day," the minister said, his cheeks as red as the stocking cap he was wearing. "I skied down the back dune of Mount Baldhead and followed the path along the beach."

He looked at the couple's chattering teeth, their eyes wet from the stinging wind. "Well, it looks like we don't have much time," he said with a wink. "Mattie, I know you had prepared some personal vows for Don, before I restate your vows."

Mattie turned to Don and grabbed both of his hands.

"You have completed me," she said. "You are the period to my sentence."

Don laughed, remembering their first kiss.

Mattie turned and looked up at Hope Dunes—the silhouettes of family and friends laughing in the warmth and light—and then turned her gaze to the winter wonder of the coastline. Pine tree boughs were heavy with fluffy snow. A cardinal sat silhouetted on a branch. Lake Michigan was frozen over for miles, icy waves suspended in midair, the beach glazed like glass. Boulders of ice had collected along the shore, like large lake stones that rolled in after a summer thunderstorm.

In the distance, beyond the shroud of clouds and snow, the horizon had broken, the sun illuminating the unfrozen waters of the churning great lake, the winter cold and sun's shards of light turning it alternating colors of brilliant blue, deep green, and steel grey.

Mattie stared at the majesty, her mouth open in awe.

"This," she said, "is where my heart and soul lives. This—this beach, this lake, this house, you, my love—is home. This is hope. This is the place I want to live and die."

"I love you," Don said, kissing his wife, their lips wet from the snow. "And I will love you forever."

As the two restated their vows—in front of each other, in front of the lake and God and their winter world—the sun broke out.

"There is always hope where there is love," the minister said. "Now go get warm before your mother kills me."

Twenty-nine

"I want to die here," Mattie said, breaking the silence.

Don looked at his wife. The moon was reflecting directly into her hazel eyes, and they reminded him of Lake Michigan on their wedding day when the sun broke through as they said their vows: alternating colors of brilliant blue, deep green, and steel grey flecked with gold.

Don wanted to protest, to tell his wife not to ruin this night, but he thought of the vows she had spoken to him fifty years ago this day.

"I know," he said. "When it's time. I promise."

Mattie nodded with conviction. "Kiss me," she said, "like that night in college."

Don leaned into his wife's ear and began to hum, "I Fall to Pieces," before kissing her deeply, passionately. He grabbed the handles of her wheelchair and dipped her back onto the two back wheels—still humming—and the two began to dance.

"*There is always hope where there is love,*" Mattie remembered the minister saying, as her husband dipped and twirled her just like that New Year's Eve so many years ago.

"Sorry we're late," Rose said, rushing in carrying trays of food covered in tinfoil. Mabel began to bark excitedly at their arrival.

"At your service," Jeri said, following, tossing off her coat to reveal a little tux and pink, sparkly bow tie. She was holding a bottle of bubbly. "Champagne?"

Mattie and Don laughed.

"That would sound great in court, wouldn't it?" Rose joked, setting down the food. " 'Yes, judge, my seven-year-old daughter was serving alcohol.' Mother of the Year, right here."

Rose turned and grabbed the bottle of champagne from her daughter's hand. "We've got a few more things to unload," she said. "C'mon, Jeri. And put your coat back on, for goodness' sake. It's freezing."

Seconds later, the duo reappeared, Jeri carrying two grocery bags and Rose carefully balancing a cake carrier. The two again walked out, returning with a small folding card table and two chairs. "Cutest caterers ever, right? I just wanted to make sure we had everything—and make it extra special—since you two hadn't had a chance to move back to Hope Dunes yet," Rose said.

"Don't worry. Dinner's all ready," Rose continued, tossing off her coat with a big shrug and turning on the oven. She slowed, tied the heirloom apron around her waist, and carried a bag over to the card table. "I just want to warm everything up, set the table . . . but, first . . ."

Rose grabbed the bottle of champagne. She removed the foil on top, leaned against the counter, and slowly began to twist off the cork.

Pop!

Jeri screamed and clapped as the cork flew across the room. Rose plucked two champagne glasses from a bag, poured some bubbly, and handed the glasses to Don.

"Thank you," he said, before raising both glasses. "A toast to the most beautiful woman in the world. Happy fiftieth wedding anniversary to the love of my life."

Don clinked both glasses, leaned down to kiss his wife, and held the glass to her lips so she could take a sip.

"Love you," she said. "And love bubbles."

Don laughed and raised the glasses again. "And to the best chefs, servers, . . ." Don stopped, his voice breaking, ". . . and friends in the world."

Rose picked up her daughter. "We feel the same way," she said. "But you haven't tasted the food yet."

"Cheers," Don said, taking a drink of champagne and again holding the glass up to Mattie's lips.

As Mattie and Don sipped champagne, Rose and Jeri worked in tandem to transform the dull card table and chairs into a beautiful setting: A white tablecloth was draped, black fabric was tossed over a chair and tied in the back with a white bow. Mattie's McCoy vase was filled with roses and placed in the middle of the table; glitter was tossed onto the tablecloth; candles were placed in silver candlesticks; black, white, and gold balloons were pulled from a bag and scattered across the room; and a beautiful place setting—of desert rose dishes—was arranged.

"The final touch," Rose said, placing a black plastic party hat on top of Mattie's head, while Jeri put one on Don. "Jeri, it's your cue."

Jeri grabbed a balloon, untied it, and inhaled the helium. "Dinner is served," she said in an elfish, high-pitched voice.

"Again, Mother of the Year," Rose said, as Don and Mattie laughed.

The lights were dimmed, the candles were lit, and the fire and Christmas tree flashed in the background. Rose pulled up Pandora on her cell and clicked on "Pink Martini," which played all the old crooners, and set it on the table.

Don pulled his chair next to Mattie's wheelchair, and Jeri took their plates and began to serve them their anniversary meal of standing rib roast, twice-baked potatoes, roasted asparagus, and homemade bread. Mabel stood on her hind legs to get a better look and bigger sniff of the roast.

"This is amazing," Don said, taking a bite and then giving Mattie one. "You're a great cook."

"I learned from my mom," Rose said, her face blushing. "And you, too."

As Don and Mattie ate, Rose watched Don feed his wife—his face full of patience, admiration, and love, hers full of strength, pride, and love—and she held back tears.

I hope I find what they have, she thought. *They embody what a marriage truly is.*

As the couple finished, Rose uncovered the cake and brought it out to the table. Don's face immediately dropped.

"No pecan pie?" he asked.

"Don!" Mattie said.

"I'm sorry to deviate from your menu," Rose said, "but it's your fiftieth wedding anniversary. I wanted to bake my mother's special wedding cake for you."

Rose hesitated and tried to quell her trembling voice. "It brings good luck," she said, "for the couple and for the person who makes it. At least that's what my mom and grandma always told me.

"I know it sounds silly, but it sums up what I think great marriages are all about," Rose continued. "Beautiful, filled with flavor and many layers, a recipe that works only because it takes hard work, effort, patience, and lots of love. And it's white. Ever hopeful."

"Show them, Mommy," Jeri said, her body twisting impatiently.

"Jeri wrote 'Happy Fiftieth Anniversary!' on top," Rose said. "I taught her how to write cursive today."

"Beautiful," Mattie said.

"It is," Don said. "I'm sorry to have sounded disappointed. This is way better than any old pie."

"And I wanted to do something special, too," Rose said.

"You did all this," Don said. "It's already special."

Rose smiled.

"I wanted to be able to give something back to you for all you've done for me and Jeri," she said, picking up the silver wedding-cake cutting set. "These have been passed down to me from my mom and grandma. I had them engraved downtown today."

Rose held the pieces out for Don and Mattie to see.

"Happy fiftieth," Don said, reading the handle of the knife. He picked up the cake cutter. *"Hope is the thing with feathers that perches in the soul . . ."*

"Oh, Rose," Don said.

"I know fifty is gold and this is silver . . . ," Rose started.

"Stop," Mattie said, her voice commanding. "You . . . are . . . hope."

Rose hugged Mattie and kissed her cheek, whispering, "No, you are. I want to add it to your hope chest." She hesitated. "I *need* to add it to your hope chest. I want it to continue with a piece of me. I hope that's okay."

"You are an amazing woman," Mattie said slowly.

"No, you are," Rose repeated, before cutting a big slice of cake.

"Delicious," Don said, inhaling half the slice.

"Yum," Mattie said, licking frosting off her lips. "Ready?"

"Another surprise?" Don asked. "I don't know if I can take any more this holiday season. The parade, the tree, the cottage, tonight. . . . Now what?"

"I'm no minister, but I'll give it a shot," Rose said to Mattie, moving her wheelchair toward the window overlooking the beach. "Don, would you join us?"

"What's going on?" he asked.

"We can't make it down there," Mattie said, looking down at the beach, "but we can re-create it."

Rose pulled a sheet of paper from the pocket of the apron. "I need both of your rings," she said. Don pulled off his band, and then wriggled Mattie's ring off her finger.

"Don, would you repeat after me?" Rose asked. "Will you, Don, have Mattie to be your wife? Will you love her, comfort, and keep her, forsaking all others to remain true to her as long as you both shall live?"

"I will," said Don.

"Repeat after me," Rose continued. "I, Don, take thee Mattie to be my wife, and before God and these witnesses, I promise to be a faithful and true husband."

"I, Don, take thee Mattie to be my wife, and before God and these witnesses, I promise to be a faithful and true husband."

"With this ring I thee wed, and all my worldly goods I thee endow," Rose read. "In sickness and in health, in poverty or in wealth . . ."

"With this ring I thee wed, and all my worldly goods I thee endow," Don repeated. "In sickness and in health, in poverty or in wealth . . ."

Rose turned to Mattie. ". . .'til death do us part."

". . .'til death do us part," Mattie said, concluding the vows.

Rose helped Don put his band back on and then Don kneeled in front of his wife and placed the ring back on her finger, Mabel wagging her tail excitedly in approval as a witness.

"Not even then," Don whispered to his wife, his throat hoarse, tears in his eyes. "Not even then."

part eleven

The Snow Globe

Thirty

January 2017

S he's getting weaker."

Dr. Edwards, the Tices' longtime family practitioner, looked at Don as they stood in the living room of the River Bend house.

Don stared at the doctor, unable to speak.

I've waited for this moment to come, he thought. *But I never thought it would.*

He took a deep breath and looked out the window over the doctor's shoulder. Snow was falling outside—prettily, lightly—as if the world were a snow globe, and God had given it a gentle shake.

Dr. Edwards pushed his round glasses up the bridge of his nose, tilted his silver head, and simply held out his arms. Don buried his head into the doctor's shoulder and began to sob.

"She's fought so hard for so long," Dr. Edwards said. "It's a miracle she's survived this long. Over five years with ALS at her age. That's simply amazing. She's fought for a reason."

Muffled footsteps echoed in the kitchen, and Rose stood helplessly— arms dangling at her sides, a kitchen towel clutched tightly in one hand— tears in her eyes. Don held out his arm, and Rose ran toward him. The doctor folded both of them into his arms.

"I thought she would go on forever," Rose said, her voice trembling.

"She will," Don said in a husky voice.

The doctor began to gather his bag and coat and head toward the front door. "Does Mattie have an advanced directive?"

"Yes," Don said. "She doesn't want a feeding tube, a tracheotomy . . . anything."

"That's our Mattie," Dr. Edwards said. "I know this is hard to hear, but hospice can be of great help, too. I spoke with her specialist. She qualifies now, and I can put the request in right away. It doesn't mean she's going to pass immediately, but her time is growing shorter. They can administer her medications, they can check her every day, they can help care for her, medically, physically, emotionally, and spiritually. I'll put in the request, if you want. Get things started."

Don nodded. "Doctor?"

"Yes."

"She does have one specific request," Don said.

"What is that?" the doctor asked.

"She wants to pass at Hope Dunes," Don said. "I promised her. Fifty years ago. Is that possible?"

Dr. Edwards nodded. "It is," he said. "Especially with hospice. It will be a bit of an effort to transport her there, but we can do that in her wheelchair, if she's strong enough, or her hospital bed. Just make sure the cottage is ready. I'd personalize it if you can. Make it the home she remembered."

"I will do that," Rose said. "I have to."

"I'll check in later," Dr. Edwards said. "Let her rest for now, gather up some strength for that move."

He opened the door, and snow blew in like a ghost. "Perfect Michigan weather," he said. "Good luck with everything."

When he was gone, Don and Rose stood there, unable to move. The trees outside creaked in the winter wind.

Her bones and her body are so tired, Don thought, listening.

"I'll make her some tea," Rose said. "In her favorite cup. I need something to keep my mind occupied today."

Rose shuffled into the kitchen. She looked out at the world, everything dusted with fresh, white powder.

It looks like the wedding cake I just made, Rose thought.

She looked back at Don, standing with his arms crossed, staring out at the snow.

Fifty years, in the blink of an eye, Don thought, his fingers twisting his wedding band. *'Til death do us part.*

Rose's heart leapt into her throat, and she could picture herself standing just like that—staring at the snow—after her parents had died, both in the winter.

"They make it through the holidays, and then they start dropping like flies," a nosy neighbor had told Rose at her mother's visitation. "Nothing to look forward to anymore."

Rose remembered staring at the woman and then looking at her mother in the open casket—her blue dress a sign of spring—and rushing out of the chapel at the funeral home.

The teakettle whistled, and Rose jumped. She placed a tea bag in the desert rose cup, poured some water, placed it on a saucer, and headed toward the bedroom.

"I don't know if she'll wake up right now to drink that," Don said. "She's already fast asleep again."

"I know," Rose said. "But she likes to have her tea ready every morning at this time."

A faint smile cracked Don's pained face.

Rose stopped at Mattie's bedroom door and peeked inside.

Still asleep.

Rose walked in—one slow, steady step at a time—and sensed a calm in the room, almost like she felt when Jeri was sleeping and the house was quiet for the night. The smell of the steaming tea—earthy and herbal—wafted into Rose's nose along with another familiar scent, like the one from her mother's "home" pillow on her couch.

Cedar, Rose thought.

For a moment, Rose thought a window might be open, and the January wind was carrying in the smell of pine and cedar trees, which always seemed even more pungent in the cold air.

But then Rose saw Mattie's hope chest, the lid open. On top sat Rose's wedding-cake cutter and knife, the silver shining and the new engraving shimmering.

The sight caught Rose by surprise, and her foot caught on the carpet, causing her to slosh tea onto the saucer.

"You're such a klutz, Rose," she said to herself out loud.

"Should see me with tea."

Rose jumped, again sloshing tea. Mattie's eyes were fluttering, her face expressionless but her voice still filled with strength, humor, and intelligence.

"Time for your tea," Rose said, attempting to make her voice sound casual.

"Bad actress," Mattie said.

Rose laughed. "Some things never change," she tried to joke.

"And some do," Mattie said, her voice now serious.

Rose took a seat in the chair beside the bed and set down the tea.

"Want some tea?"

Mattie didn't respond. She pivoted her cloudy eyes toward the window. Rose could see the snow falling in them.

"There's a certain slant of light, winter afternoons," Mattie whispered.

Rose looked at Mattie, confused.

"I'm sorry," she said. "I'm not following."

"I loved to paint on winter days," Mattie continued, the words more garbled than usual. "The light."

She stopped and skewed her eyes toward Rose. "Perfect. But doesn't last long."

Rose's heart began to race.

"Snow globe," Mattie said. "Hope chest."

Rose stood and headed to the open chest. She got onto her knees on the carpet, and began to dig through the contents. In the corner, swaddled in an old hand towel monogrammed with a cursive *B*, was a snow globe.

Rose unwrapped it and studied the snow globe.

The globe contained three trees positioned in the front—barren birches whose bark was as white as the glistening snow on which they sat. In the very back of the globe sat another tree, this one barren as well, but black, as if it were in shadow, or captured at the edge of twilight, just before the angelic trees in front were swallowed by night.

The globe sat on a silver base, now tarnished. Rose turned the globe around in her hands, and it was then she noticed two lines engraved on the base.

No, Rose thought.

They were the same lines Mattie had just uttered: "*There's a certain slant of light, winter afternoons.*"

Rose returned to Mattie's bedside and held the globe in front of her. "It's beautiful," she said.

"Shake it," Mattie whispered.

Rose gave the globe a gentle shake, and held it in front of Mattie again: Glittery snow fell softly in the globe, covering the little world in a sheet of white.

Mattie smiled, but then her eyes filled with tears, and two big drops trailed down her cheeks. Rose wiped her face with a Kleenex, and Mattie's eyes grew heavy.

"Wanna tell me about it?" Rose asked.

"Tired," Mattie whispered to Rose. "You tell me a story."

Her eyes opened, then shut, then opened again, and she watched the last of the white settle in the globe.

"Of snow," Mattie whispered.

Thirty-one

January 2000

I'm not ready!"

Rose gripped her rickety old sled, the steering column shaking in her hands.

"Not yet!"

She released her grip and pulled back the hood on her coat. Her red curls popped free, and snow immediately began to pile on top of her. She stared over the edge of Mount Baldhead, and her eyes grew as big and stormy as Lake Michigan, stretched out over the horizon.

"I can't do it," she said. "I'm too scared."

"You don't have to do it," Dora Hoffs said.

"Your mother's right," Dave said, his feet planted on the back of the sled. "You said you wanted to do this. But you don't have to do anything you don't want to do. You're only eleven. You have all the time in the world."

"That was fun!"

Rose watched a tiny figure grow larger as it trudged up the snow-covered sand dune. Finally, through the hiss of snow, Sue Lyons appeared, her sled in tow.

"You gotta do it, Rose!" Sue said, her words coming out in big puffs, like smoke. "It's like a roller coaster . . . but better!"

Rose hated roller coasters. She hated amusement parks. She wasn't big on thrills. "You go again," Rose said. "I'll watch and cheer for you."

Sue stopped when she made it to the top of the hill and caught her breath. She stared at Rose, her cheeks red, and crossed her arms. "No, you're always the one watching on the sidelines," she said. "It's time you do it . . . for you."

Rose looked at Sue, and then at her parents, before staring again down the hill.

It looks like a mountain, Rose thought. *And what's on the other side of the hill? Will I just fly into the lake?*

"You don't have to do it," Sue finally said. "But you'll never know how exciting life can be unless you dive headfirst into it."

The wind picked up and blew snow into Rose's face. She gripped the steering column, stared down the near vertical descent, shut her eyes, and yelled, "Push me!"

Without warning, Rose was flying down the dune, picking up speed, the world whizzing beside her, as if she were a space shuttle taking flight. She gripped the steering column even tighter, now realizing that would likely do as much good as steering the space shuttle with a kite string.

So Rose did the only thing she could: She screamed.

Her breath came out in a thick fog that remained frozen in place as her body careened downhill.

But, as she screamed and flew down the hill, the world around her began to slow, as if she were outside of her body and staring into the little snow globe of Saugatuck-Douglas that she kept on her desk all winter long.

In the distance, the resort towns of Saugatuck and Douglas were blurred from the snow but twinkling and glowing brightly, still drenched in their holiday lights. The harbor was frozen, geese flocking to a hole in the ice, and yachts sat in an open shelter like ghost ships.

As Rose's sled plunged down the dune, she turned and took in Mount Baldhead, framed with pine trees, boughs heavy with fluffy snow. A cardinal, the brightest red she had ever seen, sat silhouetted on a branch. It took off as she whizzed by, snow from the pine falling with a big thud.

Halfway down the dune, trees lessened, the vista opened, and that's when she saw it: Lake Michigan! It was frozen over for miles, icy waves suspended in midair.

She could make out some of her classmates, who had flocked here on this rare snow day off from school to have some fun.

To have an adventure, Rose thought.

Rose hit a little bump, and her sled hopped into the air. Ahead, as she neared the bottom of the dune, she saw the dip, which then rose suddenly like the bike ramps off which boys in her neighborhood loved to do tricks. Beyond, the lake called.

Rose screamed even before her sled took flight. She clamped her eyes shut as she felt herself go higher and higher. At the last moment, she popped them open and stretched before her was an open patch of dunes, which sat overlooking the lake. A group of parents were fanned out at the base, a safety net for incoming sledders, just in case. Rose's sled flew toward the water, but it began to slow, and, at the last minute, she pulled it, hard, left and came to a stop in the midst of the open area.

Sue whirred past, seconds later, and jumped off her sled before Rose could find her sea legs.

"Told you that was fun!" she yelled, lifting her arms into the air and doing a little dance. "Don't you feel alive?"

Rose pushed off of her sled and stood on shaky legs.

She looked at Sue, and then at the beauty of the winter scene that surrounded her.

"I do," she said. "I did it!"

Sue hugged her friend. "Told ya," she said. "Wanna do it again?"

"Yeah," Rose said. "I do."

And the two began to trudge up the steep hill, one snowy step at a time, replaying every second of their sled ride.

When Rose got home, she ran to her bedroom, changed into warm pajamas, and took a seat at her desk.

Dear Diary:

What a day! I did it! I finally did it! I rode my sled down Mount Bald-head for the very first time. I was so scared, but Sue said I could do it, and I did. You should have seen the looks on the faces of my classmates. I—

There was a soft knock on the door.

"Come in," Rose said.

"We brought you some hot chocolate," her mom said, carrying in a mug.

"Even added those little marshmallows you love," said her dad.

"Thank you," Rose said, closing her diary before cocking her head at them suspiciously. "Why are you being so nice?"

Dora laughed. "Aren't we always?"

"I didn't mean it that way," Rose said. "It's just that . . ."

"Well," her dad started, "we did want to tell you how proud we were of you for sledding today. We know how scared you were, and we know it was hard, but sometimes those things that are the hardest and scariest are the most meaningful."

Rose nodded and sipped her hot chocolate.

"It's like our farm stand," Dora said. "It's hard and sometimes scary to run our own business, but it's so worth it."

Rose set her hot chocolate down on her desk. Her mother walked over and picked up the Saugatuck-Douglas snow globe that was sitting on the desk and gave it a little shake.

"The world is prettier and safer when you live in a bubble," Dora said, watching the faux snow fall over the miniature resort towns under glass. "But it's not real. Eventually, you have to move beyond those walls that trap you in order to truly experience all the world has to offer."

Dora handed the snow globe to her daughter.

"Does that make sense?" she asked.

Rose gave the globe a hearty shake and smiled. Then she handed it back to her mother. "I think I'm done with it for a while," she said. "Do you mind putting it in a safe place? Maybe I'll just get it out every Christmas from now on."

Dora took the globe and gave Rose a kiss on the head, before walking out the door with Dave.

Rose took a sip of her hot chocolate, opened her diary, and continued to write about how exciting the world could be when you took a chance.

Thirty-two

I haven't told that story to anyone before," Rose said, picking up Mattie's snow globe and giving it a shake. She smiled as she watched the snow drift down over the trees. "Mattie?"

Rose looked at Mattie, her throat tightening. Mattie was asleep, her chest rising and falling lightly.

You scared me, Rose thought.

Rose looked at Mattie's snow globe again and reread the lines that were written on its base. She set down the globe on the little tray attached to Mattie's bed, plucked her cell from her pocket, and googled the words.

Emily Dickinson, the search results read.

Of course, Rose thought. *Her favorite poet.*

Rose clicked on a link and saw the lines on the snow globe. They were the first two lines of a longer poem about the landscape in winter, the shadows, and . . .

Rose's heart was racing by the time she finished the poem.

Death.

Does she, Rose thought, remembering what Mattie had said moments earlier, *know something we don't?*

Rose studied Mattie as she slept, snow falling outside the window behind her. Rose looked at the snow globe again, and this time her eyes were drawn directly to the single black tree. She looked at her phone again, and read the last stanza of the poem to herself again.

"*There's a certain slant of light,*" Rose said to herself, tears rolling down her face.

She knows her light is fading, Rose thought. *The shadows of her winter afternoons are growing near.*

Rose stood and ran out of the bedroom, collapsing against a wall and slowly sliding to the floor. As she cried in the hallway, the sun broke through the clouds, illuminating the house in an otherworldly light.

Rose gathered herself, stood, and peeked into Mattie's bedroom. She was still sleeping, the sun was slanted across her face—making her glow—but, in an instant, the light was gone, and shadows had engulfed her face.

"Is this how you had the chairs angled?"

Rose stood in the family room overlooking the lake and moved a burnished leather armchair just so.

"It's perfect, Rose," Don said, peeking his head into the doorframe.

Rose looked at him, her face twisted in anxiety.

"I just want it to be right," she said, nervously poking at the bags underneath her eyes.

"You need some rest," Don said.

He headed into the middle of the room and opened another moving box, this one filled with books.

"So do you," Rose said. "You can't go on like this."

Don suddenly plopped to the floor and took a seat, before stretching out flat on his back and staring up at the floor-to-ceiling lake stone fireplace that dominated the room.

"Mattie's dad and I gathered all those from Lake Michigan," he said, smiling at the beautiful polished rocks that comprised the fireplace. "Seems like another life."

Rose walked over and took a seat next to him, pulling books out of another moving box. "Life is filled with a lot of chapters," she said.

"This sort of feels like the end and the beginning," Don said, his voice trembling. "Am I wrong to say that?"

"No," Rose said, her voice resonating in the big room.

Don sat up and pulled a book from the box. He absentmindedly began to flip through the pages and came upon a yellowed, bent bookmark.

"I feel like this bookmark," he said. "Like I'm forgotten, stuck in a holding place. I'm marking my favorite passage ever in a book, but I know I can't move on to read anything else until I memorize every single nuance of this chapter."

Rose grabbed Don's hand.

"This is where she would want to be," Don said, looking at the empty space where her hospital bed was to be placed. "Staring at this fireplace. Looking out over her gardens and the lake. This house is her soul."

"And yours, too," Rose said. "This *will* mark an ending and a beginning. The next book in your life won't be remotely like this one at all, but you must remember, it's still worth exploring because the journey will change you for the better."

Don squeezed Rose's hand.

"It's strange not being with her, even for a moment," Rose continued.

"Hospice has been a godsend," Don said. "Words I never thought I would say in my life."

A soft rap on the door startled Don and Rose.

"Welcome wagon."

The front door opened, and a trio of familiar faces popped into the frame, like the Three Stooges.

"Vinnie?" Don said, surprised. "Jane? And Fern?"

Vinnie DeMuccio, Fern Reynolds, and Jane Landon walked into Hope Dunes, Vinnie carrying a cellophane wrapped basket piled with coffee, fruit, cheese, and crackers, red roses clasped in Fern's hands, while heart balloons bobbed alongside Jane's head.

"Just a few things to welcome you back home," Vinnie said. "An early Valentine's token of our love, if you will. How's it going?"

"Thank you," Don said. "It's going . . ." He hesitated and forced a weak smile. "I'm sorry. It's just been so long since I've seen any of you."

Fern walked over to Don. "It has," she said, her voice soft. "And we can never tell you sorry enough."

She looked at him and then sniffed the roses, searching for the right words. "I saw Mattie at the holiday parade," Fern said. "It was so hard. And then I was having coffee a few days later, and Jane told me you'd pulled the house off the market."

Fern's face crumpled, and she began to cry. "I'm so sorry," she said. "I finally realized it's not about us, or how we're feeling, it's about Mattie, and we forgot that. We have to live with that lost time and that regret. I just hope you might find it in your heart to accept our apologies someday."

Don looked at Fern, and then at Vinnie and Jane. "You'll have to ask Mattie that."

"We did," Vinnie said, his head dropping, his long hair falling in front of his face. "We just came from visiting her. She forgave us."

"She's always been a better and stronger person than us," Jane said.

Don lowered his head into Fern's shoulders, crumpling the roses, and she held him, Vinnie and Jane coming over to join in.

"New chapter?" Fern asked.

Don pulled free and looked at Rose, who smiled.

"New chapter," Don said. "Won't be the same, but we'll all change for the better."

Jane walked toward the empty spot where Mattie's bed would go and stared out the windows. "I always had a feeling you wouldn't sell Hope Dunes," Jane said. "I kept telling the couple who made the offer on this place all about you. When I told them you were pulling the house off the market, they said, 'It would never have been our Michigan cottage any-way. It would always be their home. We can feel them in every room.'"

Don bit the inside of his cheek and nodded at Jane.

"Now, where's that pretty McCoy vase Mattie always used for her fa-vorite flowers?" Fern asked.

"I'll get it," Rose said.

Don began to unwrap the basket, the cellophane crackling loudly, while Jane set the balloons directly on the mantel of the fireplace, beside "The Firewood Poem" plaque.

"Her favorite spot," she said. "Along with her gardens and her office."

Hope Dunes vibrated with life, and Don felt simultaneously happy and devastated as he looked back at the empty spot that Mattie would soon occupy.

And eventually leave, Don thought, working up the courage to smile. *A new chapter indeed.*

Thirty-three

Mattie shut her eyes, until her hospital bed had been lifted and locked into place. She looked out the back window of the van at the house on River Bend and, in her mind, blew it a soft kiss.

You were a bookmark in my life for just a few short months, Mattie thought. *But you led me—and Don—to an important new chapter.*

Snow was falling lightly, but it was that lazy sort of snow, the kind that took its own sweet time to fall, big flakes that seemed to enjoy every second of their journey.

The front door of the house opened, and Jeri raced into the yard along with Mabel, who chased each other in circles, leaving geometric patterns in the snow. Rose and Don followed.

They were carrying her hope chest.

The back doors of the van opened, and a rush of cold wind zipped inside. A big thud followed.

"I'll see you there," Rose said to Mattie.

"Open it," Mattie said. "Please."

Rose hopped into the back of the van. She found a moving blanket piled on one side and propped the chest open.

Mattie heard a slam as the back door shut. Slowly, a smile crossed her face.

Cedar, she thought.

Don hopped into the driver's seat and plopped Mabel into the passenger seat, the dog shaking snow all over Mattie.

"Snow," Mattie said, as the powder dusted her face, quickly melted, and trailed down her cheeks.

Don started the car and began to back out, the van beeping.

I'm going in reverse, Mattie thought. *Back to the place I never thought I'd be.*

Don carefully navigated the van out of the subdivision, past the marsh, and onto Blue Star Highway, which was slushy.

"They can't keep up with the snow anymore," Don said, the sound of the heater and the crunching tires background music to his words.

Don took a left onto Center Street and drove until Lake Michigan, literally, dead-ended the road.

"Looks like God's own skating rink," Don said to Mattie as the frozen lake stretched out across the horizon. "Looks like one of your paintings that someone put into the freezer."

"I can picture it," Mattie said.

She felt the car turn right.

"I'm glad we had this plowed this morning," Don said.

Mattie shut her eyes until she could hear the gravel of the long driveway crunch under the tires and snow.

She opened them just in time to see the wood-carved sign that had announced the name of the family cottage to visitors for years—HOPE DUNES— swinging in the winter wind on a log post attached to two stone pillars.

Mattie's heart raced.

"Hope," she whispered.

"What was that, honey?" Don asked, continuing down the drive.

Mattie didn't answer. She peered out the back window of the van and studied the beauty of the trees—pines, aspen, barren white birch, boughs and branches heavy with snow—which canopied the long drive.

"Volunteers," Mattie whispered again.

Don looked back at his wife, her eyes seemingly watching a movie, and he bit his cheek.

Mattie had been fascinated by the trees that canopied the entire length of Lake Shore Drive, both as a girl and as a landscape architect.

"It's like Mother Nature's roof," Mattie had told her parents when they walked the road into town for ice cream. "Can we do the same thing in our driveway?"

Mattie and her father had planted endless pines and birch—as well as pulled hundreds of saplings from the surrounding woods, "volunteers" as her mom used to call the tiny trees she said were ready to perform a new service. Over the years, they had grown to provide a shaded canopy, a stunning entrance to Hope Dunes.

As Mattie watched the canopy fly by overhead, she was transported back in time to when she was a teenager, and she would run as fast as she could down the driveway to greet friends and guests. As she ran, she would spread her arms, as if she were flying—able to go anywhere—and stare up at the canopy, light popping through the layers of branches, leaves, and needles.

The world was filled with hope, Mattie thought.

Mattie continued to watch the canopy fly by.

Time flies, she thought.

But as Don slowed the car in the deepening snow of the long driveway, Mattie studied the intricacies of each branch, each tree she had touched at one time in her life.

I've built a legacy, Mattie then thought.

Snow dropped from the canopy and thudded atop the van, causing Mabel to bark.

The van came to a stop, fishtailing slightly in the turnaround area by the front door. The doors to the van opened, a rush of cold air and snow swirling inside, and Jeri's stockinged head popped into Mattie's view like a Muppet.

"How was the ride?" she asked.

"Magical," Mattie said.

"Like the snow," Jeri said, her cheeks red.

Mabel hopped out of the front seat, onto the end of Mattie's bed, and then bounded out the open door, making a soft plop into the snow.

Jeri scooped up some snow in her mittened hands, made a snowball, and tossed it softly into the air. Mabel jumped and caught it in midflight, furiously chomping until the snowball had disintegrated. Energized by the cold, the black dog raced in circles in the white snow—the picture resembling a photo negative—before jumping onto Jeri's legs and barking for more attention.

Mattie watched the simple scene as her bed was lowered onto the ground.

In the background, the woods were drenched in white, snow draped off the eaves of Hope Dunes as if it were a gingerbread cottage, and echoes of kids screaming as they sledded reverberated through the cold air.

Rose and Don pushed Mattie's bed toward the front steps and up the portable ramp into the house. They navigated her to the spot in the family room and situated her bed so she could see both the fireplace to her right and out the windows to the garden and lake on her left.

Finally, Rose elevated Mattie's bed.

"Oh, my," she whispered.

Hope Dunes was decorated just as she had kept it for decades.

She peered left and then right, taking in the familiar space, furnishings, and decorations.

"One more thing," Don said, looking at Rose.

A minute later, they returned carrying the hope chest, which they positioned at the end of her bed.

"No more attics," Mattie said.

Don kissed his wife on the cheek. "No more attics," he whispered.

Just then, Jeri and Mabel raced into the home. Mabel did a few circles before shaking in front of the fire and then jumping onto the foot of Mattie's bed.

Jeri walked over and picked up the snow globe that sat on a table near Mattie's bed.

"So pretty," she said, studying the trees. "The inside looks just like the outside. See?"

Jeri gave the snow globe a shake.

Mattie, Rose, Don, and Jeri watched in silence as the snow fell in the little globe.

"I bet it's nice to be home," Jeri said, nodding, looking intently at Mattie, putting her hands on her legs.

"It is," Mattie said.

As Don and Rose busied themselves with the house, and Jeri called Mabel to play, Mattie looked out onto the winter afternoon. Her garden was covered in snow, the lake thick with ice. The afternoon light was already beginning to dim.

Suddenly, Jeri and Mabel rushed by outside, and the world filled with giggles and barking. Mattie could hear Don and Rose making an early dinner.

Yes, Mattie thought. *I can feel Don's spirit envelope Hope Dunes, which it never had on River Bend.*

"Mrs. Tice!" Jeri yelled from outside.

Mattie turned to watch Jeri toss another snowball into the air for Mabel to catch.

The fire quickly warmed the family room, and Mattie's eyes grew heavy.

I am home, Mattie thought. *Forever.*

She looked around Hope Dunes, and—just before she fell asleep—a feeling of great contentment filled her soul.

And I was wrong, Mattie thought, drifting off. *The world is filled with hope. And it always will be.*

part twelve

The Ticket Stub

Thirty-four

February 2017

I don't wanna go," Jeri said, as her mother covered up every inch of her skin for the short walk outside to the car. "I'm having too much fun. I love it here."

"I do, too," Rose said. "But I've got to make dinner for you, do the laundry, try to pay some bills . . ."

Rose looked up as she pulled on her daughter's mittens, an embarrassed look frozen on her face. The words "try to" hung in the air, suspended, not moving, like the smoke from the chimney of Hope Dunes on this frigid day.

Don looked at Mattie. "If you ever need any help," he started.

Rose stood and squared her shoulders. "Thank you," she said. "I'm fine." She tried to force a smile, but her face instead looked as if she had just sucked on a lemon. "Single working mom here. I'm used to juggling a lot of things."

Don nodded. "I'm sorry," he said. "I didn't mean to . . ."

He stopped and changed directions. "I can't thank you enough for all your help today," he said instead, "and these past few weeks. Mattie is home. I never thought this would all end up turning out this way."

This time, an embarrassed look froze on Don's face, and the word "end" hung in the air.

"Neither did I," Jeri said, breaking the tension. "I don't want this day to end, either. I'm having too much fun."

"Come on," Rose said, grabbing her daughter's hand with a chuckle. "See you both tomorrow."

" 'Night," Mattie said in unison with Don.

The door shut, and cold invaded Hope Dunes, followed by quiet. It was one of those February days that was so cold the world seemed encased in ice.

Don peeked out the window. It was four P.M. and already pitch-black.

Everything looks frozen, he thought. *Ready to break or die at any second.*

He turned to look at Mattie, who was already beginning to fall asleep in the now silent cottage.

Mattie still had good days and bad, but the good ones—when she was awake, alert, energetic—were becoming rarer and rarer. She no longer got out of bed. For the most part, she slept, Mabel napping beside her.

The headlights from Rose's car illuminated the family room and the engine revved. Suddenly, tires squealed. Don held his hands up to his eyes at the window, trying to figure out the commotion.

"Oh, my," he said, as black smoke billowed around Rose's rusted car.

Don walked over and opened the front door, and Rose and Jeri scurried back inside.

"My car's stuck," Rose said as she stood on the doormat. "Too much snow." Rose yanked off her stocking cap and knocked the powder from her coat. "My tires are too old to get any traction."

Mattie, now awake, chuckled at the unintended double entendre.

"My *car* tires," Rose said with emphasis, before breaking into a fit of giggles.

"Well, you're not a real Michigander until you have a plow man's number on speed dial," Don said. "I'll call George, see if he can come plow."

Don continued to peer out the window at the snow coming down, heavy and thick, the phone to his ear. "Okay," he finally said after a few dials. "Wow. No problem.

"George said it's getting worse," Don said. "He's too busy to get to us until morning. Looks like you're staying put."

"Yeah!" Jeri yelled, jumping up and down.

"Sorry to be an inconvenience," Rose said, taking off her coat.

"Slumber party," Mattie said in a faint voice. "Been years."

"I'll go set up the guest room," Don said, not catching his wife's words as he checked the weather radar on his cell.

Rose caught Mattie's expression, her face quickly sagging at Don's suggestion.

"How about if we just pile up some blankets and pillows and sleep out here by Mattie?" Rose asked. "It'll be fun."

"Yeah!" Jeri yelled again.

"Sure," Don said. "I think we have some sleeping bags in the garage or attic." He looked helplessly at Rose. "Somewhere. I don't even remember where we put things."

"I'll help you," Rose said. "Jeri, will you keep Mattie company while we're gone for a few minutes?"

"I'd love to," Jeri said, her voice mimicking the adult tones of her mother's.

As soon as Don and Rose had exited, Jeri plopped on the rug at the end of Mattie's bed. "Would you mind if I looked through your hope chest?" Jeri asked. "It's so much fun."

Mattie gave a weak nod.

Jeri began sifting through the chest, as she had done the very first day she had met Mattie. She tied on the apron, pulled out Mattie's rag doll, and began to have a tea party. Then Jeri began to look through Mattie's scrapbook, showing the doll the pages one at a time, before holding up the page with the sugar maple leaf that she and Mattie had preserved.

"Pretty," Jeri said. "Isn't it, Ann?"

A few minutes later, Mattie saw Jeri's rear end jutting from the hope chest. Curious, Mabel hopped off the bed and imitated Jeri's stance, nose in the chest, rear in the air.

"What's this?" Jeri finally asked, standing, blood rushing back into her face.

She walked over to Mattie. "I found it at the bottom of the chest," she continued. "It was right in the corner, stuck. Only a little piece of it was showing."

Mattie squinted, but had trouble focusing her eyes.

Jeri scrunched up her face and began to read the words to her. "Who's Judy Garlic?" she asked, reading a signature that was on the stub. "I'm sure glad my mom taught me cursive."

Rose and Don walked back into the room, arms filled with sleeping bags, pillows, and blankets.

"You don't know Judy Garland?" Don asked. "She is Mattie's favorite."

He walked over and dumped the contents of his arms onto the floor. Mabel immediately began clawing the sleeping bags into a pile in order to make a bed.

"Judy Garland was a wonderful actress, singer, dancer, and performer," Don said. "Haven't you ever seen *The Wizard of Oz*?"

"No," Jeri said.

"I was worried about the flying monkeys," Rose mouthed to Don and Mattie.

"How about *Easter Parade*?" he asked. "Or *Meet Me in St. Louis*?"

Jeri shook her head.

"Was she like Taylor Swift?" Jeri asked.

Don chuckled. "Sort of," he said.

"Why do you love her so much?" Jeri asked, looking directly at Mattie.

Mattie looked at the little girl and then out at the snow falling. "Reminds me of home . . . St. Louis, here," Mattie said, her voice weak and hoarse. "But mostly of hope."

Don finally noticed what Jeri was holding, and he walked over to take a closer look. "Oh, my gosh," he said, rubbing his finger over the singer's signature, a smile warming his face. "Honey, remember? 1963."

He waved the stub in the air. "Where did you find this?"

"In there," Jeri said, pointing at the hope chest. "Stuck at the bottom."

"How?" he asked, looking at Mattie. "Your mom couldn't have put that in there. She didn't even know."

Mattie's mouth moved, but Don couldn't make out what she was saying, so he leaned down until his ear was next to her mouth.

"I put it in there," Mattie said. "I wanted to marry *you*."

"Oh, honey," Don said, leaning into kiss his wife. He stood up and looked at Jeri and Rose.

"We hadn't been dating very long, and we sneaked away on a senior trip," Don said. "To Chicago to hear Judy."

"I wanna hear!" Jeri said.

"Me, too," Rose added, taking a seat on the sleeping bag next to Mabel, spreading out the other one and patting it for Jeri to snuggle in next to her.

Don walked over and pulled up a chair next to Mattie. He softly began to sing.

"Clang, clang, clang went the trolley,"

"Don," Mattie said, her eyes glistening. And then she tried to sing, her words coming out garbled but still framed in a happy tone:

"That's why I wish again, I was in Michigan . . ."

Thirty-five

April 1963

M y parents would kill me if they knew about this," Mattie said, looking at Don with a nervous giggle.

"They won't know about this," he said. "You're on spring break in Ft. Lauderdale with your girlfriends, remember?"

"This looks a lot different than Florida," Mattie said, peering out the car window.

The middle of Illinois was as flat as a pancake, and the cornfields ran right up to the side of Highway 55, which connected St. Louis to Chicago. The fields waved in the wind, dancing left and then right, a happy shimmy.

Don's Dodge Dart wafted in the stiff Midwest spring breeze. "No trees to break this wind," he said. "No wonder Chicago's the Windy City."

He looked at the horizon. "You can see forever out here," Don said. "Just like our future."

Mattie smiled.

"Look at the cornstalks," Don said, nodding at them and turning up Chubby Checker on the radio. "They're doing the twist, too."

Mattie laughed and began to dance to the song in the passenger seat.

"Thank you for doing this," she said. "I know Judy's not really your cup of tea."

Don took his right hand off the steering wheel and reached for Mattie's hand. "Anything for you," he said. "Anything. Even Judy Garland."

The trip to Chicago had been a dream of Mattie's, which had turned into an obsession, before becoming an elaborate ruse. For the last year, Mattie and her suitemates had been planning their senior spring break trip to Ft. Lauderdale. Every girl in America, it seems, had seen the movie "Where the Boys Are," starring Connie Francis, and every college girl wanted to head to the beach to find those boys.

But then Mattie had met Don, and one day, while on a study break, happened to read in a magazine that Judy Garland was set to perform at the grand Orchestra Hall in Chicago. Her plans instantly altered.

Although the roommates were disappointed, they understood: The only things covering Mattie's dorm room walls were posters of Judy and pictures of Don.

"We promise to keep your secret safe," her roommates said. "You're with us on spring break."

"Why do you love Judy Garland so much?"

Don's voice brought Mattie back to the present.

"How much time do you have?" she asked with a laugh.

"Long, boring drive," Don said, turning down the radio. "All the time in the world."

"I saw *The Wizard of Oz* when I was a young girl," Mattie said, cracking the window to let in the warm breeze. "It was magical. I wanted to be Judy Garland. And I believed there truly was no place like home."

Mattie turned her face toward the window, shut her eyes, and let the wind whip her blond hair around her face.

"I saw *Easter Parade* when I was eight," she continued. "I loved Easter, and I dreamed that my father would buy a place in Michigan, like he always dreamed of doing."

She began to sing.

> *"That's why I wish again*
> *I was in Michigan . . ."*

"That's a song Judy sang in *Easter Parade*," Mattie said.

"You have a beautiful voice," Don said.

"And you're a good liar," Mattie said with a chuckle.

"I saw *Meet Me in St. Louis* performed at the Muny outdoor theatre in St. Louis a few years later, and it reminded me of how much I loved where I grew up," she continued.

"You still haven't answered my question," Don said. "Why do you love *her* so much?"

"She was so talented—a great singer, actress, and performer—but there was such a fragility to her," Mattie said, watching the fields dance. "Like a child. Her voice projects such a beautiful light. If hope had a voice, it would be Judy's."

Mattie continued. "And when my parents gave me my hope chest when I was ten, they not only did so at Easter, they made a jelly-bean trail that led to it. That always reminded me of the yellow brick road."

She stopped and looked at Don. "And that reminds me of hope, too. Does that make any sense at all?"

"Yes," Don said, tightening his grip on her hand. "That's nice. So Judy to you is sort of like the start of Cardinals baseball season to me, huh? Always filled with hope."

"Oh, Don," Mattie said, taking her hand and waving at him.

"Just joking," he said. "I'm really glad I get to be a part of this with you."

Suddenly, the car lurched.

"Did we hit something?" Mattie asked.

"I don't think so," Don said.

The car lurched again, and began to sputter. The engine died, the steering wheel locked, and Don had to use all his might to pull the car over to the side of the road.

"What's going on?" Mattie asked, as the car came to a stop.

"No clue," Don said. He gripped the steering wheel tightly, his knuckles turning white.

He checked for oncoming traffic, jumped out of the car, and lifted the hood. Black smoke billowed out, and Don began to cough. Mattie stepped out of the car.

"What do we do now?" she asked.

"Wave your arms," Don said, doing just that.

Mattie began to wave her arms in front of the engine, her body engulfed in black smoke. "Not for the smoke," Don said. "Wave your arms at the passing cars to get someone to stop and help."

Mattie coughed. "Now you tell me."

Two hours later, Mattie and Don found themselves sitting in a filling station in the middle of nowhere, after an elderly couple had finally stopped and taken them to a place called Ralph's, so Don's car could be towed and, hopefully, repaired. The owner—a mechanic whose shop's name was sewn onto his blue shirt—appeared, a toothpick sticking out of his mouth.

"She ain't goin' anywhere for a while," Ralph said. As he spoke, Ralph pirouetted the toothpick round and round in his mouth. "Transmission. Gonna take a while."

Mattie groaned audibly. "We have tickets to see Judy Garland tonight in Chicago."

"Judy Garland?" Ralph asked. "Love her. My little girl, Sally, goes as Dorothy every year for Halloween. Puts our dog in a basket. Dog hates it, but, man, does Sally load up on candy. People love *The Wizard of Oz*, don't they?"

Mattie sat up, instantly feeling hopeful.

Ralph saw her expression and shook his head. "But you ain't gonna see Judy tonight, 'cept maybe in your dreams."

Tears filled Mattie's eyes.

"Sorry, ma'am," Ralph said, the toothpick stopping its spin. "I'll do my best to get you outta here before nightfall."

"I'm so sorry," Don said as the mechanic walked away. "I never imagined . . ."

Mattie buried her head in her hands and sobbed.

"Ssshhh," Don said, putting his arm around her. "I'll go see if I can find us something to eat while we wait."

Serves you right, Mattie thought. *Skipping spring break. Lying to your parents. Sneaking away with your boyfriend.*

Don showed up a few minutes later with a Coke and a Twinkie. "Sorry," he said. "That's all they had."

"This is turning out to be a great spring break," Mattie said, grabbing the snacks and heading for the door of the station. "I'm going for a walk."

"Mattie," Don said, standing and moving toward her. "Stay here. Please."

"Don't," she said, throwing open the door. "You and your stupid car."

Don watched her walk down the little dirt road in a huff, tearing open the Twinkie wrapper with her teeth and stuffing it into her mouth.

He didn't mean to, but he laughed.

Feisty, he thought, before amending that. *Too feisty?*

Don slumped into a sofa that had seen better days, its middle sagging, its cushions oil stained. He picked up a newspaper and flipped it open.

JUDY GARLAND TO PERFORM TONIGHT IN CHICAGO read the headline.

Of course, Don thought. *What a day.*

He shut his eyes and rubbed his head to stop the pounding. The noises emanating from the garage—*Zzzzt zzzzt*—didn't help.

Sounds like I'm at the dentist, Don thought. *Probably will cost just as much.*

"I'm really sorry."

Mattie's voice, soft and sweet, made Don open his eyes. "I didn't mean to say that about you and your car. I'm not usually such a brat, I promise. I'm just disappointed."

"I know," Don said, patting the couch. "Come here."

Mattie shook her head. "I'm not sitting on that," she said, scrunching her face. "You come here."

She held open her arms, and Don stood and gave her a long hug. "I love you," he said, kissing her softly.

"Me, too," she said. "Even more than Judy."

"Really?" he asked.

Mattie laughed.

"Still wanna go to Chicago?" Don asked. "See the city?"

Mattie nodded and leaned her head on Don's shoulder, and they both slumped onto the floor, where Mattie eventually fell asleep.

She smells like sunshine, Don thought, kissing her head. *Like hope.*

Four hours later, they were on their way—poorer, but at peace. The two rode in silence—radio off, neither talking—as dusk settled across the fields. There was a beauty to the scene—the colors and the symmetry—that made Mattie want to paint its loveliness.

Seal it in your memory, she thought, embedding in her mind the green of the cornstalks, the gold of the fields, the red barn and white farmhouse, the blue-black dusk and the fireball sun.

Mattie shut her eyes, and again she was fast asleep until she heard Don say, "Mattie, wake up. Look."

The Chicago skyline hovered in front of them, skyscrapers and lights engulfing the horizon.

"St. Louis is big," Mattie said, "but this is really big."

She looked over at Don, mimicking Judy. "Toto, I've a feeling we're not in Kansas anymore."

Don laughed and pulled on to Lake Shore Drive, Chicago hovering to their left, Lake Michigan to their right, a stunning juxtaposition of urban life and nature.

"It's hard to believe this is the same lake that laps on to our beach at Hope Dunes," Mattie said. "I can't wait for you to see it. And finally meet my parents."

"I can't wait, either," Don said. "As long as this remains our secret."

"Tick-a-lock," Mattie said, locking her lips and tossing away the invisible key.

Don continued to drive before taking a left and heading directly into the city.

"Where are you going?"

Don didn't answer for a while, until he turned on to Michigan Avenue. "I at least wanted you to see Orchestra Hall, where Judy performed," Don said. He pulled in front of the historic building with its arched windows over the street. People were still standing out front, talking and laughing.

"Built in 1904," Don said. "Perfect acoustics."

"Someone did their research," Mattie said, unable to take her eyes off the building.

I missed you, Judy, Mattie thought. *Maybe in another life.*

Don pulled a piece of paper from his wallet and then eased the car into the street.

"Where are you going now?" she asked. "And I hope you got two rooms."

Don laughed. "I did," he said. "I'm a gentleman. And, while we may have missed the concert, we still might make our dinner reservation."

"Dinner?" Mattie asked.

"I wanted tonight to be perfect," he said, as the car slowed in the heavy traffic. "Read the directions to me, if you don't mind. I'm not a city boy. My directions growing up were, 'Turn left at the oak tree that got struck by lightning.'"

"I don't see any trees like that," Mattie said, acting as if she were a sea captain, scanning the sidewalks and buildings—hand over her brow—with faux seriousness.

A few blocks away, Don pulled the car off the street and in front of a beautiful restaurant with a red carpet and overhang. Valets immediately opened their doors.

"Don," Mattie whispered, not moving from her seat. "This is way too nice. My outfit is all wrinkled. And it looks very expensive."

"You look beautiful," he said. "And this is your night."

Mattie smiled.

"Remember, I make a very good living as a senior groundskeeper on campus," he said, referring to his work-study job. "What's a few weeks of work for a nice dinner with my gal? It's supposed to be the best steakhouse in Chicago."

"It is, sir," said one of the tuxedoed valets, taking Don's keys. "Here's your ticket."

"Why, thank you, young man," Don joked with the kid, who was probably the same age as him.

Don walked around the Dart. Mattie nervously smoothed her sleeveless floral-print dress with a wide, white belt and poufy skirt. She pulled a compact and lipstick from her purse, touched up her face, and then took Don's waiting arm. "Now I'm ready," she said, before whispering to him, "I still smell like oil and gas."

The restaurant was decorated with white linen tablecloths and tall booths; men were smoking cigars, eating steak, and drinking martinis while women in furs sipped champagne. The restaurant was loud, almost boisterous, and Don had to shout to be heard at the front desk.

"Reservations at ten! For Tice! T-I-C-E!"

"One moment, sir," a beautiful woman in a pink pillbox hat said, picking up two menus. "Right this way."

Don and Mattie were escorted to a booth near the very back of the restaurant, near the kitchen. Doors flew open every few seconds, and waiters and waitresses rushed by with trays.

"Is there a better table?" Don asked. "This is a little hectic."

The woman smiled prettily but coldly, and gave Don and Mattie a once-over. "Only table we have," she said, setting their menus down and turning to walk away. "You're lucky we held it since you're late and we're sold out. Enjoy."

"Yeesh," Mattie said, sliding into the booth, whose padded leather back resembled a Chicago skyscraper over her head. Don moved in next to her and picked up his napkin.

"Poof," he said, flipping it as if he were a magician. "I wish I could make this day disappear."

A man appeared from the kitchen and poured two glasses of water. "Your waiter will be with you shortly," he said.

"I think I need something stronger than water tonight," Don said. "Even if we have to take a taxi to the hotel."

"Welcome," said a tuxedo-clad waiter whose jet black hair was slicked back, as if it had been dipped in wet oil, and severely parted on one side. "What may I get you to drink this evening?"

Don scanned the other tables. "Martini," he said. "And a glass of champagne for my girl."

"Of course, sir," the waiter said.

"Don," Mattie said. "You don't even drink that much. And you don't know how much those drinks cost."

"We're in Chicago," he said. "Let's throw caution to the wind in the Windy City."

Mattie grabbed Don's hand, and the two shared a little kiss. When their drinks arrived, Don raised his glass.

"A toast," he said. "I'm sorry you missed Judy Garland tonight, but I promise we will share a life filled with adventure and yellow brick roads." Don stopped, clinking Mattie's glass of champagne. "As well as a life filled with family, hope, and home."

Don took a big sip of his martini, his eyes growing wide at its potency, and began to sing, softly at first but then a bit louder, emboldened, his face flushed.

"That's why I wish again, I was in Michigan . . ."

Mattie laughed. "Someone really has been studying Judy."

"I'm sorry, but I keep hearing my name."

A face popped over the booth. Mattie screamed.

"Judy Garland?"

"In the flesh," she said. "Although my flesh is a bit red after a couple of drinks, darling."

Judy laughed that Judy laugh.

Mattie turned around in the booth and sat up on her knees, until she was nearly face to face with the legend. Judy was markedly older, but her eyes and her smile were the same as ever.

And that voice, Mattie thought.

Judy disappeared into her booth and then popped around the side, holding a martini. "My favorite booth is at the very back," she whispered. "No one knows I'm in the restaurant. Mind if I sit?"

Mattie and Don stared at her, mouths open.

"So, why did you miss my little show this evening, darlings?"

Mattie and Don both launched into their challenging day, before Mattie produced a ticket. "See? We weren't lying."

Judy flagged a waiter. "Could I get a pen?" she asked, before pointing at her glass. "And another round for the table? On me."

She looked at Don and Mattie. "You two deserve it after the day you've had."

The waiter returned with their drinks, and Judy signed her name on Mattie's ticket before tearing it in half. "Now it's official," she laughed.

"I will never forget this moment," Mattie said in a rush, staring at her signature. She hurriedly told her about seeing her movies, the Muny, and her hope chest. "I've loved you forever."

"Thank you, darling," Judy said. "And I think you've found a man who will love you forever, too."

Judy took a sip of her martini, and shut her eyes.

"Clang, clang, clang went the trolley . . ."

Judy opened her eyes and looked directly at Don. "Isn't that how you felt, darling?" she asked.

Don nodded, his mouth still agape.

Judy scooted a little farther into the booth, until her velvet jacket was touching Mattie's arms, and the black feathers atop her hat were tickling Mattie's face.

"Since you missed the concert," she whispered, "here's a little number that ends every show, just for you two angels."

"Somewhere over the rainbow . . ."

Mattie cried as the song ended, and Judy hugged her before shaking Don's hand.

"You two have a wonderful life, you hear me?" she said. "It ain't easy. But it ain't supposed to be easy, either, is it?"

And with that, she disappeared into her own booth.

Don and Mattie could barely eat their meals.

"You make everything possible," Mattie told Don as they sipped their cocktails. "Thank you."

"We make a great team," Don said, kissing Mattie. "Just like Judy and Fred Astaire in *Easter Parade.*"

Don finished his story and held the ticket stub up in front of Mattie's face.

"We still make a great team," he said, kissing her.

"What a story," Rose said, putting her arm around Mattie, as Mabel snored beside them. "I can't imagine meeting Judy Garland in person."

"I can't imagine meeting Taylor Swift," Jeri said. "I couldn't talk even."

Jeri looked at Mattie. "I wish I could watch all those movies you loved," she said. "And meet Judy, too!"

She picked up Mattie's cloth doll, still sitting by her, and began to mimic a lyric from the "Trolley Song" to Ann, mostly singing, *"Zing, zing, zing"* over and over.

Jeri stopped and tilted her head at the doll, their expressions and hair nearly identical. "I don't even know what a trolley is," she said to Ann.

"It's a shame we don't have cable set up yet," Don said to Jeri. "We're on 'the list.' Which means April, when it stops snowing."

"Hey," Rose said, her voice rising. "I think I know how to bring Judy here tonight."

She pivoted toward Don. "Where's your laptop? It's got a big screen. And you have Netflix and Internet service, right?"

Don nodded.

"We can set it up right here on the tray beside Mattie, gather around, and watch *Easter Parade*, *Meet Me in St. Louis*, and *The Wizard of Oz*," Rose continued. "We're not going anywhere until tomorrow anyway."

"Yeah," Jeri yelled, her excitement waking Mabel from her slumber.

"I'll get my laptop," Don said.

"And I'll make some popcorn," Rose said.

The three pulled chairs around Mattie's bed, tucked themselves in blankets, and watched the magic of Judy Garland. When she sang "Somewhere over the Rainbow," Jeri crawled from her mother's side, scrambled onto Mattie's bed, and nestled in beside her.

"I get it," she said to Mattie, her eyes big. "Over the rainbow. That's where you're going, isn't it? That's where we're all going one day."

Mattie's eyes filled with tears, and she shook her head.

"But it's a happy place, not a sad one," Jeri said with conviction, laying her head on Mattie's shoulder. "And you'll be able to fly again."

Don and Rose looked at one another, unable to hide their emotions.

"I love slumber parties," Jeri said, nestling even tighter into Mattie's side, before falling asleep, still clutching the rag doll and Mattie.

part thirteen

The Family Bible

Thirty-six

March 2017

Mattie Tice's dreams were always the same since being diagnosed with ALS: She was free of her body, her illness, her wheelchair; able to do anything she desired. Sometimes, Mattie dreamed she was running along the beach, other times she was knee deep in the fresh spring earth tending her garden. Other times, Mattie was dancing with her husband, swimming in Lake Michigan, or strolling the streets of Paris or Saugatuck.

But most times, Mattie's dreams were of the simplest of things: Getting up in the morning without assistance, making coffee, brushing her hair, putting on her makeup, getting dressed, petting Mabel, shutting the door behind her to leave for work.

When Mattie was young, she most often dreamed that she was falling. Now, when Mattie dreamed, she always flew free of her body, somewhere over a rainbow.

"She can still hear you," Mattie heard an unfamiliar voice say, somewhere in the midst of her dream, as she was flying. "Just keep talking to her as you normally would. She can still hear everything you say."

Am I dreaming? Mattie thought.

Mattie could feel her soul return to the room. Her eyes fluttered and slowly the world came into focus.

She was floating in the family room of Hope Dunes, hovering against the old wood beams of the cottage's ceiling, while three figures were gathered around an old woman's bed.

My bed, it suddenly occurred to Mattie.

She opened her mouth to talk—*Don!* she tried to say, *Rose!*—but no words came out.

How long have I been asleep? Mattie thought. She scanned her eyes around the room. *The last thing I remember was watching Judy Garland movies.*

Her eyes fell on the ornate grandfather clock that she had purchased long ago in Switzerland. Its hands were about to strike ten a.m. Suddenly, the clock chimed, and Mattie was amidst the mountains of Lucerne and then—in the blink of an eye—in the Swiss shop where she had purchased the clock. The shop was a joyous cacophony of chimes, dings, dongs, and whistles.

"That one."

Mattie looked down: She and Don were picking out the clock.

The clock chimed again, and Mattie was painting the clock shop.

The clock chimed again, and Mattie was back at Hope Dunes.

She could see Rose pick up the little snow globe that sat beside her bed and give it a nervous shake. Rose was wearing the apron. Ann, the rag doll, was nestled in the bed beside her, patiently waiting for Jeri to return from school. The McCoy vase occupied the middle of the dining room table, filled with flowers.

I'm wearing my beach glass pendant, Mattie thought, surveying the scene, *and my head is resting on Rose's embroidered pillowcase.*

Such a wonderful life.

Mattie felt a presence move beside her. She turned, and her mother—young, vibrant, just as she had looked when Mattie was a girl—was floating beside her.

Mom?

Such love, such memories, her mother said to her without opening her mouth. *Even those things you dreamed you would never have, they all came true. It's just never in the way we imagine it will be.*

Mattie stared at her mother. *I have so many questions for you.*

"Mattie?"

Mattie looked down. Don was sitting on the edge of her bed, whispering into her ear.

"Let me say goodbye, my love," he whispered. "I know it's selfish. But I need to see you one more time."

You are the love of my life, her mother said.

Don't go, Mom.

"You are the love of my life," Don said. "I'm not ready."

Mattie could feel her spirit alter when Don said "ready," the word coming out in three syllables—"re-uh-dee"—like it always did when he was stressed and trying to hide it.

I'll see you soon, beautiful girl, her mother said. *You're not quite ready, either. And then we'll have forever to catch up.*

Mattie could feel a pressure on her arm.

Her eyes opened. She was again in her body, Don holding her, a blood pressure cuff around her arm.

"Sweetheart!" Don said, tears in his eyes. "You're back."

Mattie nodded weakly, her eyes still scanning the ceiling of the family room.

"Her BP is still very low but stabilizing a bit."

Don looked at his wife. "This is LeAnn," he said. "Your hospice nurse. Remember?"

Mattie nodded weakly again, although she didn't remember the woman.

"Thirsty?" LeAnn asked, holding up a big plastic sippy cup filled with ice water.

"Hold on," Rose said. She walked out of Mattie's periphery and returned a moment later holding her favorite desert rose teacup. "Take a little sip," she urged Mattie. "For me."

Mattie gave a faint smile to Rose and took a tiny sip.

"Attagirl," Rose said with a wink.

"Do you need anything, Mattie?" Don asked.

Mattie's eyes again scanned the rafters of the family room. "Bible," she said, her voice barely audible, her eyes tilting toward her hope chest.

Don nodded, understanding, and opened her hope chest. He began to look through its contents and finally stood, holding a worn Bible.

He returned to her bedside and held the old Bible in front of his wife's face. The Bible's cover was brown leather—worn to an amber gold from years of use—and it was embossed with four crosses around the words, "The Holy Bible." The cover design resembled a stained glass window. The cover had come unglued from its binding and had been stitched and sewn through its spine many times. Old thread hung loose from its edge.

"Read," Mattie whispered.

Don opened the Bible, whose pages were yellow and worn. Many of them were dog-eared, folded on to themselves over and over, the creases in the pages so fragile that the slightest pressure would cause them to tear, if not disintegrate.

Don flipped through the pages.

"Corinthians 4:16–18," Don finally read, turning to one of the most dog-eared pages. "'So we do not lose heart. Though our outer self is wasting away, our inner self is being renewed day by day. For this light momentary affliction is preparing for us an eternal weight of glory beyond all comparison, as we look not to the things that are seen but to the things that are unseen. For the things that are seen are transient, but the things that are unseen are eternal.'"

Don's voice became shakier as he finished the passage. He raised his head to look at Mattie, whose eyes narrowed—changing from grey to bright green—and seemed to pierce his soul. Another faint smile crossed her lips, and she shut her eyes.

The passage I read to you, Mom, when you were dying, Mattie thought.

"Lovely," the hospice nurse said, smoothing Mattie's hair.

"I never knew," Rose started, nodding at the Bible. "About her faith."

"Her grandfather was an Ozarks preacher," Don said. "Or that's what he called himself, legend goes. I only knew him a few years, but the stories that man could tell. If this Bible could talk . . ."

"I think it can," Rose said. "What you just read. I have chills."

"We both have great faith," Don said. "She found hers in the earth, in gardening and flowers. I found mine in . . ." Don hesitated, and tears rimmed his eyes. "Her."

He closed the Bible and ran his fingers over its cover. "She was baptized in a little creek behind her grandfather's church," he said. "Didn't she ever tell you about him?"

"No," Rose said, pulling up a chair, along with the hospice nurse.

Mattie opened her eyes, and she was looking down at the three gathered around her bed. As Don began to talk, Mattie was transported back to her grandfather's creek.

Thirty-seven

July 1952

R eady?"

"No," Mattie said, before changing her mind. "Yes. Just do it."

Mattie Barnhart lifted her feet into the air and shut her eyes.

"Hold on!"

Mattie's grandfather gave her a big push, and Mattie immediately felt the wind whip her face. When she opened her eyes again, Mattie let out a mighty whoop.

She was seated in a tire swing that hung from the bent arm of an ancient, gnarled sycamore tree, which jutted from the bank and bent over Sugar Creek at a thirty-degree angle. The creek's current gently moved the branches of the tree that—when heavy with summer's leaves—dipped into the icy cold water.

Mattie soared between an opening in the tree's branches—leaves gently brushing her face—and toward the July sky. The temperature seemed to jump ten degrees as shadow turned to sun, and the cool creek fell further below. At the very top of her swing, Mattie could see the Ozarks' hills and farmland in the distance, laying out its patchwork beauty like a quilt.

Without warning, Mattie's body whipped backward, and she began her return. She shut her eyes, tightened her grip on the rope handles and knots of the swing—the tire tilting backward at an awkward angle. Mattie could feel the wind on her front and her back, and she screamed, dropped her legs, and her feet suddenly dragged through the cold creek. Mattie screamed again, until she felt her grandfather's arms around her body, slowing her swing, catching her, keeping her safe.

"Did you have fun?" he asked.

Mattie stepped from the tire swing on shaky legs, her limbs like rubber. She nodded tentatively.

"Did you have faith?" he asked.

She tilted her head, not understanding his question.

"That you would be okay?" he continued. "That I would catch you?"

Mattie nodded her head again tentatively.

"I don't believe you," he said. "Come here."

Her grandfather stepped across the rocky beach and took a seat on a big stone that had been on the beach forever. It was bleached white from the sun, and it had two indentations in it, like a chair for two, whose cushions had been worn from years of use. Mattie sat, the rock warming her legs, and looked at her grandfather.

Everyone called him Pastor Nigh—in fact, he called himself that—but he was just Grampa to Mattie. He certainly had the presence of the Almighty: tall, muscular, imposing, with a voice that boomed like thunder. He was tanned from working outside on his farm, fishing, and frogging, but his hair was white as the rock on which they sat, as blond as Mattie's.

Pastor Nigh was Mary Ellen's father. He wasn't *really* a preacher—as he didn't have a church—but he preached right here, on this stretch of rocky beach that sat at the very bottom of his land, below his farm, cows, and horses, beyond the little log cabin, beyond the bluffs that reached toward heaven. Every Sunday, a few locals—those who were deemed outcasts, those who didn't like to roll in the aisles, or those who simply wanted church to be outside on a beautiful day—would gather at the creek for Pastor Nigh's service. Sometimes there would be one person, sometimes twenty.

Mattie saw her grandfather a few times a year. It was not an easy drive down the old roads that wound from St. Louis to southwestern Missouri, but Mary Ellen made sure Mattie spent at least a summer week with her grandfather when they weren't in Michigan. It wasn't an easy emotional journey for Mary Ellen, either, as her mother had passed away years ago, when her father didn't call himself a preacher, just a farmer.

"He changed," Mary Ellen told Mattie on a drive to see him a few years back. "He told me, 'I lost everything, but I found everything, too.' He's a different person. But he's also become the father I never had. That strong, silent farmer tells me he loves me every time we talk."

"What do you see?" Mattie's grandfather asked her, his eyes scanning the water.

"A creek," Mattie said.

"You don't see the end of it, do you?" he asked. "You really don't know where it's going or where it ends?"

He stopped, and the burble of the rushing creek sang to them.

"But you know it goes *somewhere*, don't you?" he continued. "Somewhere bigger . . . to a pond, to a lake, maybe even to that Lake Michigan you and your mom love so much."

He looked at Mattie and put his hand on her shoulder. "That's what faith is," he said. "Just a realization that we are going somewhere bigger than where we are right now. That this is just the beginning of our journey, like when we take a float trip in inner tubes that starts right here."

Mattie smiled at her grandfather. "Are you really a preacher?" she asked.

He laughed, the wisps of his hair dancing in the breeze. "Yes and no," he said. "That's just what people call me because I talk freely of my faith. Some think I'm crazy, some think I'm wise."

He stopped and again let the creek talk in his place.

"I just know I miss your grandma every single day," he finally said. "I hear her in the rush of the creek, I hear her in the whinny of the horses, I hear her in the call of the whippoorwill and the moan of the bullfrogs. But I know she's in a better place. I have to believe that."

He shut his eyes. "'Now hope that is seen is not hope. For who hopes for what he sees? But if we hope for what we do not see, we wait for it with patience.'"

He opened his eyes and looked at his granddaughter. "Romans 8:24–25," he said. "From the Bible."

"So it's like me wanting to grow up really fast," she said, narrowing her eyes and looking intently at her grandfather. "And filling my hope chest up with all the things I want for my future. I just need to be patient, and be filled with hope."

"You got it," he said, smiling. "It's not about being religious. It's about knowing that life and the world are way too intricate to just end like this."

He continued. "The trees, the birds, the creek, the sun . . . *you*. It's amazing, and it all goes by so fast. I just want you to make your mark in this world, and to be a part of this world. In a blink, it's gone."

Mattie stood and hugged her grandfather.

"Will you push me again in the tree swing?" she asked. "I won't blink this time, or be scared. I'll enjoy every second."

She started toward the tree swing and took a seat. Her grandfather pushed her, and she laughed the whole way. When her grandfather caught her when she was done, Mattie looked at him.

"I had fun," she said. "And I had faith."

Then she took off running, leapt into the air, and did a cannonball into Sugar Creek.

Thirty-eight

Rose leaned into her bathroom mirror and looked at the dark circles under her eyes.

"Some things never change," she thought, reaching for some moisturizer and then for the foundation. "And some things do."

She sighed and stared at her reflection, thinking of Mattie and the story that Don had shared before she left. Without warning, she lowered her head into her hands and began to sob.

I should never have gotten so attached, Rose thought. *I knew it was temporary. I knew it was a job.*

"Are you sad, Mommy?"

Jeri walked into the bathroom, hopped on to the cushioned seat at the vanity, and looked at her mom.

"No, sweetie," Rose said, dropping her head toward the sink, acting as if she were just rinsing her face.

"It's okay to be sad," Jeri said.

Rose lifted her head and smiled at her daughter. "You're right," she said. "I am sad."

Jeri hopped off the seat and hugged her mother, squeezing her tightly.

"I'm sad, too," she said. "I told my teacher that Mrs. Tice was sick, and she asked me if I was sad."

"What did you say?" Rose asked.

"I told her I was going to miss her, because I never really had a grandma," Jeri said. "Mrs. Tice has taught me a lot of things. And she told me I taught her a lot, too."

"When did she tell you that?" Rose asked.

"Oh, we've had lots of talks," Jeri said with a big smile. "I told her I loved her, and she told me she loved me. To the moon and back."

Rose quelled her rising tears. "That's far," she said. "That's a lot of love."

"I know," Jeri said, returning to the vanity. "My teacher said that's what I will always remember. How much she loved me, and that no matter how far away she is—even to the moon—she will always be with me, even if I can't see her."

Jeri stopped and tapped her chest. "She'll be right here. In my heart."

"Your teacher is right," Rose said. "And very smart."

Jeri picked up a brush and began to run it through her unruly curls, but it got stuck before she even got started. "Ouch," she said.

The simple sight of a young girl brushing her hair lifted Rose's spirits, and she walked out and cracked the window in her bedroom. The scent of blueberry muffins and chocolate chip cookies immediately drifted inside, making her mouth water.

Even though it was barely forty outside, Rose could sense that winter was finally unleashing its relentless grasp on Michigan's coast. The sky was blue, birds were chirping, and robins were looking for worms in the unfreezing earth.

How much longer will I have this view and these smells? Rose thought. *I'm barely getting by, and I'll be losing a full-time job.*

Rose shook her head. *You're being selfish,* she thought. *Stop thinking of yourself.*

A cardinal flew onto a bare branch and tilted its head at Rose.

Mattie, she thought, remembering the one that used to greet them when they had breakfast.

A bluebird—which matched the cloudless sky—fluttered onto a branch above the cardinal.

Mom, Rose thought, remembering how much her mother loved spring and the color blue.

The birds chirped happily.

Are you two trying to tell me something? Rose thought, watching them.

She heard her mother's voice, clear as day, say, "Sunny skies ahead." Rose thought of the Bible passage Don had read earlier.

Both birds darted to the ground, landing on a tiny patch of muddy earth in the postage stamp–size front yard. They stuck their beaks into the dirt, and that's when Rose saw it: the starts Mattie had given her from her garden last summer were alive and growing.

"You are telling me something," Rose said outloud through the window, her voice causing the birds to take flight.

"Change," Rose said to Jeri, as she walked hurriedly into the bathroom. "Something blue. Something nice."

"Why?" Jeri asked. "Where are we going?"

"Church," Rose said.

"But it's not even Sunday," Jeri said, before adding, "And we never go to church."

"We are today," Rose said.

The two quickly changed—Rose in a blue turtleneck sweater, skirt, and robin's egg blue overcoat and scarf, Jeri in a sparkly aquamarine tutu over blue leggings covered with a puffy coat—and headed toward town. They turned onto Butler and headed up the town's big hill, directly toward the little white church that Dora Hoffs once attended.

"We never go by here," Jeri said when they stopped in front of the church. "You said it made you sad."

Rose's eyes dropped to look at her daughter. Then they slowly made their way up toward the church and the steeple that sat atop its roof.

"I think I was wrong," Rose mumbled to Jeri. "Come on," she said, grabbing her daughter's hand and opening the heavy, wooden double doors of the church.

"Smells like Mrs. Tice's hope chest," Jeri said as they walked into the little church, which was filled with glowing wooden pews, its soaring rafters painted white, sunlight streaming into the stained glass windows that ringed the building.

There is *something hopeful about this little church*, Rose thought, watching the colorful prism of light splay inside. *The windows change color, just like Mattie's eyes.*

"Can I help you?"

Rose jumped at the sound of Father Higgins's voice, the smooth bass echoing through every inch of the church, just like an organ.

"Rose?" he asked. "Rose Hoffs? Jeri?"

He extended his hand, and Jeri shook it politely. Rose gave him a long hug.

"Why aren't you wearing your minister clothes?" Jeri asked, a suspicious tone in her voice.

Father Higgins laughed. "It's Tuesday," he whispered in a conspiratorial tone. "We can wear jeans on regular days, just like you."

Jeri giggled.

"What brings you here?" he asked, smoothing his silver hair. "It's been so long."

He stopped and looked at Rose, his blue eyes filled with feeling. "We miss your mom," he said. "I bet you do, too. Every day. But she's in a better place now."

Rose flinched. Those words—*She's in a better place now*—chilled her.

Is she? Rose had wanted to scream at every person who said that at her funeral. *Is she really? She's dead. I'm alone. How do you know?*

Rose had thought she would find comfort in the church following her mother's death, but she had felt like an impersonator, a faker of faith.

"I can still see the pain and loss in your eyes," Father Higgins said. "The questioning remains, doesn't it? Please, have a seat. Let's talk for a second. There's a reason you're here, isn't there?"

Rose nodded and took a seat in a pew, Jeri sliding in next to her and immediately picking up a Bible in the back of the pew, next to the hymnal.

Rose began to tell Father Higgins of Mattie and her illness, her voice wavering as she told him she was in her final days.

"She has such strong faith," Rose said, talking about her family Bible. "My mom had such strong faith. Why don't I?"

Her eyes dropped and then she looked deeply into Father Higgins's eyes. "I want my daughter to have faith," she said. "And hope."

Father Higgins took Rose's hand in his. "Dear girl," he said. "You have both if you care so deeply."

He looked up at the rafters of the church and smiled.

"Have you ever heard of the Lost City of Singapore?" he asked. "The legend around Saugatuck-Douglas . . . the oldest ghost story in Michigan?"

Rose nodded her head. "Of course I have," she said, her eyes narrowing. "What's that have to do with anything?"

Father Higgins ignored Rose's question and instead launched into a story and history, much like he did in the sermons Rose had listened to every Sunday when her mother was alive. He began to tell the legend of Singapore, which was founded in the 1830s by New York land speculators who hoped it would rival Chicago and Milwaukee as a lake port. It was a busy lumbering town—with three mills, two hotels, several general stores, and a renowned bank—and home to Michigan's first schoolhouse. The town outshone its neighbor to the south, Saugatuck, which was then called The Flats.

After the great fire swept through Chicago in 1871—as well as through the towns of Holland and Peshtigo—Singapore was almost completely deforested supplying the three towns with lumber for rebuilding. Without the protective tree cover, the winds and sands coming off Lake Michigan quickly eroded the town into ruins, and within four years sand had completely covered the town, and it was vacated by 1875. Its ruins now lie buried beneath the sand dunes of the Lake Michigan shoreline at the mouth of the Kalamazoo River.

"Have you ever gone on the Dunes Ride?" Father Higgins finally asked, turning to Jeri, referencing the wild dune buggy ride throughout the sand dunes that made tourists' screams echo throughout the resort towns every summer day.

"I love it," she said. "It's so fun and scary."

"Remember when the driver stops at the top of a dune and points to the tree poking out of the sand?" he asked. "Then he says it's the top of the tree, and the trunk is actually buried miles below?"

Jeri nodded.

"That's faith," he said, turning to look at Rose. "That's hope."

Rose tilted her head and looked at him.

"When you think you're buried, when you think you can't see light anymore, if you just keep believing and reaching, then hope will appear, just like that tree.

"It's okay to search, to seek, to be lost, and to question," he continued. "That's part of the journey. But do you want to remain buried in the dark, or do you want to see that blue sky again?"

He smiled at Rose and tightened his grip on her hand.

"Much of the lumber that was used to build this church was salvaged from Singapore's ruins," he said, his voice soft but still rumbling through the church. "Your mother and your friend Mattie are like that lumber. They are strong. They are leaving a legacy. They have built a solid foundation for you and Jeri."

Father Higgins looked toward the altar. "Your mother was always so worried about you," he said. "She wondered why you always doubted yourself, let others come first. I told her it was because you were actually stronger than everyone else, you just didn't realize it yet."

He looked at Rose. "Do you realize it now?"

Rose dissolved into tears. "I miss my mom," she said. "I'm going to miss my friend so much."

"They'll always be with you," he said.

"May I?" he then asked Jeri, taking the Bible from her little hands. He flipped through its pages, stopping at Job 14:7. "'For there is hope of a tree, if it be cut down, that it will sprout again, and that the tender branch thereof will not cease.'"

Father Higgins gave Rose a hug and then leaned over and shook Jeri's hand goodbye. "I hope to see you both again soon," he said, standing. "And, Jeri, I'll wear something a little more appropriate, okay? I'll leave you two alone for a while. Light a candle. Say a prayer. Talk to your mom and your friend."

He exited, his footsteps echoing through the church, until all was silent. Rose stood, took Jeri's hand, and together they lit two candles, one for their friend, and one for their mother and grandmother.

Then Rose and Jeri walked to the front of the church, knelt in front of the altar, bowed their heads, and prayed.

When they emerged from the church and into the light, Jeri and Rose joined hands and walked in silence until they reached Lake Effect Coffee. They ordered a latte and hot chocolate, and two blueberry muffins, and—despite the chill in the air—walked outside to the garden and took a seat under an arbor of pine and aspen.

As Jeri sipped her hot chocolate—marshmallows covering her lips—she looked up into the branches, the blue sky smiling upon them, and said, "I feel like that tree on the dune buggy ride."

Rose smiled at her daughter and took a big bite of her muffin, her lips blue from the berries. "So do I," she said.

Thirty-nine

"Why don't you go get some fresh air?" LeAnn said to Don. "Take a walk. It's a beautiful day."

Don lifted his head from the back of the chair that sat next to Mattie's bed. There were bags under his eyes.

"What if . . . ?" he started.

"She's not going anywhere," LeAnn said. "She'll wait for you. Trust me." She smiled and rubbed his back.

Don bit his cheek. *Hospice workers are angels on earth,* he thought.

Don turned his gaze to LeAnn as she placed a small clip on Mattie's finger to monitor her pulse. LeAnn was tiny, with dark hair and eyes—almost like a blackbird—but she carried herself with the strength and elegance of an eagle. When Don looked closely, he noticed that she, too, was exhausted, that heavy dark bags drooped beneath dark eyes.

It's as if that's the only place she can carry the weight of her emotions with a job like this, Don thought.

"Okay," he said. "But I'll be quick. And then you need to take a break."

He stood, leaned over, and kissed Mattie. "I'll be right back," he said. "I love you."

Mattie's body shifted slightly, and the beach glass pendant she was wearing around her neck tumbled free of her pajama top. The sun shining through the windows caught the beach glass, and it glowed, splaying light onto Mattie's chin and face like a kaleidoscope.

You've always been filled with light, Don thought. *My sunshine.*

"Scoot," the hospice nurse whispered, shooing Don with a wave.

Don took a few steps and then stopped.

He walked out the back door of the cottage, onto the screened porch, where he stopped, unsure if he should leave or not. As the door to the screened porch slammed shut, the little bell that Mattie's mom had made for it years ago tinkled, and the wind chime Mattie hung in the corner sang in the breeze. Don took it as a sign that it was okay to go.

She's everywhere, he thought.

Don zipped up his jacket as he took the stairs to their beach. It was an atypical March day in Michigan, meaning it wasn't snowing or overcast. It was clear and bright, crisp but warm by Michigan standards. Still, Don's eyes watered as the chilly wind off the lake met his face with a slap.

Don stepped into the sand, which was still icy and packed, like the ground after a hard frost. He walked toward the water. Although a layer of ice still covered the coastline, Don could see the lake was beginning to thaw. Great cracks had already formed in the ice at the shoreline, and Don could see the waves gently undulate the frozen layer, making the surface appear as if it were lava, or ice cubes in a cocktail.

Don kicked up a patch of beach, turning it over to uncover the softer sand, and sat down. He let the cold sand trickle through his fingers as he watched the lake come alive once again after a long winter's slumber.

Mattie won't awaken, though, Don thought. *She won't see another summer.*

Don's heart shattered, and he lay back on the sand, his tears turning the sky into a broken mosaic.

Don wished he could freeze time, just like winter had the lake—stop everything from moving forward, just a little while longer.

Time will march on, he thought. *Life will continue.*

He thought of the first holiday season with Mattie after her mother had died. From now on, his life would be filled with lasts and firsts as well. The first Fourth of July without Mattie, the first year of her gardens without their creator, the first sugar maple leaf to fall.

It's not fair, he thought, before another cliché entered his head. *She'll be in a better place soon.*

In the years following Mattie's diagnosis, Don had been angry not only at God but also at every single person who insinuated that his wife would one day be better off dead.

But Mattie had made him realize that his anger was misplaced.

It's not about you, Mattie told him many times. *You're being selfish wasting all of your strength and emotion over something you can't control. This is no way for me to live. And one day, I* will *be in a better place, free of this body.*

She had stopped and looked intensely at Don. *That's enough,* she had said. *Conversation over.*

"You are the strongest person I will ever know," Don said into the lake breeze, tears streaming down his face. "You are grace incarnate."

He sat up and let the wind sober him.

Mattie, of course, had her funeral planned, years ago, down to every last detail. She wanted to be cremated, her ashes scattered amongst her gardens, on the beach, and in the lake.

I want to be part of Hope Dunes forever, she'd said.

Mattie had picked out the poem she wanted Don to read, the one that would be in her program.

Emily Dickinson, of course, she had said.

The poem was titled "Asleep," and Don had memorized it long ago just so he could get through the service without making a fool of himself. He shut his eyes, and began to recite it to the lake, ending with:

> *While color's revelations break,*
> *And blaze the butterflies!*

"You are a blazing butterfly, my dear," Don said. "It's time to fly again."

Don stood and walked to the shoreline. Small boulders of ice dotted the beach as far as the eye could see. The sun made them shimmer like diamonds, and it illuminated their interiors, bright and blue shining forth from their frozen outsides.

Don smiled. *Just like you, my love,* he thought. *I can still see all of your beauty.*

Don walked up to one of the round ice balls and knocked on it, as if for luck. He was about to turn away, when something flashed and caught his eye.

No, he thought, falling to his knees to get a closer look. *It can't be. It's a miracle.*

Buried at the bottom and frozen along the outer wall was a piece of beach glass, similar to the one Don had been unable to get his hands on last fall. Don turned, scanning the beach, and eyed a small rock with a pointy end. He picked it up and began to chip at the ice.

"C'mon," he said, blowing on the ice and continuing to chip away at it. "I need bigger tools."

He flew up the steps and returned moments later, out of breath, with an ancient ice pick, one that Mattie's father had gifted him.

"There's a reason you gave this to me, Joe," Don said, beginning to chip away.

As Don worked, he began to sweat, so much that he shed his jacket and began to huff. He slowly began to chip and pick, ice flying into his face as if he were playing hockey, until fifteen minutes later a chunk of the outer wall finally fell free into the sand. Don chopped the layer until the piece of glass was free.

The glass was iridescent blue, like ice itself, and nearly as large as the pendant Mattie wore. Don lifted his head toward the sun and laughed like a crazy man. That's when something finally occurred to him—something he had forgotten in his despair—and he tore off running, flying up the beach stairs, until he was at Mattie's bedside.

"Are you okay?" LeAnn asked.

"Look," Don said to Mattie. "Just like when we met."

He took Mattie's hand and placed the cool beach glass in her palm, enclosing it with his own hands.

"Remember what you first told me? Your father said you have to search long and hard to find love—just like beach glass—but sometimes finding it is as easy as simply being aware of what's right in front of you, keeping your eyes open during the search. Because—*boom!*—like beach glass, it will be right there."

Don stopped, bit his cheek, and willed the tears from rising. "We found each other," he said, his voice trembling but strong. "Somehow, we found each other. And somehow I found this. How's that for a birthday gift? You've got one coming up, remember? You didn't think I'd forget, did you?"

He leaned down to his wife's ear and whispered, "I am a better man because of you," he said. "I have known unconditional love, and I will never stop loving you."

He hesitated, began to cry, and then burbled through his tears, "How's that for a platitude?"

Don turned, and LeAnn was waiting, arms open. She held Don. "There, there," she said.

After a few seconds, LeAnn's body jerked upright. "Look."

Don pivoted, and Mattie's hand—weakly, nearly imperceptibly—tightened around the beach glass.

Forty

Don and Rose held hands in silence beside Mattie's bedside.

"She's transitioning," LeAnn had said a few hours earlier.

Over the past few days, LeAnn had prepared Don and Rose for Mattie's decline, explaining that the process of death was akin to closing a major league baseball stadium after a game: One section of lights goes out at a time, until, finally, it is dark. The hospice nurse constantly checked Mattie's feet and legs, nodding to herself, understanding silent signs Don and Rose did not.

Mattie had not verbally responded to Don in two days, and she was now on morphine.

"You push that button every twenty minutes, hear me?" LeAnn had told Don. "She doesn't need to experience any pain."

Much like Mattie, Don and Rose were living in a temporary, transitional state, one that wavered much like a dream, where nothing seemed real but everything was.

As word had trickled out, friends had brought food. "Casserole queens," LeAnn jokingly called them. "They comfort with food. It's the only way they know to help."

The kitchen and refrigerator were overflowing with food—casseroles, lasagna, ham and beans, turkey, roast beef, chicken, cookies, cakes and pies—but no one felt like eating.

Now, it was quiet. Mattie's machines and oxygen had been removed. The only sounds filling the house were of the lake and wind, or from squirrels scampering across the roof.

Rose thought of Jeri at school.

Was she at recess? Rose wondered. *Was she working on a spelling assignment? Was she thinking of Mattie?*

Rose could picture all of the children on the playground, unaffected by the world's troubles, by a life passing.

"I feel as if I need to do something," Rose said.

"You're here," Don replied. "That's everything."

Rose's agency had requested that she start another job, but Rose felt as if she'd not finished this one.

"I can't," she told her boss, who was more than understanding, but said, "We might not have an opening for you after this."

"I know," Rose said. "But I can't leave. And please don't charge them for my time. I'm here as a friend, not an employee."

Rose tightened her grip on Don's hand and then reached for the family Bible nestled next to Mattie's body.

Rose nervously flicked through the pages, noticing how many pages had notes scribbled in the margins.

"I lost faith for the longest time, you know," Rose whispered, looking at Don, an ironic smile crossing her face. "Until I met Mattie. She taught me to be strong again," Rose said. "To have faith . . . in myself and beyond."

Rose hesitated, and her lips quivered. "She reminded me I was important," she continued. "She taught Jeri that her confidence is a good thing."

Rose stopped. "I won't cry, I promised myself," she said, before continuing. "But you both gave us a family again."

Don hugged Rose. "You did, too," he said. "You know that, don't you?"

Rose shrugged and then nodded. "Thank you."

Rose looked down at the Bible. Out of all the pages, she had once again turned to the page Don had read days earlier.

"'For this light momentary affliction is preparing for us an eternal weight of glory beyond all comparison, as we look not to the things that are seen but to the things that are unseen,'" Rose read. "'For the things that are seen are transient, but the things that are unseen are eternal.'

"I like that," Rose continued. "I believe that. I *have* to believe that."

Rose lay the Bible down next to Mattie again.

"It's too nice of a day to have the house shut up like this," Rose said. "Mattie would have a door cracked open for some fresh air."

She stood and cracked the door that led to the screened porch. Noises suddenly invaded the home—hawks crying, birds chirping, someone yelling on the beach—along with the smells of outside, of the earth warming, of spring . . .

Of hope, Rose thought.

Rose turned and looked at Mattie, the rag doll that Jeri had nestled against her seeming to hug her still body. Without thinking, Rose walked over, pulled Mattie's hope chest into the center of the room, and opened it. Another smell invaded Hope Dunes: cedar.

Rose knelt to her knees and began to rustle through the contents of the chest.

Everything in here has a story and a history, Rose thought. *Each of these heirlooms has taught me something not only about Mattie and her family but also about myself. They are living lessons.*

Rose lifted the apron from the chest and tied it around her waist absentmindedly. She trailed her fingers over the blueberry stain that dotted it.

I have a history with this incredible woman and this family, Rose thought. *It's my legacy to continue her story.*

Rose stood, and Don smiled, nodding at the apron.

He scanned the room: All of the items from Mattie's hope chest—from her childhood and her life—surrounded her. Her doll and Bible were with her. The snow globe shimmered beside her bed on a table, which also held the McCoy vase, filled with hyacinths, and the painted picture frame of Mattie, Rose, Jeri, and Don; a desert rose teacup, still filled with tea, sat on her tray. Rose was wearing the apron, Mattie was wearing her beach glass pendant, and her white-blond head was resting against Rose's embroidered pillowcase.

You're home, Don thought. *Surrounded by everyone and everything you ever loved.*

A breeze suddenly raced into the family room, and grew stronger, rustling the curtains on every window. Don looked at Rose and then LeAnn, who came scurrying over.

She checked Mattie's pulse and her blood pressure. LeAnn smoothed Mattie's hair, bowed her head, and said a short prayer.

"I'll leave you alone for a bit," she said. "It's okay to tell her it's time to go. Let her know you'll be okay and that you love her. I'll be in the other room."

Don looked helplessly at Rose, and she sat beside him again. They held hands and said a silent prayer. Rose stood, hugged Mattie, and whispered, "Thank you for giving me a family again."

She turned to Don. "I'll leave you alone now," she said. "It's time for you two to be alone."

When the room was quiet, Don took his wife's hand again. "You have been my best friend and the love of my life," he whispered. "What a life we had, huh?"

He stopped and squeezed her hand before giving it a kiss. "You gave me more than any man could ever ask for," he continued. "You gave me hope. And there is no greater gift."

Don leaned into his wife's ear and whispered, "It's okay to go now, my love. Fly free of this body. I will miss you every single day until we're reunited, but I know you will always be with me." He stopped and looked at Mattie's hope chest family heirlooms. "And I will always be surrounded by your presence. Now go. Give your mom and dad a big hug for me."

Don hesitated and took a deep breath. "And tell our children that their mom will be with them now forever. I love you, Mattie."

Another breeze—this one even stronger—rushed into the family room and ruffled Mattie's hair. As Don smoothed her hair back over her ears, Mattie's eyes fluttered.

At first, Don thought it was simply the medication, or a reflex from Mattie's dying body, but she opened her eyes just enough to look at Don, her hazel eyes dim but still filled with light. A weak smiled trailed across her lips. Don's eyes flooded with tears as his wife locked eyes with him. Her gaze flickered toward the open door, and the beach beyond, before moving heavenward. Don stared into her eyes.

Her gaze then went toward the foot of her bed, where Mabel lay and had not left her side for days.

Don followed the movement of Mattie's eyes until, finally, the reflection of her hope chest, and all its contents, shone brightly in them.

Mattie took a pained breath, and her lips parted.

"Cedar," she said.

"Yes," Don said.

Mattie shut her eyes, and Don waited for her to open them again. Her shallow, inconsistent breathing slowed and then suddenly stopped.

No, Don thought. *Mattie.*

Don felt for his wife's pulse. He lifted his hand to his mouth, covering it to hide his sobs. Mabel rose from the foot of Mattie's bed and walked gingerly toward her face. She put her nose against Mattie's, and stood silently for a moment, as if listening for a breath. Mabel turned and looked at Don, let out a small whine, and then pawed at her. Mabel put her nose against Mattie's once again, and then gave her a little kiss before laying down directly on her chest.

Don sobbed quietly and petted the dog. And then, as he had done for years, Don crawled into bed next to his wife, gave her a kiss, and put his head on her chest.

"Good night, my love," he said.

Forty-one

Mattie's soul was light and free. She gave Don a silent kiss, and then Mabel. She watched Rose and LeAnn rush into the room and then stop when they saw Don lying in bed beside her.

Mattie was floating at the top of the family room and then, suddenly, she was outside, in the branches of the cedar tree, whose arms reached toward the heavens.

"How big do you think this will get, baby girl?"

Mattie turned, and her father was beside her.

"As big as my hopes and dreams?" she asked.

He hugged her.

"Mattie?" she heard. "Are you ready?"

Mattie's mom appeared beside her.

"I am," she said. "Can we take one last walk?"

Mattie's mom nodded.

"Go on, sweetheart," Mary Ellen said. "You can do anything now."

Mattie smiled and took off, her spirit a flash of light.

She soared over Hope Dunes and then flew down the long, gravel driveway, zipping under the arbor of trees. She stopped at the end of the drive and gave a little kiss to the wooden carved sign, HOPE DUNES. Mattie then exhaled mightily, smiling as the sign swung on the log post.

Mattie heard a herald of giggles. The school bus had stopped on Lake Shore Drive. Jeri bounded out, jumped up, and tapped the wooden sign, making it swing again, and sang as she ran down the driveway.

Mattie took off again. Her mother and father grabbed her hands, and they soared over the majesty of Lake Michigan, into the clouds, and then up, up, up.

Forty-two

Thank you for doing this with me," Don said to Rose a few weeks later. "It means the world. And it would mean the world to Mattie, too."

"I'm honored," Rose said.

"I thought this would be appropriate," Don said, holding out a desert rose teacup.

Rose peered into the teacup. It held some of Mattie's ashes.

"I think she would love it," Rose said. "Where do we start?"

Don and Rose headed out of the cottage and toward the big cedar behind Mattie's garden. Mabel stood at the door, hesitant, and then looked behind her, waiting.

"It's okay, Mabes," Don said, his voice trying to sound singsongy but instead cracking at the dog's heartbreak. "She's not coming."

A male cardinal, as red as Santa's hat, watched the scene.

"No," Rose said. "She's already out here."

"Come on, Mabel," Don said, crouching and clapping his hands for the dog to come. Finally, Mabel ran to him.

As Don and Rose began to spread a few of Mattie's ashes at the tree's trunk, the cardinal lifted its head in song.

"*Hope is the thing with feathers that perches in the soul and sings the tune without the words and never stops . . . at all,*" Rose said. "I will never forget that poem. Or her."

The two walked in the midst of Mattie's garden. Pockets of snow still stood in the shadows as well as in the crevices between the lake stones that bordered the garden. The latticework and trellises that were the canvas for many of Mattie's vining flowers—and which Mattie and Don had left, thinking they would never return—had taken a beating over the winter. Their paint was peeling, some had broken.

Don looked at the layer of decomposing leaves and shook his head.

Mattie would never have allowed it to look like this come spring, he thought.

"We have some work to do," Don said to Rose.

We? Rose thought happily, her emotions rising into her throat. She smiled. "We do," she said.

Don kneeled and brushed aside a layer of leaves. "Look," he said, his voice rising. "Over here."

Rose kneeled, too. Beautiful white snowdrops, snuggled close to the ground, were beginning to emerge.

The two stood and began to scatter Mattie's ashes around her garden.

Don protected the teacup with his hand and headed toward the stairs that led to the beach. He stopped at the first landing—the place where he and Mattie had stood many times to watch the sun set or take in the glory of the coastline in fall—and tossed some ashes into the breeze. Don continued, one warped step at a time, until he was on the sand.

Rose followed him to the shore, and Mabel sprinted past her, chasing down a group of seagulls enjoying the season's silence. Mabel began to bark as the birds took flight, before digging wildly in the sand.

"Ice is breaking up early this year," Rose said. "Lake will be warmer. Going to be a beautiful summer."

Don looked at her, his face blank.

"It *is*," Rose said. "Not the same—never the same—but still beautiful. You need to forge on somehow."

She stopped and looked out over the water. "I'm glad you decided to keep Hope Dunes," Rose continued.

"*Mattie* decided to keep Hope Dunes," Don said. "With your help."

"She did it for you," Rose said. "So you could continue. You have so many good years left and so much love to give the world. You honor your wife by doing that."

"I know," Don said. "I just need a little time."

He shut his eyes for a moment, the tide providing a calming rhythm. "I feel so empty right now. I didn't just lose my wife, I lost my soul, my conscience, my heartbeat, my debate partner, my lover, my friend, . . . my everything," Don said. He stopped and mumbled to himself. "Someone once said Mattie and I were codependent. Maybe he was right. Maybe that's why this hurts so much."

Rose took a few steps through the sand and put her hands on Don's shoulders. He turned, and she looked him right in the face.

"It's not being codependent," Rose said. "It's being blessed."

She lifted her hands to Don's face and gave it a gentle shake. "I can only imagine your heartbreak after being with her for fifty years," Rose said. "And I can only imagine your love, too. Do you know how rare that is these days?"

Don shook his head and bit the inside of his cheek.

Rose continued. "You had what I dream of—what everyone dreams of," she said. "We get one chance on this earth. One short little stop to get things right, and too few of us do. We focus on everything that is unimportant. You and Mattie focused your energies on making the world a better and more beautiful place. You loved each other with all your being."

Rose stopped and looked at Don, as the lake breeze caught her hair and tousled it around her head. "And if that ain't gettin' it right, I don't know what is."

Don removed his hand from the teacup, took a few of Mattie's ashes, and offered the desert rose cup to Rose.

"I know how much you loved Lake Michigan, my love," Don said.

They tossed the ashes into the lake, but the breeze caught them, and the ashes came flying back into their faces.

Don coughed and then laughed. "Mattie always had a rather dry sense of humor," he said.

Rose laughed and wiped her face.

"This still doesn't feel right, does it?" Don asked.

Suddenly, he grabbed Rose's hand, and they took off running down the shoreline. Mabel joined them, barking at their exuberance.

Don lifted the teacup into the air as they ran. He gave it a shake. The wind off the lake caught the ashes and they streamed into the sky. The breeze caught them and gave them a shake. As Don and Rose ran, they watched as some of Mattie's ashes fell on the beach, some flew into the lake, and some kept floating higher and higher.

Don and Rose stopped and looked skyward. The ashes soared, grey against blue, until Don and Rose had to squint to see the specks.

"Looks like birds on the horizon at sunset," Rose said. "Flying to get home before dark."

Rose gave Don a big hug, and the two headed back to Hope Dunes, tossing sticks for Mabel as they walked the shore.

"Want some tea?" Rose asked as they shed their coats upon returning.

"Not really my thing," Don said. "Mattie loved her tea. I love my coffee."

He tilted his head and suddenly rushed into the kitchen, Mabel trailing. Don began to rustle through the cabinets. "Here it is!"

Don lifted a sleek machine—all curves and silver, nozzles and knobs—from a shelf. He set it on the counter, releasing an "Oomph" and rubbing his back as he did so.

"Do you happen to know how to make a latte?" Don asked. "Mattie got me one of these fancy espresso machines a few years back. She said I was spending too much money on toffee lattes at Lake Effect, that I was keeping Vinnie in business."

He plugged in the machine and then stood back, hands up, as if it were a nuclear bomb he was about to detonate.

"As you can tell," he said with a laugh, "I never quite figured it out. Funny, isn't it? I can fix the engine on my vintage T-bird, but I can't figure out a coffee machine."

Rose's laughter echoed in the kitchen. "And I can raise a child but can't figure out how to order anything off Etsy."

Don doubled over, laughing, and the two began to inspect the machine. The two had just jokingly tried to place an entire bag of coffee into the little metal grounds basket when Jeri rushed in the door from school.

Mabel barked and jumped into the little girl's arms.

"How was it?" Don asked. "How was the Ice Bucket Challenge?"

Jeri tossed her book bag on the counter, and then Don lifted her up until she was sitting beside it.

"Cold," Jeri said, bouncing up and down, her red curls following suit. "I got ice dumped on me outside. It was a special assembly, not recess, even though it was on the playground."

She stopped and waved at Mabel who was sitting on the floor, barking to be with her.

"And then the teacher and principal got ice dumped on them, too."

Jeri stopped. "Glad you and Mom told me to bring a change of clothes," she said. "I was so cold and wet."

Jeri continued to bounce, recounting her day. "And I raised $762 for ALS," Jeri said. "But my teacher said what was best of all was that I raised . . . raised . . ."

Jeri stopped, her eyes wide. "I can't remember the word," she said.

"Awareness?" Don asked.

"That's it!" Jeri said. "And I got to put out pictures of Mattie and tell the school how much she meant to me. And how awful ALS is, and how we have to work to find a cure."

She stopped and looked at Don. "If it's okay with you, I want to bring her hope chest to school for show and tell next month."

"I'd love it," he said. "Mattie would love it, too. Can I come?"

"I'd love it," Jeri said with a smile, mimicking Don. "And it's too heavy for me to carry anyway," she added with a giggle. "Hey, can I have a cookie? I worked really, really hard today."

"Maybe in a second, honey," Rose said, returning to the coffee maker.

Jeri finally noticed the espresso machine sitting on the counter, a whole bag of coffee jutting from it.

"What are you trying to do?" she asked.

"Make a fancy coffee," Don said.

"Why don't you just go get one in town?" Jeri said, her lips curling into a smile. "And they have the best cookies ever."

"You're one smart cookie," Don said, reaching over to mess up her curls. "I have an idea. Why don't we all pile into my T-bird and go into town?"

"Is there room?" Rose asked.

"Well, Jeri will have to sit on your lap," he said. "I'll go really slow and take the back roads. And, if we put on coats and scarves, I can put the top down. It's a pretty day."

"Yeah," Jeri yelled. "Mommy?"

"Okay," she said.

The three loaded into Don's T-bird and headed into town for coffee and cookies, the top down on the convertible despite the chill in the air. Don took Lake Shore Drive toward Saugatuck, a panoramic view of Lake Michigan to their west.

"Look," Rose said.

Don slowed the car to a stop and squinted to see what Rose was pointing toward.

"There," she said.

He followed her finger. Birds—no bigger than tiny specks—were flying across the horizon.

"Where are they going?" Jeri asked, finally spying what the two were watching.

"Home," Don said.

epilogue

The Hope Chest

Easter 2017

I found it! I found it!"

Jeri zipped around the burgeoning gardens at Hope Dunes and directly toward a dyed pink egg nestled in the crook of the cedar tree.

Don and Rose laughed as she jumped up and down in her sparkly pink princess dress, holding up the matching pink egg for them to see.

"I wish she would wear a proper Easter dress," Rose said, sipping a glass of "Easter fizz," an orange juice and sparkling soda concoction her mother used to make for her every Easter.

Don smiled. Don had hidden the eggs and prepped the brunch before the three had gone to church. Now, he was grinning even bigger than the Easter bunny as he watched Jeri race around the yard hunting eggs.

He looked over at Rose, who was laughing as she watched Jeri run around, basket in hand.

I have a daughter and a granddaughter, Don thought, the reality nearly overwhelming him. *I lost my wife but—through her strength—found a family.*

It was a stunning Easter morning. The lake, fully unfrozen, shimmered in the near distance, while a hillside of blooming daffodils complemented the sun. And, in the midst, a pink bunny was giggling, hopping around, gathering eggs.

"My mom used to hide eggs for me," Rose said, her voice wistful. "Thank you for doing this. I think I'm finally starting to feel like myself again."

She looked over at Don. "I'm starting college again next year," Rose said, her voice a bit sheepish. "To become a nurse . . . finally."

Don jumped, just like Jeri. "That's great," he said. "I'm so proud of you."

"Just two night classes a week at the community college," Rose said.

"You *will* do it," Don said, his voice confident.

"And I start a new assignment tomorrow for a gentleman in town with Parkinson's."

Rose looked at Don. "Which means I'll need a little help with baby-sitting," she said. "And, you know, some tutoring."

Don's eyes filled with tears. "Of course."

"Want some more coffee?" Rose asked.

Don nodded.

"Back in a sec," she said.

As Rose walked away, Jeri looked toward the porch, where Don's face was watching from behind the screen. Don looked to make sure if Rose was gone and then secretly pointed toward the next secret location—a squirrel hole in an old oak—and Jeri giggled, racing off to the next hiding spot, her basket bursting with bright green plastic grass, chocolates, and colorful eggs.

"Perfect Easter," Rose said, returning with his coffee. "Looks like *The Wizard of Oz* with all the color, doesn't it?"

The dogwoods and redbud were in bloom, white and pink dotting the emerging green. Although the trees were yet to get their leaves, tulips encircled them—a crayon box of colors—and hyacinths bloomed. Burgeoning trillium in white and pink dotted the woods. The earth smelled alive.

"Mattie's father told me he decided to buy a place in Michigan on Easter when she was still a little girl," Don said. "Something about Easter, isn't there?"

"Hope," Rose said.

Jeri's happy shrieks echoed throughout the yard, and she ran toward the screened porch, then rushed inside, breathing heavily.

"You are too excited," Rose said, taking her napkin and wiping down her daughter's face.

"It's Easter!" Jeri screamed.

"I have one more surprise for you today," Don said, unable to hide a smile.

"No," Rose said. "You've already gone to so much effort today. Please. It's too much."

"It's never too much," Don said. "Isn't that why grandparents spoil their grandchildren?"

Rose's lips quivered with emotion.

"Follow me," he said.

Don led the duo into the family room of Hope Dunes, and Jeri immediately gasped: A trail of jelly beans meandered past the lake stone fireplace and then into the dining room.

"Where's it go?" Jeri giggled.

"Follow it and find out," Don said.

"Follow the yellow brick road," Jeri sang. "Like that movie we watched with Mrs. Tice."

The little girl then altered the lyrics. *"Follow the jelly bean road!"*

Jeri suddenly took off in a flash—Easter basket still in the crook of her arm—Don and Rose scampering to keep up, the trail of jelly beans leading under the dining room table, up the stairs, and then into the guest room where smack-dab in the middle sat a large package wrapped in colorful cellophane.

"That's a big Easter basket," Jeri said, her eyes wide.

Don laughed. "Open it," he said, kneeling down in front of her. "I'll help you."

"What is it?" Jeri asked as they continued to unwrap.

"Oh, my gosh," Rose said, when the gift was unveiled, her mouth falling open. "It's Mattie's hope chest."

Rose felt wobbly and sat down on the floor next to her daughter.

"An Easter gift," Don said. "Mattie's parents gave this to her on Easter when she was a little girl. She told me she wanted to pass it on . . . to Jeri."

"Don, no," Rose said. "We can't. It's part of your family."

"So are you," he said.

Rose burst into tears, stood, and hugged Don.

"This is mine?" Jeri asked, running her hands over it. "I don't know what to say."

"Thank you," Rose said.

"Only that you'll love it as much as Mattie did," Don said.

"I will," Jeri said, nodding. "I promise."

"And I promise that your mom and I will help you fill it before you're all grown up."

"With what?" Jeri asked.

"Well, a hope chest is filled with lots of things," Rose said, as if reading Don's mind. "Just like all those things you played with of Mrs. Tice's. But they're more than playthings. They are special keepsakes for you when you grow up, go into the world, and maybe get married one day. They all have a special history."

"A hope chest is filled with things like blankets and linens to keep you warm," Don added, recalling what Mattie's mom told her all those years ago. "It's filled with household items, like glasses, dishes, kitchen towels, and bakeware, so that your future house is truly a home. It's filled with memories, like scrapbooks and family pictures, teddy bears and dolls, so that you can pass those along when you are married and have a family. It's a way to connect your past with your future."

Rose smiled and looked at her daughter. "But mostly, a hope chest is filled with love, and the hopes and dreams that parents—and grandparents—have for their daughters and granddaughters, all the things that Mr. Tice and I have for you."

Don sat on the floor next to them.

"Would you mind calling me Grampa?" he asked, looking at Jeri before looking to Rose. "If that's okay, I mean. 'Mr. Tice' just seems too formal."

"Okay," Jeri said before her mother could say a word. "Grampa!"

Jeri turned to the hope chest.

"It's so pretty," she exclaimed, touching the chest.

"See those beautiful spring flowers on the front?" Don asked. "Mattie's father carved them into the chest specially for her. They were all of her favorite flowers: tulips and daffodils and dogwood blooms. They loved to work in the garden together."

Don looked at Jeri and continued. "And Mattie and I wanted to add some things just for you, to personalize it, really make it yours.

"See the top?" Don asked. "I added some polished stones and made a frame for this picture of us with Mattie. I shellacked it onto the wood so it will be there forever."

"That's the picture of us from fall," she said. "With the leaf!"

"Open it," Don said.

Jeri stood and tried to lift the lid.

"It's stuck," she said. "I think it may be broken."

Don smiled. "Oh, I forgot," he said.

He grabbed one end of the chest, nodding at Rose to grab the other. The two tilted the chest off the floor. "See that?" he asked Jeri, as the key glimmered in the light. "Grab it."

"What is it?" Jeri asked.

"See the lock?" he asked. "There's a special key—the only one like it in the world—that goes with it, that only you will have. So you need to keep it in a secret place, and Mattie always kept her key taped to the bottom of the chest."

"Why?" Jeri asked.

"Her mother told her it was the last place anyone would ever look," he said, "because it's the most obvious."

Jeri giggled. "I have a secret hiding place now," she said. "And a secret key!"

"Open it," Don urged.

Jeri inserted the key and then lifted the lid. The scent of cedar filled the room.

"Smells like we're in the woods," Jeri said. "I love that smell."

"Look inside," Don urged.

On top of Mattie's heirlooms sat a gift wrapped in pink tissue, tied in velvet ribbon with a big bow on top.

"I did that," Don said proudly. "Open it."

Jeri gently untied the bow and ribbon, and then peeled the tissue back to reveal a pretty white dress with little pink bows.

"Mattie's mom made that Easter dress for her," Don said. "Mattie wanted you to have it. She even had someone alter it to fit you."

"It's so pretty," Jeri said. "And I love pink."

"Try it on," Rose said. "We'll be right here."

"Okay," Jeri said, running into the bathroom with her dress.

, "Thank you," Rose said. "You are too kind."

"There's something in there for you, too," Don said. "From Mattie and me."

Rose shook her head. "No," she said. "Don, really. Stop."

"Go on," Don said. "Please."

Rose leaned into the hope chest, and an envelope with her name sat folded in the arms of the cloth doll, which sat atop the folded apron and pillowcase.

Rose tentatively reached inside, nabbed the envelope from the doll's arms, and slowly began to open it.

Inside it was a card with a beautiful watercolor of a cardinal perched on a pine, the lake in the background, the image of a flower—a bleeding heart—open and tender in the foreground. Inside, there was a poem and another envelope. The poem began:

> *If I can stop one heart from breaking,*
> *I shall not live in vain*

"Mattie had the card made just for you," Don said. "That's one of her watercolors. The poem is by . . ."

"Emily Dickinson," Rose said, finishing his thought, the card trembling in her hands. "It's so beautiful. Thank you."

"One more," Don urged.

Rose could barely open the second envelope. She pulled a piece of paper from it.

A legal document, she thought.

And then she read it and immediately collapsed into tears.

"No, no, no," she wept. "I can't."

Tears bounced off the paper, and Rose bent over the hope chest, sobbing into it, her cries muffled.

"We wanted you to always have your family home," Don said, "just like you encouraged us to keep our family home."

"You paid off my mortgage?" Rose continued to sob, her shoulders shaking. "Don, it's not right."

"It is right," he said. "You said too few people ever get it right, this journey on earth. Mattie got it right. I want to get it right."

He stopped. "We wanted to do this for you," he said. "You deserve the chance to have a great life. And we all need a little support . . ."

Don hesitated. ". . . from family."

"Are you okay, Mommy?" Jeri asked, coming out of the bathroom.

"Yes," Rose sobbed. "These are happy tears."

She dried her eyes. "You look so beautiful, honey," Rose said. "It fits perfectly. Do a twirl for us."

Jeri twirled in Mattie's Easter dress and then walked over and picked up the rag doll. Then she looked into the hope chest and pulled out a plaque.

"What's this?" she asked.

"It's a 'Home Sweet Home' plaque for *your* future home," Don said. "Mattie's mom wrote the poem on it just for her, and her father engraved the plaque. Now it's yours."

Rose took the plaque from her daughter's hands and read it aloud.

Hope Is Only One Short Letter From Home
H is for Hope
Now and for always

O is for the Overwhelming love
I have for you

P is for the Practical items
That will make your house a home

E is for the Eternal memories this chest will provide
Every time you open it up

You are my hope, and my home, in this world
My daughter, my love

"And, look," Don said, "on the other side of the plaque, Mattie's father engraved the word 'home' and trailed her name down from the *m*. See what I did? I trailed 'Jeri' down around the *e*. Mattie always told me that hope is only one short letter from home."

"I know a perfect place to hang this," Rose said, her voice still shaky. "Our home."

"Thank you!" Jeri said to Don. "I love my dress! And I love the hope chest! When can we start filling it up with new stuff?"

"We have all the time in the world," Don said. "We'll have it overflowing by the time you meet the man of your dreams."

Don stopped and pulled Jeri close. "Can I tell you something important?"

Jeri nodded.

"Always remember that hope is something you carry with you forever, not only in this chest but also in your heart. So look inside it and inside yourself when you need hope the most, and it will guide you and remind you of what was and what is to be. That's something Mattie's parents told her and she told me."

Jeri looked thoughtfully at Don, considering his words.

"Okay!" she said. "But I don't think there will ever be a time when I'm sad. I have tons of hope!"

Jeri popped a chocolate into her mouth, hugged Don and her mom, and skipped out of the room with her Easter basket, the bows on her new dress twitching.

"Later, gators!" She giggled, leaving five chocolaty fingerprints on the inside of the frame of the door. She called back, "I'm hungry. When's brunch?"

Don and Rose laughed, and she leaned in to hug him tightly.

"Thank you," she said. "For everything."

"No," Don whispered. "Thank you."

Before they left the room, Don stopped and began to shut the lid on the hope chest.

"Don't," Rose said, interrupting him. She inhaled deeply. "It needs to remain open. We all do."

Don smiled and nodded.

He turned, leaving the hope chest wide open, and the two walked downstairs, the scent of cedar drifting out of the room and trailing behind them, enveloping Hope Dunes.

Acknowledgments

The past year has been filled with the highest of highs and the lowest of lows, and I would—literally—not be here without the love and support of my family and friends.

Huge, heartfelt thanks to my literary agent, Wendy Sherman, who has been my guide, go-to, gatekeeper, and biggest supporter since my first book. We just celebrated our tenth anniversary together; however, while tin or aluminum is the traditional gift, a roll of Reynolds Wrap just doesn't seem quite right for the woman who has such great taste. How about another book (or ten) together instead?

Huge, heartfelt thanks to my editor, Laurie Chittenden, as well. She, too, helped shepherd my first book into existence, and I'm humbled and honored to work with her again on my fiction. She is funny, smart, kind, insightful, and not only makes my work infinitely better but also champions it without fail.

I couldn't ask for a better publisher to work with than Macmillan, St. Martin's, and the entire Thomas Dunne team: Tom, Pete, Lisa, Katie, Melanie, Laura (and so many others), thank you for your expertise, support, guidance, and belief!

Carol Fitzgerald, you are a force of nature and a wonderful sounding board. You are a Web site rock star, as is your entire team (and you make me laugh harder than almost anyone).

Jenny Meyer, you've helped bring my work to the attention of the world, and I can never thank you enough. #unsungheroaward

No book I write would *ever* be complete without the love and support of my rescue dogs, Doris and Mabel, who steadfastly follow me to my writing office every single day, nestle at my feet, remind me to take breaks, tell me I'm brilliant, kiss me when I cry, and never leave my side. Every morning, they wait as I get my coffee, ready to accompany me on my short commute. "Ready?" their faces seem to ask excitedly. "Let's do this!" I always reply. And we do. Together.

And I would not have become a writer without the guidance, love, and support of my mother and grandmothers or the unwavering belief and inspiration of Gary Edwards, who makes life an adventure, allows me to view the world with the innocence of a child, helps me see the beauty in every butterfly and raindrop and flower. Your reflective light inspires me, warms me, and allows me to continue to reach, reach, reach for the stars.

For those who ask how I became an author and want to do the same, I believe in these practices: Live—and write—without fear. Follow that voice that calls to you. Write. Every day. Believe in your talent. Never give up. Write. Every day. Write. Every day. Edit. Edit. Edit. Write and edit some more. Believe. And never give up. Ever.

There is no magic key (like the one on the cover of this book) to becoming an author. There is talent and perseverance. Writing (and publishing) is not a craft fair. It takes the same dedication and gut-wrenching hard work that you put into every other aspect of your life. You hold that key. And only you are able to unlock that door. My mother once told me that life is as short as one blink of God's eye, and we are all given gifts to make that brief journey truly miraculous, but too few ever do or truly understand that truth before—*blink*—our journey is over.

And, so I repeat, as inspiration and warning: No fear. Channel your unique voice. Write every day. Believe. And never, ever give up. I can already hear that door unlocking . . .